LECTURE CANCELLED

When I got to the second floor, I turned to where the English Department offices were. I wasn't practicing police skills; I was just going to listen to a very distinguished professor rant and rave at the decay of humanist values in a rock 'n' roll world. I've listened to people rant and rave before.

Professor Warren's door was ajar so I took a deep breath, knocked, and pushed my way in.

Professor Warren lay sprawled on the floor. There was a lot of blood. I'd seen that much blood once before, so I knew Professor Warren would never have to worry about minor annoyances like rock music again. And neither would I, for a while.

Avon Books are available at special quantity discounts for bulk purchases for sales promotions, premiums, fund raising or educational use. Special books, or book excerpts, can also be created to fit specific needs.

For details write or telephone the office of the Director of Special Markets, Avon Books, Dept. FP, 1350 Avenue of the Americas, New York, New York 10019, 1-800-238-0658.

AMENDS
for
MURDER

M.D. LAKE

AVON BOOKS ◆ NEW YORK

AMENDS FOR MURDER is an original publication of Avon Books. This work has never before appeared in book form. This work is a novel. Any similarity to actual persons or events is purely coincidental.

AVON BOOKS
A division of
The Hearst Corporation
1350 Avenue of the Americas
New York, New York 10019

Copyright © 1989 by J. A. Simpson
Published by arrangement with the author
Library of Congress Catalog Card Number: 89-91272
ISBN: 0-380-75865-2

First Avon Books Printing: November 1989

AVON TRADEMARK REG. U.S. PAT. OFF. AND IN OTHER COUNTRIES, MARCA REGISTRADA, HECHO EN CANADA

Printed in Canada

UNV 10 9 8 7 6 5 4

To Mary Trone
for her encouragement
and her generosity in sharing
her knowledge of mysteries and publishing

One

The day Adam Warren was murdered, I'd been working the middle watch, from four to eleven, for a week. Since rookies aren't assigned night patrols right away, that was my first time. It didn't bother me because, unlike most women I know, I've always liked being out alone at night.

I got to work late that afternoon, changed into my uniform in the women's lounge, and hurried down the backstairs to try to make the end of roll call. As I passed the full-length mirror on the landing I slowed to look myself over, which is what the mirror's there for, and I liked what I saw. My hairdresser takes his time, and he'd taken more than usual that day, but he knows how to cut curly hair so it looks good even under a uniform hat.

The other cops were all heading out to their assignments when I came into the squad room. One of them, Lawrence, asked me if I wanted him to wait so I could get a ride in his squad car, but I said no, I'd walk to where my beat started, just a couple of blocks down the street. Sergeant Hiller didn't say anything about my being late, probably because it was the first time. I was a very dutiful cop in those days. In the navy, women like me were called "Nancy Navy," and I was well on my way to earning the same reputation on the campus police force. I didn't know if they had a name for it: "Cathy Cop," maybe.

My assignment was the Old Campus, on the east side of the river. I've always loved that part of the University, with its oddly shaped buildings engulfed in ivy, and the elms and oaks that live quietly within themselves summer and winter.

1

I'd spent most of my own student days on the Old Campus, and avoided when I could the New Campus, designed for an age of brutality.

Sergeant Hiller told me what I'd missed at roll call. Friday nights aren't usually quiet in the spring and early summer, but he thought this one would be. It was the last day of final exams and most students had already taken off for wherever they planned to spend the summer, while the summer students wouldn't be arriving for another week. Of course there'd be fraternity and sorority parties on the edge of campus, but the campus itself should be pretty calm.

"Keep an eye out for thieves," Hiller added. I suppressed an urge to laugh, since keeping an eye out for thieves kind of goes with the territory of being a cop. Sergeant Hiller's a nice guy. He worries about all of us, not just the rookies and not just the women. Besides, several months before, in April, a custodian had surprised someone trying to steal a computer from one of the Law School offices and ended up in the hospital.

I glanced into Ginny Raines's office on the way down the hall but she'd already gone off duty. Ginny and I were moving in the direction of a friendship. At least, I hoped so. She'd been a campus cop a lot longer than I had—she was the first woman hired—and she'd helped me get adjusted. There were only three women on the campus police, Ginny, Paula Henderson, and me.

As I walked past Ron, the dispatcher that night, I tossed him a wave. He had a phone to his ear. "Somebody'll be right over to take care of it, sir," he said. He signaled me to wait. "In fact, she's on her way." He put a hand over the mouthpiece and said to me, "You're the somebody, Peggy, so stand by," and then, back to the phone, "Yes sir, and then she's to come straight to your office in Frye Hall. Got it." He hung up and made a face at the phone. "That was Professor Warren," he told me. "Adam Warren. I don't suppose I have to tell you who he is."

No, he didn't. Although he was only a professor of English, Adam Warren was so distinguished that even the football coach might have recognized his name.

"He's upset," Ron went on. "The frat boys across the street from his office are making too much noise again."

"It's after four," I said. "What's a big shot like Warren doing on campus so late on a Friday afternoon anyway? When I was a student, they all headed for their summer places around noon."

"He's reading exams—or trying to—he says. Rock and roll's destroying his concentration. I could hear Springsteen in the background as he was talking. Funny, Bruce doesn't destroy my concentration." Ron scratched his head and tried to look worried about that, but worry doesn't come easy to him.

We have an agreement with the fraternities, worked out after many years of noise and complaints from the faculty in Frye Hall and other buildings on that edge of the campus: they're supposed to play their stereos quietly and keep their speakers indoors until five o'clock, so they won't disturb the faculty and those students who don't need rock and roll to stay awake in class. After five they can make all the noise they want within reason and we don't harass them about it. The boys usually keep the bargain, but today was the last day of school and they'd started early. I'd heard the music myself as I biked to work.

"Why don't I just go tell them to hold it down for another hour or so?" I asked. "I don't need to go soothe Professor Warren, too, do I?"

"Do it, Peggy," Ron told me, "because he wants you to. Deal with the noise first, but then go over and let Professor Warren chew you out for ineptitude. Look intrepid, dedicated, and contrite." Ron was on a fierce self-improvement regime and his normal vocabulary had been one of the first things to go. "You're good at looking contrite," he added, "which is the only reason we hired you." He gave me a sunny smile, perhaps to tell me he didn't mean it. "Remember, our budget's coming up for review next month. We don't want complaints, especially from someone like Warren."

So I went. I didn't mind, because Frye Hall was a part of my beat anyway and I could just as well start there as anywhere else. Besides, it might be interesting to see Professor Warren again. I'd taken a class from him in my senior year, just after he got back from his stint in Washington, and I'd liked him as a teacher. I was pretty sure he wouldn't remember me, even though I'd gone to his office once to ask about an assignment I'd missed, and we'd talked for a minute or two.

I walked down College Avenue. As I approached Frye Hall the rock music began to get louder until, by the time I reached the first fraternity house, it sounded like a concert was in progress. It might not have been so bad—for someone who liked rock music, at least—if all the houses had been tuned to the same radio station or playing the same record or tape, but one seemed to be tuned to the teenybopper station, another to the hard-rock station, and a third was apparently playing something that celebrated the end of the world in a very unpleasant way.

Large speakers were set in windows and facing out onto the frat-house lawns, and beneath them the boys were milling around in their customary defensive clusters, as if awaiting an attack by a gaggle of sorority girls. I don't care what anybody says, frat boys all look alike. They're like jigsaw-puzzle pieces; they need all the others to add up to anything.

As I approached them I could hear voices from deep within each cluster giving orders and making muffled catcalls. The boys at the center are the leaders, those on the perimeters are the expendable ones and therefore the most exposed.

"Turn 'em down," I said, speaking directly to the first boy I came to. "It's not five o'clock yet. You've got half an hour to go." I spoke pleasantly, even gave him a smile. One guy to another.

"Ah, hey, Officer, ma'am," came a mocking voice from the dark, soft center, "it's the end of finals. Loosen up, go tell the old farts across the street to take their finals up to their cabins and grade 'em there, where we can't bother 'em."

"Turn them down," I repeated patiently, enunciating a little more precisely, "or I'll send somebody to collect them. We need new speakers at headquarters. These sound good enough."

"Thank you, ma'am. Hey, I thought that being a lady and all, you'd understand. You're a great disappointment to me personally. Rhodes! Go do what the lady says." One of the boys peeled off the perimeter and, more appropriately than he probably realized, goose-stepped into the house. I forced myself to stand there on the lawn until the volume sank to a fraction of its former self.

The boys outside the two other fraternity houses across from Frye Hall had had more time to prepare for me and rehearse their lines, but the results were the same in the end and not significantly more hilarious. A kind of peace settled over College Avenue in my wake.

I crossed the street to Frye Hall and went around to the main entrance, on a path that begins its winding stroll through the Old Campus there. It was hot and humid and I was sweating by the time I'd climbed the front steps and entered the building.

Inside, though, it was cool and dark. Old ceiling lights ran the length of the hall, but only every other one was on, a result of the University's efforts to cut costs. A dark-haired woman passed me as I started up the stairs; she gave me a quick glance and then looked away. I was used to that: women in cop uniforms are still fairly unusual on campus. When I got to the second floor, I turned right, to where I knew the English department offices were. I wasn't practicing police skills, I was just going to listen to a very distinguished professor rant and rave at the decay of humanist values in a rock-and-roll world, before starting my patrol. I've listened to people rant and rave before.

The door to the office next to Professor Warren's was open. I glanced in and saw a man sitting at a desk, his back to me. He was obviously absorbed in whatever he was doing and didn't turn around. The name on the wall beside his door said he was Lee Pierce, and I knew who that was: the University's poet. I'd never attended one of his readings, but I'd seen him occasionally, walking around Lake Eleanor near where I live.

I stopped at Professor Warren's door. It was ajar, so I took a deep breath, knocked, and pushed my way in.

Professor Warren lay sprawled on the floor. There was a lot of blood. I'd seen that much blood once, a long time ago, long before I'd ever thought of becoming a cop, so I knew Professor Warren would never have to worry about minor annoyances like rock music again. And neither would I for a while.

Two

Even though I knew he was dead, I stayed where I was and called his name. He didn't move, of course, so I went closer and saw the mess something had made of the back of his head. I'd forgotten I was a police officer; I didn't think about the danger that might be in the room still. I went to him and knelt beside him. I took his arm, felt for a pulse knowing there wouldn't be one, and waited until I was sure.

There was so much blood. It was red in his white hair, but almost black where it had spread over the dark oak floor like a glittering evil halo around his head, and puddled against a pack of cigarettes and a book sprawled open and facedown like the man himself.

I felt sick. I scrambled to my feet and looked around in panic. I had enough sense not to use the wastebasket, nearly full of crumpled paper that might contain clues, and threw up in an empty corner of the room instead. When I was finished, I wiped the water out of my eyes with my fists, then stood a moment, and finally drew my gun, uncertainly, stupidly. If whoever had killed Warren had still been in the room, and wanted to kill again, I'd have already been dead.

The office was cluttered, with books and papers stacked on every available surface and piled on the floor. The ceiling light was off, but the afternoon sun was still bright in the room. The windows were shut, but even so I could hear the sound of the rock drums across the street, like a throbbing pulse. The boys hadn't turned the volume back up yet, but it wasn't hard to imagine what it would sound like in Warren's office when they did.

A door in the wall beyond Warren's body was partly open. I went over and opened it all the way, looked in. It was a large bright room even with the lights off, with a long table running the length of it and computers standing at intervals on the table. It contrasted sharply with the dark oak and the clutter in Warren's office behind me, and with Frye Hall itself.

A computer was lying on the floor, upside down, an IBM desktop. I knew it was an IBM because that's what a label on it said, and I knew it was upside down because that's how I had to read the label. A keyboard lay next to it, still attached by its cord. The computer monitor sat on the long table, staring at me blindly, its black cord dangling over the table's edge.

I went back into Warren's office, stepping over Warren's body, and then out into the semidarkness of the hall to the office next door, Lee Pierce's office. It occurred to me that maybe he hadn't noticed me earlier because he was dead, too, that maybe I'd stumbled onto a massacre of poets and professors in Frye Hall. I went in quietly and stopped just inside. Pierce was just getting up, but still writing on a piece of paper on his desk. He saw me out of the corner of his eye, continued writing for a few seconds more, and then turned. When he saw the gun in my hand, he raised his eyebrows, the way some people do when they're surprised or pretending to be.

"What's the matter with you?" he asked.

It was the first time I'd pointed my pistol at anybody in earnest, and I wondered what I was supposed to do next. He wasn't moving toward me, both of his hands were in plain sight, and he was a reasonably famous man, at least around here. I didn't know what I'd do, however, if he came toward me and wouldn't stop, so I was glad he stayed where he was.

"Ah," he went on, "there's a girl under that uniform. And quite a pretty one, too. The ladies room is in the basement, two flights down. You won't need your gun." He'd recovered his composure, if he'd ever lost it.

"Professor Warren's been killed," I told him, finding my voice. "Call 911. Tell them that."

He looked shocked enough then, and I liked that.

"Adam?" He took a step toward me and I moved the pistol up a degree or two. "I don't believe you. Where is he? In his office?"

"Stay here. Call 911." Calling 911 would bring the city, not the campus police. I intended to call my own headquarters on my portable as soon as I got back to Warren's office.

Someone in Warren's office screamed. I spun around and ran back there. Another body lay sprawled on the floor, not far from Warren's, this one a woman's. She was dressed in a yellow skirt, with a matching blouse and socks, and tennis shoes. She looked like a child dressed as a butterfly for the school play.

Lee Pierce had followed me. I shouted at him to do what I'd said and waited until he disappeared, then I ran to the woman, knelt, and without thinking about it, put my pistol down on the floor beside her head. I felt for a pulse and this time found one. I shouted, "Are you all right?" into her face as I'd been taught to do. Her eyelids began fluttering rapidly and then slowed and steadied. She stared around the room, at me, at my pistol, and finally at what she could see of Warren's body behind me. Her eyes opened very wide and came back to me.

"I'm a police officer," I told her. She nodded, then moved fingers with long nails painted a bright red to her neck, fumbled with a gold chain. "My pills, please," she said. I reached into her blouse and pulled out a locket with the head of a young girl carved on it in ivory. When I opened the catch, a tiny pill fell out. I knew what it was, because my mother has angina, too. I put it in her hand and she took it between nails like bloody chopsticks and poked it into her mouth.

A noise made me look up. Lee Pierce was standing at Professor Warren's feet, half-turned to us. I hadn't heard him come in. When he saw me looking at him, he gestured dramatically at the body and declaimed, "Oh, weep for Adam Warren, he is dead!" parodying a poem I'd had to read for Warren's class, by Keats or Shelley—one of those two. Then he added, presumably to me, not the dead man, "D'you know you've got hair like a bouquet of fire?"

I scrambled to my feet, then bent and picked up my pistol. I was doing really well.

"What would you be without your gun?" he asked, smiling into my eyes. But his eyes weren't smiling at all. It looked as if he were fighting hard not to cry. "Is Doris going to be all right?" he asked, turning away from my stare. He peered down at the woman on the floor with an expression of concern on his face. "Was she here when you found Adam's body?"

"Please go back to your office," I told him. It felt strange, speaking to a professor that way, even with the *please*. I asked him if he'd called 911, and he said he had.

"Who did that?" he asked, pointing to the mess I'd made in a corner of the room, as he started for the door. He saw the color come into my face before I could stop it and stared at me for a moment in what seemed to be real surprise. Then he laughed and said, "It looks like a clue, Officer."

"What's going on in here?" a voice asked from the door. Several people were trying to get into the room all at the same time, craning to see inside.

Feeling overwhelmed, I put my pistol back in its holster.

"Please," I said, raising my voice, trying to keep it steady, "everybody stay out. Let Professor Pierce through."

I moved aside to give him room. The woman on the floor started to scramble up, but I told her to stay where she was.

"Professor Warren!" she said, her voice loud and trembling. "He's not really dead, is he?" She was sitting up, staring at the body.

"Of course not," Lee Pierce said, stopping and turning back. "He's just resting, Doris," he intoned. "Resting between battles."

A tall pale man in a dark suit, standing in the door, said, "For Christ's sake, Lee, shut up and get off stage!"

Pierce's voice lost its control then as he whirled and flared, "Shove it up your ass, Art! I feel worse about this than you do. Adam Warren was my friend. I loved the man." He shoved his hands into the pockets of his jacket and leaned into the crowd at the door. They made room for him.

"He's going to be *all right,* isn't he, Miss—? He's going

to be *all right?*" the woman on the floor asked. Pierce had called her Doris.

"O'Neill," I said, crouching beside her again. "My name's Peggy O'Neill. No, he's not going to be all right. He's dead. I'm sorry." I took her hand. I should have been a nurse, not a cop.

"Just like in the song," she said, and settled her head back on my arm and stared up at the ceiling. "Peggy O'Neill! Isn't that nice? *Dead!* Adam Warren's dead! What next? What next?"

Three

"Next time," the homicide lieutenant said, "make the call yourself. That's why you were issued that portable on your belt. Tell them to send a squad to secure the entire building." He looked directly at me with blue eyes that had no particular expression in them at all. "That poet, what's his name, Pierce, just told them to send over an ambulance, that there'd been an accident. That held everything up."

I didn't say anything, just sat there and looked as if I were willing to learn, a useful technique when you're dealing with an unknown quantity that might turn out to be a zero. His name was Hansen. He was probably in his late thirties, about my height, and with blond hair turning white in places.

I was grateful to him for not dwelling on the mess I'd made in a corner of Professor Warren's office. One of the lab men had tried to give me a rough time about that. He apparently had no trouble with battered corpses and the smell of blood, but throw-up made him wrinkle his fat nose. Lieutenant Hansen had given him a look he seemed to understand, and he got back to work.

Now Hansen was telling me that I was supposed to go by the book. The trouble with the book is that it doesn't tell you what to do when there's blood all over the place, real people who might be murderers crowding you, and butterflies in tennis shoes fainting when you least expect it. The book doesn't smell of blood. I didn't think Hansen would be interested in these thoughts, however, so I kept them to myself.

We were sitting in the office of the English department's secretary at the end of the hall. The secretary, Doris Parker, wouldn't be needing it for a while. She'd been taken to the hospital for observation by one of the cops, protesting as she was led away that she was all right.

From where I sat I could see uniformed and plainclothesmen going in and out of Warren's office, halfway down the hall. The flashbulbs going off intermittently inside resembled heat lightning at dusk. Now and then, other people—faculty and students—would poke their heads out of office doors to check on what was going on and then just as quickly pull them back inside, like small forest creatures that feel safest in trees.

I told Hansen how I'd found the body. He listened patiently, occasionally made a note on the pad in front of him on Doris Parker's desk. But mostly he doodled: sailboats, canoes, cats. Quiet things. Or maybe just things that were easy to draw. His blue eyes were crinkled at the corners. Laugh wrinkles, my grandmother would have called them, but he wasn't laughing now.

Although the windows were open and a fan was blowing, the office was still hot, and I was tired and feeling depressed and I wanted to get out of there. We'd been interrupted once, to go out and feed the television cameras what passes in that medium for news, and that just depressed me all the more. A plainclothes detective came in to ask Hansen a question and then looked at me and asked, ''You the campus cop who puked?'' Hansen told him to go away and the man did before I could add something of my own that would have made me feel dumber.

Hansen turned back to me. He wanted to know times: when the volume on the frat boys' stereos had gone down, when I'd entered Frye Hall, when I'd gotten to the top of the stairs. I couldn't be very precise about any of that. The only exact time Hansen had was when the dispatcher, Ron, had logged in Warren's call, at 4:16.

I said, in a surly voice: ''I remembered to look at my watch after I'd discovered the body, thrown up, drawn my pistol. Those things don't take much time, they probably took me less than a minute. It was four-twenty-seven.''

Hansen looked up from his doodling. ''I'm glad you have your priorities straight,'' he said. His blue eyes seemed to find something funny about me. "Then Warren was killed," he went on, "sometime between four-sixteen and, say, four-twenty-five, which is about when you started up the stairs to the second floor. You think he'd been dead awhile before you found him?"

I said I didn't feel any violence in that room when I came into it, that it was too still in there for the murder to have just taken place.

Hansen gave me an odd grin that I understood perfectly. I felt myself turn red.

"Really?" he said. "You're claiming psychic powers? You're a cop for the 'New Age'?"

I told him no, I didn't have psychic powers and didn't believe in them either. I didn't know what I'd meant by what I'd said. I was just tired.

He wasn't reassured. "No premonitions," he demanded, "no lurid visions, no claim to second sight?"

"No," I said, and found myself grinning in spite of how I was feeling.

"Thank God for that! Then I assume you just agree with Shakespeare, who wrote something about murder shrieking out. Well, I suppose even that shriek dies down after a while, and that's the quiet you noticed."

I said I thought Warren could have been killed anytime after he made the phone call to the campus police.

"You're wrong," he replied. "There must have been a lot of noise. The noise of the hammer striking and of Warren falling, a computer and keyboard hitting the floor in the room next to his. And all the other noises that killers make killing and victims make dying. Somebody should have heard some of that, but apparently no one did. Lee Pierce, in the next office, didn't hear anything, he says. Professor Fletcher, whose office is just across the hall and a few doors down, didn't hear anything either. So either one of them is lying— or both of them, for that matter—or else Professor Warren was killed while the boys across the street were still playing their music at its loudest, before you made them turn it down. Rock and roll claims another life."

He asked me to tell him again what Lee Pierce was doing when I passed him on my way to Warren's office and what he was doing when I went back in there. The first time, I told him, he'd been sitting at his desk.

"And the second time," Hansen said, "he was just getting up from his desk?"

"Still writing as he did, yes."

I told Hansen I'd seen only one person in the hall that I might be able to recognize again, the woman who'd reached the bottom of the stairs as I started up. My eyes were just getting used to the darkness, but I thought she was about my age, in her late twenties perhaps. Smaller than I, with dark straight hair cut short. She'd been wearing glasses, too, and slacks or jeans and a T-shirt, but if she was a student, she was an older one.

"Any writing on it? Messages?"

"On what?"

"The T-shirt."

"No."

"That's too bad," Hansen said, then asked, "You want to know what Lee Pierce was writing while he was standing there at his desk?"

"Not, I suppose, a confession."

"No. A note for a poem. At least, that's what I think it is. Listen." He flipped back a few pages in his notebook. " 'To find the flame again, somewhere in the alphabet.' " He looked up suddenly. "You think that's a poem?"

I stared at him for a second and then laughed, in spite of how tired I was, at his attempt to play dumb. And then he laughed, too, the smile wrinkles working at the corners of his eyes.

"Well," he said, suddenly all business again, "let's see what we've got. Distinguished professor murdered, skull crushed. Computer found on floor in nearby computer room, upside down. Murder weapon a hammer belonging to English department. Usually kept in that cabinet back there." He aimed a thumb over his shoulder at a white metal cabinet standing next to the window behind him. "What does this suggest to you?"

He seemed to really want to know.

"It looks as if somebody was trying to steal one of the

English department's computers," I said. "But maybe that's just how it was meant to look."

Hansen nodded. "But you have been bothered by a rash of computer thefts this year, haven't you?"

"We've lost over a hundred thousand dollars' worth of computers," I replied, "more than twice as much as last year. Ripping off computers has replaced stealing ten-speed bikes. In some ways they're easier to take than bikes because the people who use them don't own them, so they're not always very careful about locking them up."

Hansen wanted to know if we had any idea who was behind the thefts. I told him we suspected that while some of them might have been the work of amateurs who wanted to acquire some advanced technology to try to improve their grades, a professional ring was probably involved, too.

There wasn't any pattern to the way offices were entered. In some cases the thief or thieves had come through open windows. In others they'd smashed locks. And in quite a number of cases they'd simply walked in, in broad daylight, taken the computers, and walked away with them. One theory was that students were recruited to steal computers to finance a drug habit, a trip to Florida, an education, or all three.

Hansen listened and said, "Then nothing about Warren's death couldn't square with the theory that it was a computer thief. Warren caught one in the act and got killed for his trouble."

I shrugged. Apparently, though, it wasn't a convincing shrug.

"What don't you like about it?" he asked me. When I hesitated, he added, "This is your territory, not mine. What's bothering you?"

"If it was a thief," I replied, wanting to rise to the occasion, "it was an unusually dumb one. When you steal a computer in broad daylight, you do it during breaks between classes, when there's lots of people milling around. A serious thief would have waited until summer school starts, next week."

"Unless he was strapped for cash," Hansen suggested.

"Or she," I said, sticking up for my own sex. Then I remembered something else I'd been wondering about. "Do you know why Warren's office had a door leading into the computer room?"

"What's strange about that?"

"It just seems odd to me. How come his dark and dusty office opens into a bright new room full of computers and printers?"

"I'll see if I can find out," Hansen said, and searched around on Doris Parker's desk until he found a list of telephone numbers. He dialed one of them and asked whoever answered my question and then waited, listening. His eyes rolled up at the ceiling, then down at me. He winked. I decided I liked him.

He finally thanked the speaker and hung up, turned to me, and said, "That was Arthur Fletcher, the guy you say exchanged angry words with Lee Pierce in Warren's office. He's assistant chairman. According to him, the English department only stepped into the computer age last fall, when it purchased five of the things. Doris Parker uses one, and the others are used for word processing by the faculty and graduate students. They needed a computer room, so the room next to Warren's office was requisitioned. Professors can tolerate more dust than computers, apparently, so the room had to be completely remodeled. Warren was one of the first faculty members to learn how to word-process, after he returned from Washington. He was supposed to be working on a book and was often in the computer room."

"But how come his office has a door leading into it?" I asked.

"No mystery about that, if you believe Fletcher. The computer room used to be a classroom and a long time ago a professor could step straight from his office into his classroom without having to risk being buffeted by unwashed students in the halls."

"So Warren could have gone in there from his office," I said, "and surprised the thief. But I don't see why a thief would kill him, even so. It's just not worth it. Why not just drop the computer and run? Warren wouldn't have gone chasing after anybody."

"You don't think so? I've seen him on television a few times; he didn't look old and decrepit to me. But the thief might have been someone Warren recognized, a student or former student.''

''Maybe,'' I said, ''but how'd he—or she—get hold of the hammer, then get behind Warren to use it on him?''

''The hammer was already in Warren's office. Before Doris Parker was hauled off to the hospital, she identified it for us, said Warren had borrowed it from the file cabinet sometime last week to hang a picture. He was redoing his office, she said. Then he forgot to return it. Another reason for putting tools back when you're through with them.''

''And the other question?''

''I don't know the answer to that one,'' he said, shrugging, ''but we have to leave something for the murderer to tell us, don't we? Otherwise we might leave him speechless. Maybe Warren got careless, maybe he didn't believe that violence exists anywhere but in the books he loved so much, the classics, and he turned his back on the thief after he'd caught him—or her,'' he added with a little seated courtly bow. ''That's another reason, by the way, why I'm so eager to talk to this young woman you saw on the stairs. I'm hoping somebody in the building can tell us who she is, if she doesn't come forth on her own.''

''Where'd you find the hammer?'' I asked. I hadn't seen one on the floor anywhere near the body.

''In the wastebasket, sunk under a mass of bloodstained paper.''

I grinned. At least I'd had the presence of mind not to throw up in the wastebasket.

Hansen returned my grin, as if he knew what mine was for, then stood up and stretched. I could hear a bone creak somewhere. ''Anyway,'' he went on, ''we've got a murder weapon and suspects and that's a help. What's a murder without a weapon and a few suspects? For starters, the entire faculty and staff of the English department, your mystery woman, all the students, and somewhere out there a computer thief who may have felt strongly about anonymity. Oh,'' he added, ''and you, of course.''

''Me?''

''Sure. You had opportunity, didn't you? Motive, maybe. Didn't you say you'd taken a course from him once?

What grade did he give you? We only have your word for it that he was dead when you came into his office.''

"And then I threw up to confuse you," I said, playing along to reward him for his effort. "Anyway, I got a B. He's a tough grader—was, I mean."

"Well, we'll see. Was he married? Divorced? Living with somebody? Straight or gay? We'll find out."

He tried to put his arm around my waist, the way some men will do. I stepped away, suppressing the urge to try a low elbow strike into his guts. He didn't seem to notice. "You're new at this, aren't you, Officer O'Neill? We're not dealing with the ordinary, run-of-the-mill campus flasher today. And not with the ordinary campus thief, either, paying his way through law or medical school on the proceeds of high-tech theft. No, not your ordinary campus thief, not anymore." As he spoke his voice became grimmer and grimmer.

We walked out of Doris Parker's office together. "You were lucky," he said. "Lucky you didn't arrive when the killer was still there. It takes a lot to hit a person in the head with a hammer once. To go on doing it—that takes something more, and whoever can do that is capable of anything. Remember that, will you, in case you bump into somebody in the dark who's got something expensive in his hands that doesn't belong to him."

"We need a new pronoun," I said.

"I know," he replied, without missing a beat. "For him and her, when you don't know which it is." For some reason, I wasn't surprised that he knew what I'd meant.

We passed Adam Warren's office. The door was half-open. There was a chalk outline on the floor where Warren's body had been, but the body wasn't there anymore. I caught a glimpse of a plainclothesman sitting at Warren's desk. He looked up when Lieutenant Hansen leaned in to tell him he'd be back shortly.

We went down the stairs and out into the heat and brightness of the summer evening in silence. I didn't know why Hansen was following me, but I was glad to be with him a little longer. He stood there next to me on the steps, gazing out. Then he turned and gave me a sudden smile, a beautiful smile, and said good evening. He reached out—to give my arm a squeeze I think—but changed his mind and walked back into the building. I watched him go, wondering how a homicide cop could keep such a lovely smile.

Four

When I got back to headquarters, Ron looked up from the paperback he was reading and said, "Next time, Peggy, use your portable. I thought it was a crank caller at first. He had the voice of—sorry!"

I'd had more than I could take and it showed then. It was almost seven, I was hot and sweating, and my throat was still raw from throwing up. I'd performed badly under stress, so I went on performing badly under stress for a few seconds longer and then ran up the stairs, taking them two at a time, leaving Ron staring after me.

I cried for a while, on the old couch we'd inherited from the men's lounge when they got their new one. I let the images tumble through my head: Professor Warren's body sprawled there on his office floor as if asleep in his own blood, and then alive at his desk, looking up as I came in to ask him something; in his classroom making a dry joke and the time he woke up a student who'd fallen asleep with a deep sudden silence followed by a stare of ice; Doris Parker on the floor with Lee Pierce standing over us, reciting a parody of a poem at the body of a man he said was his friend. And Hansen, Lieutenant Hansen, with his hooded eyes watching me with something that might have been sympathy and might have been amusement, but was probably both, as his hand unconsciously doodled something quiet in his notebook.

Paula Henderson, another of the University's female cops, came in then, heading for her locker. When she saw me, she changed directions and came over and put one of her long brown arms around me. After a while I thanked her, grateful for her arm and her silence, and went to the bathroom, something I'd been wanting to do for a long time. I peed and washed the sweat and tears off my face, ran a comb through my hair, put on my hat, and went back downstairs. In the mirror on the landing I gave myself a long stare, but there was no expression on my pale face at all and my hair looked funny under that stupid hat.

Sergeant Hiller called to me as I passed his office. He had a kid who looked about thirteen in with him, slumped in a metal chair against a wall.

"Where're you off to?" Hiller asked.

"Back to my beat," I told him. "I didn't really get started."

"Ah, not tonight, Peggy. Stay here with me for a while—learn something about real police work. Jesse said he'd finish your patrol. Now look at what I got here! A master criminal, nabbed taking reflectors off bikes in front of the library. The kid's got more reflectors than spokes on his bike. A tough case, Peggy. I'm going to need all the help I can get with it."

The boy slumped further down in his chair, perhaps under the weight of Hiller's banter. I looked at him with distaste. Bike reflectors today, I thought gloomily, and computers or whatever's the hot seller—robots? personal helicopters?—tomorrow. And murder, if anybody gets in his way.

"Thanks anyway," I told Hiller. I gave him an appreciative smile and left his office.

"So be a hero," he called after me.

The night was quiet, the Old Campus nearly deserted, and most of the buildings were dark and empty. I strolled my beat in the light, hot night, wandered randomly through buildings. It wasn't pleasant anymore.

I ended my patrol where it had begun that night, at Frye Hall. I planned it that way.

Across the street, the fraternity houses were lit up and crowded with people inside and out. The street looked like the midway at the state fair. The boys had been joined by their opposite numbers from the sorority houses, and the big speakers in the windows were blaring out rock music as loudly as the expensive fruits of Japanese technology could pump it. I was glad I was going off duty. Soon there'd be reports coming in of fights and drunkenness and kids falling out windows, and later, sorority girls would be coming into police headquarters to find out if they'd been raped, others to describe how they had been.

I let myself into Frye with my passkey and retraced my earlier route up to the second floor. The halls shone softly in the dim light under a fresh coat of wax, the classrooms were full of chairs newly arranged in attentive rows. The silence was much louder than the muted noise of the music outside. Frye Hall was an old building, solidly built. Nothing creaked in it.

I glanced at Lee Pierce's door, paused at Warren's a moment, moved quickly on.

On the other side of the hall and a little way down, light shone through the frosted glass in a door. I looked at it as I passed, thinking it was moonlight. The plate next to the door said the office belonged to Arthur Fletcher. I stopped when I saw something move in there, a shadow crossing the light. It could have been anything, nothing. I started to reach for my portable, to call the dispatcher—I'm capable of learning—when a sudden noise behind me made me catch my breath and spin around.

It was Fletcher. I took a step back.

"I didn't mean to startle you," he said. "I didn't see you until I was almost on top of you. It's these damned dark halls."

He was a very quiet walker, if he hadn't meant to startle me. He'd come down the stairs behind him, which led to the third floor.

"I think there's somebody in your office," I told him, my voice shaky.

He looked at his door, then back at me. "I stayed to work late," he explained, ignoring what I'd just said. "Grading final exams. Adam's death is going to put extra work on all of us, I'm afraid, with summer school starting soon."

His hair and eyebrows were almost black and his complexion was white and seemed to shine in the dim hall. When I'd seen him that afternoon in the doorway of Warren's office, he'd been wearing a dark suit. He was wearing the same trousers now, but he'd removed the tie and jacket. His shirt was patched with sweat from the heat and humidity in the building.

"I guess you don't believe in ghosts," I said.

"Apparently you don't either," he answered. "This afternoon you looked as if you could use a night off."

"That's why I came back," I said, and stayed there waiting for him to open his door.

"It's all right, Officer," he said, realizing what I was doing. "I'm just returning from the men's room. There's no surprise waiting for me in my office."

He stood there until I moved on. I gave his door another look, then said good night and started up the stairs he'd come down. When I looked back, he'd disappeared into his office and the door was closing.

I waited for the noises that killers make killing and victims make dying, heard nothing, and continued on up to the third floor, which was even hotter than the second, and took a turn around the hall up there.

When I'd proven whatever it was I needed to prove to myself, I went back downstairs. The light was still on in Fletcher's office—a desk lamp, not the overhead light—and I could hear soft voices, Fletcher's and a woman's, coming from inside. I shook off the temptation to knock. Instead I went on downstairs, let myself out a side door, and walked back to headquarters through the heat and noise of College Avenue.

"Lots of excitement today," the night dispatcher greeted me, his voice neutral, his eyes curious.

I agreed with him.

"Quiet now, though," he said. He was just settling in for the night with a thermos of coffee and a paperback mystery. "I don't guess it'll stay that way much longer."

"No," I said, "I suppose not."

I had my bike. I pedaled back up College Avenue, toward home. I had to swerve suddenly to avoid a fraternity boy who jumped out at me from the sidewalk, waving a spilling can of beer.

Five

I didn't sleep very well. I got up early, put coffee on, and while it was brewing checked my answering machine for messages. I usually do that when I first get home from work, but last night hadn't been usual. I pressed "Messages," and after the machine cleared its throat, my aunt Tess's voice flared at me.

"You're never home," she complained. She'd learned to talk to an answering machine from being forced to talk to mine. She was self-conscious about it at first, but she adapts quickly and unfortunately it no longer cramps her style. "Probably shacked up with some man. Well, that's none of my business and after you've spent four years in the navy I don't suppose there's much left over for Mr. Right anyway—assuming you'd recognize him when he came along, which I doubt." She took a breath after that salvo, but not a long, deep one because she always thinks she's going to run out of tape. "Well, if you ever do get home and remember to check your messages, call me. It's about your father's car. I've found a buyer for it. The blind mortician—you met him years and years ago, before he went blind." There was a click as she rang off. She never says good-bye.

I didn't recall ever having met a mortician, blind or otherwise, but I assumed I had if Aunt Tess said so. The only other message was from Al, the man I'd be shacked up with if I were shacked up with anybody, which I'm not—and if people other than Aunt Tess still used that term, which they don't. He asked me if I was free for lunch and, if so, to be at Eleanor's by the Lake at noon. I said okay, forgetting, not for the first time, that the conversation wasn't live. Al's a veterinarian, with an office near the lake. He didn't say anything about me and Professor Warren's murder, which probably meant he hadn't heard about it. That didn't surprise me at all.

I was up early enough to watch the morning news, so I poured myself some coffee and turned on the TV. After a while they ran an interview with Lieutenant Hansen filmed earlier that morning and the much shorter one they'd made with me the afternoon before. Hansen said he had no suspects yet and no idea why Professor Warren had been murdered. He mentioned the computer thefts on campus as a lead they were pursuing, although he was confident that the campus police had done an excellent job with the resources at their command. I listened intently there, trying to tell from his tone how enthusiastic he was over the notion that a computer thief was responsible for the murder, but I couldn't tell. There were several people he wanted to interview, he went on, and he hoped people with any information that could be of help would come forth voluntarily. His eyelids were like hoods against the glare of the camera lights and the wrinkles at the corners of his eyes were emphasized, so that he looked like a benevolent lizard. His voice stayed neutral, dry, practiced at giving the vultures enough to still their hunger at least temporarily, without losing too much of his own flesh.

The camera flipped back in time to the afternoon before, and to me.

I tried to find meaning in the sight of the Peggy O'Neill I was then, fresh from discovering a violently murdered man, but couldn't. I just looked surly, the way people do when they know other people are going to profit from their misery and there's nothing they can do about it. My hat was on crooked, too, and my new haircut looked like shit. Comic cop. I hoped Dennis, my hairdresser, hadn't seen this.

"How long have you been on the campus police?" the interviewer, a woman, asked me, and stuck her mike into my face. She was trying to look intrepid, as if she'd gone through hell to find me and bring this interview to her viewers.

"Almost four months." My voice sounded raw because that's how it had felt.

"Do you plan to continue after this?"

"Continue what, after what?" I enjoyed watching myself trying to be as helpful as possible, but slow.

"Continue being a campus policewoman—is that what you call yourselves?—after making this shocking discovery and almost falling victim to the killer yourself?"

"Yes."

"Could you tell our viewers, in your own words, what you did when you discovered the corpse of Professor Adam Warren?"

"I puked," I told her viewers.

The camera switched quickly back to her, and in that way missed the look Lieutenant Hansen, lurking at my side, had given me.

Lee Pierce appeared on the television screen then, introduced as the internationally acclaimed American poet, as if there were just the one, and he expressed his shock and horror at seeing the body of his old friend and colleague lying there in a pool of blood. He looked as if he'd been crying, but tears became him. The camera thought so, too, and feasted on his face.

Next appeared the president of the University and the dean of the College of Arts. The president has long and remarkably white teeth and, coincidentally, perhaps, his name is Wolf. Some people still think he's Little Red Riding Hood's grandmother, but their number is dwindling.

He announced that University flags would fly at half-mast for thirty days to honor the memory of Adam Warren, the distinguished professor whose tragic death cut short a brilliant career in midstride. He went on to remind us that for several years, Adam Warren had played an important role in strengthening the humanities nationally, as head of the President's Commission on the Arts and Humanities, and that the University had rewarded him for his scholarship, teaching, and service by making him a University Scholar, an honor reserved for only twelve members of the faculty at any one time.

I went to my refrigerator and got out milk. More suspects, I thought: every member of the faculty with a shot at a vacancy in the Scholars' ranks.

The president, however, had another theory. He concluded his remarks by lamenting the fact that a man of Professor Warren's achievements had been cut down by a petty thief. He seemed to think either that thieves should limit their killings to less distinguished fish, or else men as distinguished as Professor Warren should be killed by grander thieves. In any case, he left no doubt that the police, working hand in hand with the campus police, would find the culprit shortly and bring him—or her, he added, for sometimes he was sensitive to the demands of Affirmative Action—to justice.

Maybe so, I thought, but it would help if he'd give us back the four cops we'd lost in the last budget cut.

The dean of the College of Arts appeared next, a large man with a gloomy crack in his face that serves as a mouth. As he spoke I poured milk over Shredded Wheat and cut into the resultant mess with the side of my spoon. My phone rang.

"What a *jerk!*" the voice at the other end said, and my heart, not soaring that morning anyway, sank further. It was George, the Incomprehensible Mistake.

"Hi, George," I said.

"And a woman, too! You'd think a woman would have some understanding, *empathy.* But you really took care of her: 'I puked.' That shut her up!" I realized that George was talking about the television interviewer. "You were just great," he went on, into the silence. "I don't know how you could handle it like that, after the shock of finding that body. Jesus!"

I chewed cereal. It's hard to talk with your mouth full of Shredded Wheat.

"Let's have breakfast. Lunch. Name it."

"None of the above," I named.

"Hey, come on, Peggy," he said, hurt. "I want another chance."

George got his chance while I was in rookie school, when I let him move in with me after we'd been going together for several months. I'm still not sure how it happened—maybe because rookie school was such a bruising experience and I needed all the comfort I could get, I wasn't thinking straight. Each time he moved something of his into my apartment, a voice inside me told him to take it back where it came from, but I didn't say anything to him until, one day, George was there with everything he owned. Incomprehensible.

He was doing postdoctoral work in learning disabilities in children—a case, I've since thought, of mutual attraction. The affair lasted until I graduated and interviewed for a job on the campus police force. George had never approved of my going into police work anyway. What's the point, he'd wanted to know, when he was going to get a fat plum of a position at a top-ranked university someplace soon and then my training would be wasted? Besides, he'd added, I didn't look good in blue.

I look very good in blue. That's one reason why I chose the navy over any of the other services after I got out of high school—although I got fooled on that one when the navy changed to black while I was still in boot camp. Luckily, I look good in black, too.

Then George crept at me from the psychological point of view at which, given his education, he was adept. I'd grown up in a home dominated by an abusive and, when he was in the mood for it, good-natured alcoholic father, he reminded me. My mother whined, wrung her hands, prayed a lot, and hoped the neighbors didn't know anything. The neighbors, watching the destruction from behind blinds, drapes, trees, bushes—whatever was handy—knew everything. Not having known any real structure while growing up, George droned on, I'd been naturally, if neurotically, drawn to the structure, the organization, the security guaranteed in advance by the military. So first I'd joined the navy and now I wanted to join the campus police. I liked to say *sir*, and to please people.

Some of George's words were longer than those, and some of his sentences more complex, but reduced to plain English it was all just baby talk. There are so many ways of saying *sir*, so many kinds of structure, and the varieties of uniform are endless.

I'd attended some of the parties George was invited to by members of his department. The psychology faculty thought highly of him, and the wives gave preliminary approval of me even though I didn't drink or play bridge. They thought

I was well mannered, because they couldn't read my ill-mannered mind.

My relationship with George fell quickly down around my ankles and puddled there, which made it difficult to walk. The end came the day I arrived home in my new cop's uniform and George asked me what I called the thing I had on my head.

"A hat," I said. "And someday I might refer to it as an 'eight-pointer,' to distinguish it from the thing I'm going to wear when it's cold, which I'm going to call 'bunny ears.' "

"Jargon,' he said. "The metalanguage of people who need to belong to an exclusive group. That's so sad."

"Metalanguage? You mean mumbo jumbo?"

"I mean metalanguage," he said.

"George," I told him then, "I want you to pack your things and move out. I'll even help, if you like."

Something in my tone of voice, perhaps, led him to suspect that our relationship was in trouble, and nothing in the scene that followed did anything to relieve him of his concern. He took it badly. He was still taking it badly.

"You had your chance to become a campus cop's husband," I said into the phone, trying to make it light, "and you blew it. You mean you've changed your mind?"

"C'mon, Peggy," he wheedled. "I've just got a job offer, at Brown. They've probably got a campus police department there. See? I'm changing. If you want to work for a while, go ahead. We were good together, honey. Good in bed, too, really good in bed!" He laughed into the silence that followed that.

George's lovemaking often made me think of that ad they used to post in buses to remind young men to register for the draft: quick, easy, and the law.

"Water under the bridge, George. Sorry. I never go back."

There was another silence that got longer, which was one of the tactics he used to win arguments, or at least keep them going until he could find a way to win them. I was supposed to fill the silence with words that he could sit back and pick apart, the way you pick apart flowers.

I kept the phone loosely at my ear and watched the television news, unfolding without sound on the kitchen counter.

A child's body lay huddled on a street in some ruined foreign city. The leaders of three countries appeared on the screen one after the other and expressed mute concern, perhaps over the child's grades.

George cleared his throat after a time and said, quietly and steadily, as if closing a coffin, "I hope you don't regret this, Peggy," and hung up.

I went over and turned off the television, went to the bathroom, and took a shower. For some reason, I started humming Bob Dylan's "Don't Think Twice, It's All Right." It's about a guy who's traveling on because some girl treated him badly—a sequel of sorts to a song my father liked a lot, about a ballerina who chose fame instead of the poor loser crooning the song.

Boys can get very petulant at times.

Six

If the city police made any progress in the case, they didn't share it with the media. After a spate of articles on crime on campus, a few letters to the editor from concerned parents, the story of Adam Warren's murder began to drift further and further back into the newspapers and later and later into the television newscasts until, by the following Wednesday, it wasn't there at all. Professor Warren had been a distinguished man in his field and even, for a time, a national figure, but that was a while ago and even then he didn't move or shake things.

My colleagues on the campus police force were pretty evenly divided on who had done it. Some thought it was a computer thief who'd panicked, found the hammer lying there, and killed Warren; others thought the killer was someone in the English department or at least in one of the departments housed in Frye Hall with a grudge against Warren. Ordinary campus cops like me didn't get much from our superiors either. Maybe because they weren't getting anything from the city police.

Wednesday morning was unusually hot for June. I spent it on the shore of Lake Eleanor, a couple of blocks from where I live. It was crowded and noisy with people sucking all the summer they could get into themselves, storing it the way the rhubarb and the asparagus do to help them survive the long, deep winter months their conscious minds have already forgotten. It was a windless day, great for swimming in the still-cold water, but the sailboats and wind surfers weren't going anywhere. Frisbees floated on thermals of rock and roll that blasted from colorful boxes stuck in the sand, and lovers sizzled in oil like french fries.

My friend Al was trying to capture some of this with his watercolors. Al's a veterinarian and he paints like one. We'd been lovers since a week or so after George moved out in February. I was just lying in the shade, staring up into the darkness of a tree outlined against the brightness of the sky. Al doesn't like to talk much when he's trying to paint, so I had time to think.

I was thinking about Professor Warren.

I'd taken a course from him the first semester of my senior year, a literature course, to satisfy a requirement for graduation. I like to read, which was a good thing.

Warren wasn't the best teacher I'd ever had, but he knew his subject and could usually explain it in ways that made clear to us what it was and why it might be important. He enjoyed the sound of his voice and the way he put words together, and so did I.

He was a few minutes late coming to class one day. The woman sitting next to me turned to me and said she'd bet me five dollars he wouldn't show up at all.

I asked her why.

Because, she told me, she'd seen him in his office just before the bell rang with a woman in his arms. "I mean," she elaborated, "I just started to walk in on them, like, to deliver this paper." She pointed to the paper on the desk in front of her. It was two days late. "I mean, the door wasn't shut, I just, like, nudged it open and there they were!" She was just coming down from a deep summer tan. She used the word *like* as a kind of spring that propelled her from one part of a simple idea to another. "Guess who the girl was!"

"I don't know. His wife, maybe?"

"Oh, right! I mean, guys kiss their wives like that, like . . ."

She broke off as Professor Warren walked into the room, sat down at his desk and pulled a paper clip off his little stack of note cards. He seemed a bit rattled, but maybe it was just my imagination. The woman sitting next to me leaned over and whispered in my ear, "It was his teaching assistant!"

For about five seconds, as Warren was starting his lecture,

I looked at him with something other than professional student interest. The thought of faculty members having affairs with their students had always seemed sort of disgusting to me. It doesn't seem fair, somehow—like fishing at a trout farm.

He'd introduced his TA to us the first day of class—she was going to read and grade his examinations, he'd told us, and if we had any complaints or problems, we were supposed to discuss them with her before coming to him—but I hadn't seen her since. I couldn't for the life of me remember her name; I just remembered that she was tall and strikingly beautiful, with hair that fell to her waist and a perfectly oval face. Professor Warren was around fifty at that time, but he seemed in good shape, especially for a man who smoked as much as he did. He brought the smell of cigarettes into class with him, and sometimes a little smoke too, as if he'd stubbed out his cigarette just outside the door.

Al looked up from his watercoloring. "What're you thinking about?"

"Oh, you want to talk now, do you?"

"Only because some beach bully came running by and kicked sand on my lakescape," he replied. "It was your fault. He saw you staring intently at his outsized, oily biceps, and he wanted to let you know that he thinks you're super, too."

"I wasn't staring at anything, at least not at anything that exists anymore. I was thinking about Professor Warren. The police don't seem to be getting anywhere with finding out who killed him. I'm thinking of giving them a hand."

"That's good," Al replied. "They'll be grateful." He started packing away his watercoloring stuff in a wicker basket. "Why?"

"Because I think I've got a lead of sorts," I told him. "And because with you away on vacation I'm going to need something to keep busy." And because I'd started waking up at night, scared by dreams of a white-haired corpse lying in blood—sometimes in Adam Warren's office and sometimes on my bedroom floor. I didn't tell Al that, though. He was leaving later that afternoon for a two-week vacation in Arizona, where his kids live with their mother, and he didn't need my problems to worry about.

"I thought it was just a thief," he said, "a student supporting a drug habit or something. He'll be lying low for a long time. You'll have a computer-thief–free campus. You think you know who done it?"

"No, I just want to try to do something on my own, see if something I know that the city cops might not is important. I kind of botched it when I discovered the body," I added.

"No risks, though, right?"

"No risks," I repeated.

"I hope not. In my capacity as a veterinarian, I know that curiosity does kill cats. Happens all the time."

"I'll be careful," I said.

"Fine. In the meantime, how about lunch? Give the murderer a few more good hours before you pick up the scent. My plane doesn't leave until four, so we've got plenty of time."

Not plenty of time, because I had to leave at 2:30 if I wanted to bike to work, but enough if we had lunch at my place instead of a restaurant. We strolled up the hill from the lake to my apartment, holding hands, and I did get to work on time, but just barely.

Seven

I waited until after the lunch hour the next day and then biked to Frye Hall and went up to the English department office. Professor Warren's name was still on the wall next to his door, but at least his office hours had been removed.

The only thing I had to start with was a student's story that she'd seen Warren kissing his TA in his office over a year and a half ago. That wasn't much, and maybe the police already knew all there was to know about Warren's private life. Well, I thought, if they did, I'd find out soon enough.

Doris Parker looked up from her typewriter, her fingers still flying over the keys, her receptionist's face in place. Then she recognized me, gave me a smile that changed almost immediately to concern, and her typing speed slowed. Her eyes glittered in their dark rings like mica, but not with any emotion I recognized.

"Hello,' I said. "You look like you've recovered."

"Why, thank you!" she answered. "Oh yes, I'm just fine now. I shouldn't have fainted like that and I'm very sorry I did. It was just such a shock, seeing Professor Warren that way, so unexpectedly. Happily, my pills were handy. Not that I needed them, of course. I didn't faint because of my angina! But it's always best to be on the safe side. I always keep them there in my locket. You're a very resourceful young lady."

Her chattering was a kind of music that seemed to mean nothing more than itself.

Doris Parker was around forty-five, and she'd probably been very nice looking once, before disappointment began to nibble away at her. Her wide mouth had a life of its own, full of resentment when its owner wasn't forcing it into a smile. She was dressed in shades of pastel green—blouse, skirt, barrettes in her hair. Even her watchband was green.

I told her how sorry I was that the department had lost Professor Warren. He was a brilliant man, I said, and a good teacher.

"How do you know that, Officer?" she asked.

I explained that I'd once taken a course from him and enjoyed it.

"That's very kind of you to say. Yes, he's going to be missed. He was a professor of the *old* school, a gentleman." She smiled, seemed pleased with her words, as if she'd written them out and then memorized them. "But," she went on, "we have to be strong. There's no sense dwelling on our sorrow. Wipe out and pass on! I learned that as a child. Wipe out and pass on! I thought frequently of those words when my Marilyn went away. I read about you in the student newspaper," she said, suddenly changing the subject, "when you were first hired. I was one of those who didn't think women should be police officers, even on a university campus where so little happens. Now I think so even more strongly."

"Marilyn?" I asked, jabbing a name into her torrent of words in hopes of stopping the flow. It hadn't made news when I was hired, so Doris must have been thinking of Ginny, who came first, or even Paula Henderson, our first black cop.

"This is Marilyn," Doris said. She picked up a portrait in a white plastic frame on her desk and smiled at it before handing it over the desk to me. "Isn't she beautiful?"

The photo had faded some in the sunlight that fell through Doris's windows. It was one of those double portraits where the same pose taken from two angles stares off in different directions, as if the one were dreaming the other, a happy dream. I really think you have to be wall-eyed to appreciate them. Marilyn looked a lot the way her mother must have looked at that age, at sixteen or seventeen—at least in a faded photograph she did.

"She was taken from me at Christmas," Doris said, reaching up for it. Her eyes, still flickering with mica, were studying my face, as if looking for appropriate signs, but I didn't know what signs to make.

"I'm sorry," I tried. From the way she spoke, I couldn't tell whether her daughter had died, been committed, sent to prison, or removed from her mother's custody for her own good. I waited for an explanation, but didn't get one.

She replaced the portrait on her desk, dropped her hands into her lap, looked up at me, and asked, "How may I help you?"

I asked her for the name of Professor Warren's TA two years before, in the fall quarter.

"Why?" she asked. The smile that wanted to please was still on her face, but only through neglect, and her eyes had become wary.

I told her I was helping the city police with their investigation and we were looking into all the dead man's recent associations. I was making inquiries about some of the people who had worked for him over the years.

"You're here on official police business?" she asked.

"Why don't you call Lieutenant Hansen," I told her, "the man who was here from homicide. Perhaps that would save us both some time. I don't have his number, but homicide's in the phone book. I was on my way to work and thought I'd just stop in and ask, rather than make an extra trip."

"I thought," she said, her eyes not leaving mine, "the police were satisfied that Adam Warren was killed by a thief—trying to steal one of our computers."

I told her that that was the most likely answer, but we were obligated to pursue all possible lines of inquiry.

She thought about it, her hands in her lap, the fingers of her right hand twisting a ring that wasn't there on her left hand.

"I suppose it's all right," she said, without conviction. She got up and went to a file cabinet. Her socks were green, too, I noticed, but her tennis shoes were the same ones she'd been wearing in Warren's office. Doris Parker was sensible, about some things at least. She lifted out a folder and brought it back to her desk and thumbed through it. She reached for a pen and notepad and wrote down a name, then handed it to me.

The teaching assistant's name was Susan Carpenter. I remembered it as soon as I saw it.

"Do you have her address?" I asked.

"No. She left no forwarding address."

I thanked her and turned away and then remembered something else and kept turning until I was facing her again. She hadn't expected that and so I received in the face what had been aimed at my back: a sneer, and eyes flickering with malice.

It took me a moment to recover from my surprise. By then the expression was gone, banished so smoothly and swiftly that I almost thought it had been my imagination. "I remembered something else I wanted to ask you," I said.

"Yes?" She gave me the smile I'd gotten when I first came into her office, her receptionist's smile.

"Would you tell me why you happened to come into Professor Warren's office when you did that afternoon?"

"Lieutenant Hansen has already asked me that question," she replied. "Didn't he tell you?"

"No," I said.

"I went there to get the hammer Adam—Professor Warren had failed to return to my file cabinet," she said. "I had written him two notes, requesting that he return it, but to no avail." She gave me a triumphant smile, as if to say Adam Warren had been taught a lesson he'd never forget, and swiveled back to her typewriter.

Eight

As I started down the hall I saw Arthur Fletcher. He was standing at his office door about to go in, looking at me curiously as if he'd seen me somewhere before. It had been almost a week—six days, to be exact—since he'd scared me in Frye Hall the night Professor Warren had been murdered. On an impulse I stopped and asked him if I could talk to him.

"You're the young lady who discovered Adam's body, aren't you?" he asked, and then, remembering our last encounter, smiled and said, "I suppose I owe you something after the way I made you jump." He was wearing dark slacks and a navy blazer, which must have been hot, but went well with his black hair and his complexion that was as pale as my own.

He sat down at his desk and gestured to a chair beside it, asked, "What're the police up to? Are they sending lovely young women to get close to us? Make us let down our guards and say something we wouldn't say to them? Is that it?"

"It looks that way," I agreed.

"Well," he went on, fishing for something in his coat, "I try not to gossip, even about the dead. But we're not always able to live up to our ideals, are we? Often we're lucky just to have a few left. So fire away, fire away." Before I could do that, he shot a glance at me and added, "I take it the police have decided not to take the easy way out, blame the murder on a computer thief."

"You don't think it was a computer thief?" I asked.

"I didn't say that," he replied, "I just think there are other

39

avenues to explore. A computer thief is just a little too convenient, isn't it?''

''For example?'' I asked.

''What?''

''What other avenues are there to explore?''

He got flustered at that. ''I didn't mean,'' he said, his eyes jumping around his office. ''It's just that . . .'' He dug into his pocket, fished out a pipe. ''You wouldn't be here,'' he said finally, ''if there weren't.''

I gave up on that line of questioning and said I'd gotten the impression that Lee Pierce didn't like Professor Warren very much, and I wondered if he could tell me why.

''Perhaps I can,'' he agreed. ''But before I do, maybe you'll tell me why you're asking me a question the police—the homicide police—have already asked.''

I hadn't had time to work up an explanation for such an obvious question, but that was okay. I'd learned to lie at a good school. I told Fletcher that we often returned with the same questions later, hoping to pick up something we'd missed the first time around.

''Hoping to catch us in a contradiction,'' he said, ''is what you mean.''

''Yes,'' I replied, grateful for his support.

''Lee Pierce,'' he said, ''Lee Pierce.'' He sucked on the name as if it were one he had once known but could no longer place, like a candy flavor from childhood. ''Lee's a suspect, is he, is that it? But of course, we're all suspects, aren't we? You'll be asking Lee the same questions about me, too, I shouldn't wonder, if you haven't already.'' He looked at me hopefully. I looked at him hopefully, too, and waited.

''The entire faculty had access to Adam that afternoon, of course. So I'd better get my licks in, too.''

He searched in his coat pocket, this time finding matches. He didn't seem at ease, even in his own office.

''Yes,'' he said finally, ''I suppose we can all agree that Lee didn't demonstrate what we might call appropriate behavior on the occasion of Adam Warren's death. Well, that was Lee at his worst. He and Adam were once good friends—as Lee never tires of reminding anybody who'll listen. They saw a lot of each other for a number of years. They were neither of them married, you know."

Fletcher met my eyes and read something in my face.

"Oh, no, no, no! Nothing like that. No, there was never any question in anybody's mind of *that*. The city police asked about that, too. It wasn't so. Not that it would have mattered in the least." He got busy with his pipe, now that he'd brought together the two things necessary for its functioning.

"I've heard," I said, "that Adam Warren hustled students." That wasn't exactly a lie, just skirting the edges. Arthur Fletcher dropped his box of matches. Such things happen. The box and four or five of the wooden matches lay in his lap. He swore softly and left them there. When he finally looked up at me, the surprise was still in his eyes.

"The police—city police, I mean—didn't raise that question, not with me at least," he said. "Are you just fishing?"

"No," I said.

"Students, then," he said, fishing himself. He waited for me to bite, I waited for him to go on. "Student gossip." He laughed, trying to find this theory comfortable. "You mustn't believe what you hear from students. Or from faculty either, for that matter," he added.

"Then it's untrue," I said. "Warren never got involved with his women students."

Fletcher didn't know what to say or where to look, so he began picking the matches in his lap up, one by one, and putting them back in the box. "Frye Hall is a small town," he said when he'd finished that task. "A narrow, ugly small town. We all know something of what the 'neighbors' are up to, sometimes try to guess the rest. Or don't try."

"That's an answer?" I asked.

"I don't know the answer,' he snapped. He tried to meet my gaze, decided he'd rather look out his window. He'd forgotten his pipe.

"You said Warren and Pierce had been good friends for years. How long, do you remember?"

"Oh, I don't know." His eyes came back to me, as if this subject were easier. "Three years? About that. I can't say exactly. It started when Adam came back from Washington, from his stint on the president's humanities commission. Yes, because Lee Pierce came up for promotion the following year, and Adam put all his weight behind it. If Adam hadn't been here to push for it, Lee wouldn't have made it.''

"Why not?'' I asked, surprised. "Pierce is a famous poet. Why wouldn't the English department be eager to promote him?''

Fletcher finally got his pipe going, seemed to be feeling more comfortable now. "Lee burned out a long time ago,'' he said. "I never thought he was much of a poet to begin with but, officially, the date established—by others, not just me—for when Lee burned out well and good was some days before he began writing the poems that went into his last book. What's it called? *Skiing the Burning Valium*?'' He laughed unpleasantly. "No,'' he added, "that was his first book.''

His first book was called *Skiing the Burning Valley.* Even I knew that, although it had appeared sometime in the sixties.

"He won that big literary prize when he was still in his twenties, back in the sixties when anything that was easy enough to read was good, and since then it's been downhill into silence. *Skiing into Silence*—maybe that's what he'll call his next book. Blank pages. He spends a lot of time in bars shooting off his mouth, with young would-be poets, mostly women, hanging on his lips.''

For a moment I thought Fletcher had forgotten I was there. He'd lost his professor's mannerisms and spoke in a voice heavy with disgust.

I waited for him to continue. When he didn't, I said, "And Professor Warren was the only faculty member who supported Lee Pierce for promotion?''

"Well, he couldn't have gotten Pierce promoted alone, could he? We're still a democracy, after all. But the chairman's in a pretty powerful position, and Adam carried a lot of clout. He swayed a few votes, did a little coercing among the junior faculty, bullied a bit. He'd brought Pierce into the department in the first place, before he went off to D.C., and wouldn't admit he'd made a mistake.''

"But then their friendship went sour,'' I prodded him, "Warren and Pierce's, after Pierce got his promotion.''

"Yes, and I have no idea why. But I started to *see* it for the first time right after school started up again after the Christmas holidays, last January. They ignored each other when they passed in the hall. Others noticed it, too. Nothing really serious—nothing open, you understand. An outsider might not have noticed it, if he didn't know them from before."

Fletcher jammed his pipe into his mouth, sucked, and took it out again, gave it an angry stare. He transferred the stare to me, as if the nasty taste in his mouth were my fault, and asked, "What else can I do for you, Miss O'Neill—*Peggy* O'Neill, is it?" Suddenly a grin started to spread across his face, and I braced myself. "There was a song popular on the radio back when I was a kid," he went on remorselessly, as I knew he would, "about a girl named Peggy O'Neill." He tried a snatch of melody, got it right, if a bit off-key. I waited patiently, as I sometimes have to do when dealing with people of his generation and older. The song is much older than Arthur Fletcher, but unfortunately it enjoyed a revival at about the time I was born. " '. . . And *that's* Peggy O'Neill!' " he finished, with a swoop and then a self-conscious chuckle. "Any relation?" he asked.

"I'm her granddaughter," I said, playing along without much enthusiasm.

"Well," Fetcher said, suddenly serious again, "watch out for Lee Pierce when you interview him! Or have you already?" He waited for my answer; I made a noise that sounded something between yes and no. "He likes women your age. And redheads. And now that he's Irish again, he likes them Irish, too."

"You mean he's not Irish?" I recalled seeing in the student newspaper items about Lee Pierce visiting Ireland to give readings and lectures on poetry.

"Oh, he's Irish enough. More than enough, at least when he's drunk. Lee's an enthusiast, you know, always looking for something meaningful to hang on to. In the sixties, he was an interpreter of the experience of living in the Far West—the closest he could get to the Far East without having to go there. For his second book he was a cowboy, interpreting redneck America. And now he's found his Irish roots.

I don't know what sort of book'll come out of this metamorphosis. Nothing, most likely. Maybe that's what he'll call it, too: *nothing*."

If the murder victim had been Lee Pierce instead of Adam Warren, I'd have my number-one suspect, I thought. On the other hand, Arthur Fletcher seemed to dislike Adam Warren, too. Maybe Fletcher didn't like anybody.

"Why nothing? He's still writing, isn't he?" I was thinking of the snatch of poetry Lieutenant Hansen had read to me, that Pierce had been writing when I found Warren's body.

"Oh, I recall seeing something a few months ago, in some obscure journal," Fletcher replied. "Pretty thin stuff, in my opinion, even for Lee. A poem about itself. Worse than that, a poem about poetry about poetry. Masturbating," he added, looking at me to see if I'd be shocked at the word, "in the hall of mirrors."

It was an interesting image. I got up to go, then remembered something else I wanted to ask Fletcher about. "Professor Warren's office looked as if it had been ransacked."

Fletcher shook his head. A Lieutenant Hansen or Jensen of the city's homicide division had asked him about that, too, he said. Well, Adam Warren had never been very tidy, even before going to Washington, but it had gotten much worse since he returned. It was hard to walk around in his office.

"I looked through Adam's office," Fletcher said, "with two cops watching me like hawks. It was pretty messy but, surprisingly, not as bad as it had been the last time I was there. Adam had obviously been trying to carve some order out of the chaos." He got up abruptly and said, "And now you'll have to excuse me. Summer school starts next week and I'm not ready for it yet. Adam's death has upset everything around here." He shepherded me toward the door.

"Did Doris Parker get along with Professor Warren?" I asked as I opened it.

"Doris?" he repeated, startled. "Of course. From eight A.M. until four P.M., with two fifteen-minute coffee breaks and a half hour for lunch, Doris gets along with everybody. She goes by her job description, and unless there's something in it about murdering professors, she wouldn't do it. Besides, Doris liked Adam—if she's capable of liking anybody. He always did and said the right things, at least around her. She's a strange bird, have you noticed that? She's been in the department longer than I have—longer than any of us except Adam. They gave her a party last year—the other secretaries in the building, I mean—for her twentieth year. I signed the card," he added, as if he were proud of it. "You may have noticed that she dresses rather brightly?"

I said I had. I'd never forget the sight of her lying in a yellow puddle in the room with Professor Warren's body.

"It's just another service Doris provides us," Fletcher explained. "Let me see if I remember how it goes." He closed his eyes, recited: "Red is for Monday, green is for Tuesday, she's blue on Wednesday, orange on Thursday and yellow on Friday. Once you've broken her code, you never have to wonder what day it is."

"She gave me the impression," I said, "that something had happened to her daughter."

Fletcher turned back to his desk and rummaged around on it for his pipe. When he found it, he started searching his coat for his tobacco.

"What happened to her daughter?" I persisted.

He turned back to me. "She was killed," he said, and started filling his pipe.

"How?"

"Hit-and-run accident. It was very sad." I wanted to ask him if he'd signed a card for that, too, but decided against it.

"It happened at Christmas, she told me," I said. "Did they catch whoever did it?" I had to raise my voice a little so he could hear it over the noise of his concentration.

He looked up at me as if he'd already forgotten who I was. "I don't think so," he said finally. "No, I don't suppose they did."

Nine

I live four miles from the University, so I ride my bike to and from work when I can. Maybe it's not the most sensible thing for a woman to do late at night, but most of the neighborhoods I bike through to get home are safe enough. Besides, why should women have to live with a curfew? It would make more sense if men did. I don't advertise my coming and I bike through the bad neighborhoods fast. And when I get to the really unsafe ones, I ride on Central, which is well lit and where the only real danger comes from the drunk drivers. At Lake Eleanor Drive, I use the bike path, and that's where the biggest menace of all is—the bikers who brush past silently like oiled saw blades.

It was a hot night and so humid that only a storm could bring relief, and heat lightning flickered far to the west, as if there were a giant drive-in movie on the other side of the lake somewhere. I was looking forward to a cool shower and then to sitting in front of the fan and watching that night's episode of "Fawlty Towers," which my VCR taped for me while I worked. The VCR was my second high-tech purchase after I got hired by the campus police. The first was my answering machine.

I have the lower half of a duplex. It's an old, white stucco house, but well kept up and I'd been lucky to find it. I'd looked at several small tacky apartments and I was on my way to look at one more when I'd seen a woman pounding an APARTMENT FOR RENT sign into her lawn. I stopped on impulse and asked her if I could see the apartment, although I was sure I wouldn't be able to afford the neighborhood.

She'd looked me up and down with old-landlady eyes and asked me what I did for a living. I told her. "Then I won't have long to wait," she'd replied, "if I have to call the police because there's a rowdy party going on downstairs." When I saw the apartment, I wanted it—you can even see a piece of Lake Eleanor from one of the living room windows. She'd asked me what my monthly salary was and I told her and she told me what the rent would be. It was on the high side for a rookie cop, but a lot lower than I'd expected. It's the nicest place I've ever lived in.

I had my bike half up the front steps and was opening the porch door when I heard somebody on the sidewalk behind me. It was Lee Pierce.

"Here, let me help you with that," he said.

"Thanks, I can do it myself," I told him.

"I'll help you anyway." Without waiting for an answer to that, he lifted the back wheel of my bike and carried it up the steps behind me. When I got the bike on the porch, I turned back and said thanks. He was on the top step, the screen door resting against his arm.

"May I come in?" he asked. "Believe it or not, I sometimes walk around in this neighborhood. I don't live far from here."

I believed he sometimes walked around in the neighborhood because I'd seen him. I also believed he lived fairly close by, on the other—the really expensive—side of the lake, because I'd looked up his address. However, that didn't mean he was here by chance tonight.

He looked almost comic, smiling up at me, as if he'd followed me home from school and was working up the courage to ask me for a date.

"To tell you the truth," he went on as I was thinking of how best to tell him no, "I looked you up in the phone book. But I do walk in this neighborhood, and tonight I thought I'd combine business with pleasure. I was going to ring your doorbell, if I'd seen a light on."

"What business?"

"Art Fletcher mentioned that you'd been to see him today," he said. "Told me you're helping the police with Adam's murder. I assumed you'd come looking for me, too, to try to charm out of me whatever I wouldn't tell them. I wouldn't want to miss that pleasure, Peggy, but I'm leaving in a couple of days for Ireland. It is Peggy, isn't it? I didn't just dream that?''

Word spreads fast through Frye Hall, I thought. It surprised me that Arthur Fletcher was on gossiping terms with Pierce.

''Well?'' Pierce said, ''May I come in?'' He flashed me a choir boy's smile that must have worked for him a lot. I let it work this time, too.

''Sure,'' I said. I remembered what he'd said about my hair in Adam Warren's office: a bouquet of fire. That was pretty good, for a poet.

Lee Pierce was as good a candidate for Warren's murderer as anybody else, at least in my book. On the other hand, Warren's murder didn't look like the random work of a maniac, so what did I have to be afraid of? I didn't think I'd learned anything yet that would make me a threat to Warren's killer. I couldn't imagine why Lee Pierce was standing at my door asking to come in, but I could only think of one way to find out.

As he passed me in the hallway, I looked him up and down. I'm five-foot-nine, so he must have been close to six feet. I'd worked hard at hand-to-hand combat in rookie school—I'd enjoyed it, frankly—and did well, even against men working for jobs on ''real'' police forces. I'd also studied karate for a few months in the navy, a quick course in self-defense for women that seemed a sensible thing to do to pass some time. Among other things, I'd learned to break a broom handle very fast with one barefoot kick, and that was supposed to be more than enough to break a man's leg.

Lee Pierce didn't look as if he'd done much to keep himself in shape. I knew he was forty-three and he didn't look any younger than that to me. His eyes were red-rimmed, as if he hadn't been sleeping well lately, but they weren't bloodshot. They were remarkably clear and light blue. When he didn't think I was looking at him, however, or when he forgot I was there, a switch seemed to go off somewhere inside him, leaving exhaustion. He had long hair of no particular color, and he needed a haircut.

I let him throw his raincoat over a chair by the living room door. He dropped his hat on top of it, one of those soft tweed hats you used to be able to buy only in Ireland, but that're sold everywhere now.

I opened a window, set the fan in it to stir up the hot air, and offered to make coffee. "If that's all you've got," he replied without enthusiasm.

"I've got sparkling water, too," I said.

Hope died in his eyes and he chose coffee. I ground some beans and started the coffee maker.

"I like these old houses," he said, drifting around the room. "You're lucky, you've got a view of the lake, too." He went over to the couch, dropped onto it, and leaned back into a corner. When I came back to the living room, he was looking at my answering machine, on the end table next to the couch.

"Things like this spell the end of civilized discourse," he said, giving it a sad smile, and before I could reply that people had probably said the same thing about the telephone, he asked me if I had an ashtray. He had a pack of cigarettes in one hand and a throwaway lighter in the other.

I told him I didn't allow smoking in my house. As a host, I was batting zero. Until about a year ago, I would have felt bad about it. Before that, I would have let him smoke. We progress slowly.

"Quitting smoking's become an epidemic," he said, with a laugh that didn't hide his annoyance. "Everybody's doing it."

He dropped the pack of cigarettes on the coffee table, fell back again into the corner of the couch, and grinned his boy's grin. I watched him out of the corner of my eye, over the kitchen counter, as I poured the coffee. He was watching me, too, as if he knew I was watching him. It would have looked quite funny to a watchbird, watching us.

"You're a detective, then," he said. "I had the impression you were just a patrolman, or patrolwoman—is that a word? New at your job."

I told him I'd been a campus cop for almost four months, but didn't say anything about being a detective.

The Monday after Adam Warren was murdered, before I'd

decided, at least consciously, to stick my nose into the case, I'd stopped by the downtown library and read around in Lee Pierce's poetry, just out of curiosity. I'd read his first book, *Skiing the Burning Valley,* when I was still in high school. My brother had left it behind when he'd run away from home. He was sixteen at the time, it was the late sixties. The book had been a kind of sacred text—one of a series of such texts that changed swiftly, sometimes overnight, like the gurus and pop psychologies of the time. The poems spoke knowingly of drugs, gods, and loving. *Skiing the Burning Valium,* as Arthur Fletcher had called the book.

Burning Up/Burning Down had been Pierce's second book, the one for which he'd won the Eli Mortenson Younger Poets Prize. It contained a lot of poems from all the right places: Vietnam, the streets of L.A., the slums of Chicago, barrios, and Indian reservations. I liked a few of them, but most of them were too full of the song of Lee Pierce, and he wasn't Walt Whitman.

I couldn't find anything between *Burning Up/Burning Down* and his last collection, *Letter Poems to Friends and Foes,* published nearly a decade later. Nothing in that collection had interested me at all, but a lot of other poets had liked it, to judge by the blurbs on the back cover. They were long poems that read like private letters, with the private references letters have, as if Pierce were talking over the reader's head to more interesting people across the room. The University had hired him the year after that book appeared, and he hadn't published a book since.

I handed him a cup of coffee. I'd never had such a distinguished visitor in my apartment before, I reminded myself, and what do I know about poetry anyway? I'd never had a murder suspect in my apartment before either.

Pierce put his coffee cup down next to his cigarettes and then pushed the cup aside. "Well," he said, "let's get it over with. Seduce me into betraying my best friend—or myself. I take it that that homicide man—Hansen?—doesn't buy the computer-thief theory?"

"Tell me why you disliked Adam Warren so much," I answered, ignoring his question.

My question didn't seem to surprise him. He said, "I didn't

behave very nicely over Adam's body, did I? Well, maybe you can't understand it, Peggy, but that was just my way of protecting myself. Besides, Adam tricked me, getting himself killed that way.''

"Tricked you?"

"Yes, tricked me. I didn't want him to die. I needed him, wanted to show him something.''

I waited to hear what the something was.

"My next book, Peggy!'' As he said it he lurched forward, placed his hands on the coffee table, and stared across at me. "You want to know why our friendship went sour, Adam's and mine? Did Art Fletcher tell you that? Christ, it doesn't take Miss Marple to get the dirt out of that hypocrite.''

Thanks, I thought. "What did happen?'' I asked.

Still leaning at me, Pierce replied, "Adam lost faith in me, Peggy. Do you think that's a motive for murder?''

I shrugged, said it might be for some people.

"Well, you're right, it is! It's more than enough for a man like me, a writer who has to dig for every word, like a prospector looking for gold. Do you know what I'm talking about?''

His eyes left mine suddenly and he stared down at the coffee table. He'd asked me a question, but apparently it was just rhetorical. "Adam shouldn't have died when he did,'' he said quietly.

"Adam Warren wasn't the only one who seemed to lose faith in you,'' I said. "I've heard that you wouldn't have gotten promoted if Warren hadn't pushed for it.''

Pierce stared at me. "Art told you that, too, did he?''

"I've talked to other people in your department besides Professor Fletcher.''

"Who?'' When I didn't answer, Pierce gave an angry laugh and said, "I don't suppose he told you how much *he* hated Adam.'' He was having trouble keeping his voice steady. "Fletcher opposed anything Adam wanted to do for the department. Oh, I'll admit that Adam could be a little rough at times in dealing with opposition, but Christ, Art was asking for it. He set himself up as leader of the department's Young Turks, tried to get himself elected chairman when Adam resigned. He didn't make it.''

"But wasn't he acting chairman while Professor Warren was in Washington?"

"Yes, *acting*. And with that advantage, he still couldn't get elected chairman after Adam resigned. Adam saw to that. They made him assistant chairman instead—the booby prize."

"Why did Professor Warren resign so suddenly?" I asked.

"He just got tired, tired of being sniped at by Fletcher and his band of mediocrities. They blamed Adam for what they saw as the department's going downhill. They sat around in their offices and reminisced about the good old days, whenever the hell they were, and plotted. Adam knew what was going on, of course, and it hurt him—more than he'd ever show. Finally he just got tired of it, tired of the backbiting, the bickering. He wore out."

"He resigned as your friend, too," I told him. "Or was that your doing?"

"God, Art must really hate my guts." Pierce's shoulders slumped, as if the man he'd just been trashing had dealt him a mortal wound. He was still staring down at his hands, which were playing with the cigarettes I wouldn't let him smoke.

"You can only take so much," he said, sitting back on the couch. "I don't blame him for losing faith in me, Peggy." He glanced at me, then quickly over at the window, where the fan was pulling in air that was getting cooler. There'd be a storm soon. "I was looking forward to the day I could prove him wrong, come into his office and throw my book down on his desk and say, 'Look at this, Adam, let's watch the vultures feast on this one!' Have you read any of my poems, Peggy?"

"The first book," I told him. "Years ago. I still don't understand what you mean by Warren having 'lost faith' in you."

"Don't you? I showed him some of the poetry I was working on; he didn't like it. I could tell he didn't; he just returned it to me without saying much about it. As if he were disappointed."

"When was this?"

"When did Art tell you it was? I thought Fletcher knew everything."

"Not everything I know came from Fletcher."

"Or everything you *think* you know. It was a long process, Peggy, a long, slow process. And then we had a fight. It was *my* fault, I finally got angry at him and said some things I shouldn't have."

"When?" I persisted.

"Late last year."

"At Christmas."

"Does it matter?" he asked. "Yes—I suppose so." He stared at me directly with his light blue eyes, waited a moment, and then asked, "Why?"

"Just wondered." Arthur Fletcher had told me he'd first noticed the hostility between the two men right after Christmas break. I decided to try an idea on Pierce that I'd tried on Fletcher. "Professor Warren hustled students," I said.

That startled him. "*Art* told you that?" he asked, as if he found it hard to believe.

"No, he didn't," I said.

"No," Pierce said, and laughed shortly, "I guess you're telling the truth there. And I don't suppose you're going to tell me who did, are you?"

I shook my head.

"Then it would have to have been a student. You've been busier than I thought. It would be more accurate to say that students hustled Adam." He shrugged. "So what? Adam wasn't married and he wasn't a monk."

I took that to mean yes, Adam Warren hustled students. I asked Pierce if he knew any of their names.

"I could probably remember some of them," he replied, "given enough time—and the inclination. But I don't have the inclination. Sorry."

He went back to playing with the pack of cigarettes on the coffee table, batting it lightly back and forth between his hands. I assumed he needed one and felt a pang of guilt for standing in the way of his pleasure.

He sank back into the couch. "You've only read my first book," he said. "That's too bad. A piece of crap, actually. I wrote it a long time ago, when I was just stretching my muscles, getting ready for the serious work ahead. My first-born child," he added, "but there are still things about it I like. I wonder if you'd like my later work, too."

I hadn't said I liked his first book, but I didn't correct him. Instead, I offered him more coffee, but without much enthusiasm. There was nothing else I wanted from him, so I wanted him to leave.

He turned down coffee, but didn't get up. Instead, he asked me if I lived here alone. I hesitated too long before answering to lie about it, so I admitted that I did. He heard the hesitation, smiled, and asked me why a single woman needed such a large apartment. I shrugged and answered that I didn't know. I didn't want to tell him why I liked it so much, the pleasure I get from being able to walk into any room at any time and know that it's mine, that nobody else is in there waiting for me, waiting for something from me. The previous tenant had been an interior decorator who'd put expensive wall-to-wall carpeting in every room. It was thick and soft and blue and I liked being able to walk anywhere in the apartment naked and flop down on any floor at any time. I do that a lot, just to remind myself that I can.

For some reason, I thought of George. I'd almost let him take that away from me. I shuddered at the realization of how easily I could be tricked, trapped.

"What was that about, Peggy?" Lee Pierce asked softly. He'd stood up.

I tried to laugh it away, said, "Nothing, just a ghost. A small one." I stood up, too.

"You're a loner, aren't you?" he said. "So am I." He came in my direction, stepping around the coffee table, and I took a step back. He stopped. "What are you doing, getting involved in all this? It's just a mess. Let the cops—the *real* cops, I mean—straighten it out. Do you really care who killed Adam? Would it matter if somebody killed off the whole damned English department? Every last one of us? Leave it alone, Peggy, it's none of your business. Christ, you have green eyes, and a face meant for smiling. Do you ever smile, Peggy?"

"Sure," I said, and stretched my mouth into a grin that showed every one of my teeth, some of which are straight, some not. I have amusing teeth.

He laughed, thought I was being funny. He took a step closer, so I took another step back and then decided not to do any more retreating. "Far enough," I said, still trying to keep it light. "I'm tired, it's been a long day." He took another step, then stopped.

"It's been a long time since I've met a woman like you," he said, as if I hadn't spoken. "I know that's a tired old line," he added, seeing in my green eyes and face meant for smiling that it was, "but I mean it and I don't know how else to say it. Maybe," he went on, perhaps trying to hypnotize me, "I like you just because you don't pretend you've read my poetry and because you're not a poet. You're not, are you?" he asked, pretending to be afraid.

I said I wasn't and he said he was glad. "I'm tired of poets. Men poets and women poets. I'd like to spend some time with someone who doesn't even pretend to know my work, who won't try to talk knowingly of Eliot, or Pound—*or* me. Would you have dinner with me sometime, Peggy, after all this is cleared up, after whoever murdered Adam has been caught? Or before, for that matter? Why not live dangerously, why not let a murder suspect take you to dinner? Or come to Ireland with me. I'm leaving Saturday, right after the memorial service for Adam."

"No."

"Well, dinner then?"

"No."

He took it like a man—one who's just been turned down by a woman who doesn't know anything about modern poetry. He stepped back and blinked, tried to laugh, and failed miserably.

He walked to the door, then turned around and said, "I loved Adam Warren the way a son loves his father. Adam was a father to me." He shrugged into his raincoat. "I came here tonight to try to help you. I didn't have to do that, did I? Especially since I don't believe you're working with the city police. I think you're meddling in something that's none of your business."

He carefully arranged his hat on his head and gave me a last long look. "I didn't want Adam to die," he added, and then said it again, "I didn't want him to die."

Out on the porch, he turned and said, "I don't know what your problem is, Peggy, but be careful. And don't believe everything you hear, either. Especially from students.'' He finally got the opportunity to light one of his cigarettes. ''That's going to be a big, dirty job, interviewing every student who ever chased after Adam Warren. There were a lot of them, and there's a lot of bitterness, too. And maybe, somewhere among all those jilted coeds, you'll find who killed Adam. Whoever it is can't be too stable, do you think? So be careful. You wouldn't want to scare up any ghosts, with hammers in their pretty little hands. You'd be safer sticking with computer thieves. Good night.''

He closed the porch door behind him as he left and I watched as he went down the walk to the street in the dark green light that comes just before a really serious storm. He didn't look back.

I closed the door against his cigarette smoke before taking a deep breath and letting it out slowly, as if I'd been holding my breath for a long time. I locked the front door, put the chain on, and went to take the shower I'd promised myself on the way home, what seemed to have been a long time ago. A sudden crash of thunder, not far away, shook the house, and a few seconds later, the rain started splashing on my windowsill.

I closed the window. As I did a police siren started up somewhere far away. Police sirens always seem to start up just as summer storms begin. I have a theory that you can tell how far away a storm's center is by counting the seconds between the first crash of thunder and the first police siren. I have quite a lot of strange theories. People who live alone and like it, do.

Ten

The next day was Friday, a week since Adam Warren's murder. I got to work early that afternoon and waited for roll call in Ginny Raines's office, a hotbox she shares with a detective who was working the dog watch in June. Ginny's a corporal, a rank they created to keep from having to promote women to sergeant.

I told her about my interviews with Doris Parker and Arthur Fletcher and the visit Lee Pierce paid me the night before. As I talked I found it hard to ignore the look of disbelief that grew and grew on her face.

When I'd finished, she said, "You don't really believe in this, do you, Peggy?"

I replied that I didn't know what she meant.

"You don't really think Warren's murder could have been premeditated—someone's cold-blooded work—possibly somebody in the English department," she explained. "Right?"

"I don't know what to think," I said, bewildered by her questions and her tone. I echoed what Professor Fletcher had said, that the computer-thief theory was too convenient.

"The point I'm trying to make is this," Ginny said, finally letting her voice go, almost hollering. "If you really believe a member of the English department might have done it, you wouldn't let a prime suspect into your goddamned apartment! You'd be just a little bit scared. The fact that some unknown person deliberately struck Adam Warren with a hammer not once but many times would make you pause before you let Pierce into your apartment. Did you pause, Peggy?"

"Well, a little," I said, trying out a grin. I'd only seen Ginny this angry once, when she was dealing with someone accused of rape who was trying to explain that the woman just didn't know her own mind.

She didn't grin back. "Good," she said. "That's a start. Now how about going just a little bit farther with common sense? Let the city police handle it, Peggy. That's what they're trained to do. We're not. The robbery people think it's a ring, one that uses needy, hardworking university students to steal for them. And homicide's working on it, too, of course. Between robbery and homicide, this case'll be solved sooner or later."

"You don't sound very convincing," I said.

"Damn it," she exploded again, "what I sound like doesn't have anything to do with it! Besides, what the hell's your interest in the case anyway? So you took a course from Adam Warren. So what?"

I gave her my standard reason, that it was me who'd found Warren's body, that I hadn't handled it very well.

"You don't sound very convincing, either," she observed, looking at me closely. "It that really all there is?"

"As far as I know," I answered. I asked her what progress she'd made in her investigations on campus. I knew she'd been assigned to work on it.

"Not much," she admitted. "We thought we had a lead, but it didn't go anywhere."

A year ago, she said, they'd caught an ex-student in the act of stealing a computer. He'd been given a fine and a suspended jail sentence and then he'd disappeared. Apparently left town. A dead end. At the time, the campus cops had suspected he was a part of a ring, but they couldn't get anything out of him.

"The city cops," Ginny said, "have pretty well taken over the investigation. I've heard Bixler talking about it—yelling, I should say. He's pissed, he thinks he's being slighted, that the downtown cops aren't letting him know what they're doing. That makes perfect sense to me. Which brings me back to my point. Find something else to do in your free time. Don't you have any hobbies?"

"Well," I said, "I'm thinking of taking up cooking. How about coming over to my place for dinner—"

I was about to invite her over for dinner on Tuesday, my night off, when the intercom above her desk squawked. "O'Neill in there with you, Ginny? I want her. In my office. Now!"

It was Lieutenant Bixler's voice—the voice of the Rooster. He talks like that when he deals with women officers: *I want her, now!* The sultan, calling for a wife. To be fair, he treats the men the same way, if they're sufficiently his junior.

Ginny gave me a worried look. "That doesn't sound very good," she said.

I agreed and went.

Bixler's office was on the west side of the building, the hot side at that time of day. He'd bought an air conditioner with police funds several summers ago, Ginny had told me, but the University wouldn't pay for the electricity it consumed, so he had to take it back. He hadn't been a gentle man before that defeat. He wasn't a gentle man afterward, either.

I paused outside his door, drawing on all the skills I'd learned as a child to disguise how nervous I felt, then entered.

Bixler was a balding, self-important man who parted his hair across the back of his head and then combed it forward. This made him look like a balding, self-important man with a strong wind at his back. Men and women alike called him "Rooster." I sat down in the chair he indicated and, instinctively, put my knees together and my hands in my lap. A childhood of parochial school, especially when it's followed by four years in the navy, will do that to a person. Angry with myself, I crossed my legs and sprawled just a little. I put my look of innocence on my face and stared him in the eye. I had to squint, which must have ruined the effect, since he was standing with his back to the room's only window, and the sun was streaming through it.

"Have you been reassigned since I last looked?" he asked, his voice sweet. I got tenser, felt the sweat trickling down my ribs, not all of it on account of the heat and humidity.

"No."

"No. No, that's right," he agreed. "That's right on the

nail! You're a patrolman, aren't you? A patrol *person,* I mean." He stretched *person* out quite a bit. The department had tried that one out for a while several years ago, before my time. Nobody liked it. *Police officer* sounded good to us. So did *cop.*

Bixler pulled a handkerchief out of his pants pocket and blotted his face. A sponge would have been more effective, I thought.

"A rookie patrol person," he continued, "a cop in uniform, a campus cop in uniform." He appeared stirred by his ability to find synonyms with which to define my professional identity. "You're not a detective," he went on, deciding now to explore the world of antonyms, "a *city* cop, a municipal cop, a homicide detective. Are you?"

He really wanted an answer. The way I was slouched down in the chair was beginning to feel too much like the way I was beginning to slink down inside myself, so I sat up straight. "No," I said, "I'm not a city cop."

"There's been a complaint," Bixler said finally, after examining my reply for any whiff of insubordination. He lifted a sheet of yellow paper from his notepad, let it fall. "You've been passing yourself off to the faculty and civil-service personnel of the English department as a bona fide investigator, working for the homicide squad of the metro police on the murder of Professor Warren."

"That's not true," I protested. "I only said I was helping them—assisting."

"And you hoped they would draw the right—or wrong—conclusions. That's good, Officer O'Neill. Very, very bright." Then he cut loose. "You can't go to hell for an itty-bitty little lie like that. But you can get your butt fired off this police force if you do any more 'assisting'! Do you understand that?" He loomed over me like a red wet beach ball somebody had aimed at my face. I tried not to duck.

I said I understood. He went back to his desk and sat down, mopped his face some more as if he'd done a hard afternoon's work. "Did you learn anything?" he demanded.

"What?" I wasn't sure I'd heard correctly.

"Did you pick up anything that might be of interest to homicide? Anything I could pass on to that homicide man,

Hansen?'' His tone said he didn't like asking me this very much. "Sometimes things fall through the cracks in a regular investigation," he said. It was the first intelligent thing he'd said since I'd come in, so I assumed he was quoting Hansen.

"Do you want me to call him and tell him?" I asked innocently.

"You don't seem to get it, O'Neill," he roared. "You're out of it. You were never in it. Anything you tell me, I'll pass on to Hansen. That's how he wants it. More important, that's how *I* want it." I don't think I've ever heard Bixler speak a sentence that I couldn't finish for him.

I repeated most of what I'd learned from Arthur Fletcher, and added that I thought Fletcher disliked both Adam Warren and Lee Pierce. I made the mistake of telling him what Pierce had told me about how Warren had prevented Arthur Fletcher from becoming chairman of the English department.

"Where'd you get that?" Bixler asked, startled. He'd been taking notes and, simultaneously, trying to act uninterested in what I was saying. "You've talked to Pierce, too?"

So it wasn't Lee Pierce who'd lodged the complaint against me. That left either Doris Parker or Arthur Fletcher.

I told Bixler about Pierce's visit to me the night before. He listened, his mouth open. When I'd finished, he said, "You're dumber than I thought, O'Neill, letting a murder suspect into your house. Jesus! Women cops!" He shook his head, wiped his face again. "So Warren blocked Fletcher's bid for the chairmanship," he said, reducing what I'd told him to a headline, probably to make it easier for him to digest. "What else?"

"Nothing," I replied. I didn't think Bixler would be interested in what Lee Pierce had said about me—that I had green eyes and a face meant for laughing.

"What did the Parker woman have to say?" he asked.

"I just asked her about some of the people Adam Warren worked with," I told him. "There wasn't anything there."

"People Warren worked with," he repeated, shooting me a suspicious glance up from under fat eyebrows. "For instance?"

"Graduate students," I replied. "Teaching assistants."

"Why?"

I shrugged. "I thought I had to start somewhere," I said.

He looked disappointed. "You holding anything back?"

"No," I replied. My eyelids don't flicker when I lie.

He nodded. "All right. I'll report what you've told me to Hansen. It's not much and they probably have it already. Pierce really said that, huh, about Warren keeping Fletcher from becoming chairman? I wonder if homicide got that." I could see him also wondering how he could take credit for finding it out, if it came as news to Hansen. Bixler's eyes refocused on me. "You can go, O'Neill. But remember what I said. I mean it. Here's where it ends for you. Understood?" He didn't wait for me to nod, so I didn't. "Instead of getting into mischief, you might spend some of your free time studying proper police procedure," was his parting shot.

I went back to Ginny's office to retrieve my hat and she looked at me and said softly, "Your normally pale complexion, which I envy, looks like milk of magnesia at the moment."

The walls are thin. I strung together a long series of silent curses, trying out some combinations I'd never heard before, but used my lips expressively enough so that Ginny appeared to get most of them. She hid her eyes behind an arm and I started out the door to find out what I'd missed at roll call.

"Hey," she called after me. When I turned back, she said, "I like your idea for a new hobby, cooking. If that was an invitation, before we got so rudely interrupted, and if it's still open, I accept. When?"

Eleven

I spent my time for a week working in the little garden my landlady lets me have in the backyard, reading, and walking around the lake, usually alone. I got a postcard from Al, from Flagstaff, Arizona, but he gave no return address, so I couldn't send him anything in return. I would have worked on my tan, but I don't tan, I just burn and peel, burn and peel, all summer long. I called the Y to register for a karate class that started in July. For some reason, I wanted to work on my high elbow strike—the one to the face—and my round-house kick. For a beginner, I'd once had a very good round-house kick.

Tuesday was my night off. I found a recipe for a cold steak salad and made it for Ginny. I served it with iced tea and some kind of expensive French crackers, and we ate it on my front porch. Even Ginny thought it was great.

Ginny's short and dark and tough. She grew up on a farm a couple of hundred miles north of here, about ten miles—a million miles to a child—from the nearest town. Her life had been about as different from mine as two lives can be and I listened with very mixed emotions as she told me about it. One part of me said her childhood sounded boring as hell—suffocating—and another part of me was saying, "Yes, that's how it's supposed to be."

I grew up in Los Angeles and, until I left home and joined the navy, had assumed that there were mountains, ocean, and smog everywhere. Ginny grew up thinking that there were plowed fields and prairie, lakes, animals, and clean air everywhere.

She'd also assumed that good, concerned neighbors, people who'd known you forever and cared about you, were everywhere, too, and it came as a shock when she discovered she was wrong. That had happened when she came here to go to the University, she said, and that was what made her such a tough cop.

I had a hard time not smiling. My experience of neighbors had been different. We never had the same neighbors very long when I was growing up—we moved too often for that— and my brother and I, and probably our mother, too, were glad of it. Neighbors were quick to find things out, in my experience, but not because they were eager to help.

She asked me what had brought me here from California and I told her I had an aunt living here. When I was little, Aunt Tess used to come out to California to visit us and my brother and I thought she was both strange and wonderful.

"She read movie magazines," I told Ginny, "and when she came to visit us, she'd be dressed the way she thought movie stars dressed. Sometimes, meeting her at the airport, we didn't recognize her. Once she got settled, she'd take the bus to Hollywood and spend all day walking in the area around Hollywood and Vine, and come back to our house in the evening excited about how many movie stars she'd spotted. Of course, there hadn't been any movie stars in that area for about thirty years—she'd just seen other tourists who read the same movie magazines she did and were dressed the same way she was. But we never told her that."

Ginny laughed. "And the other tourists spotted her as a star, too, of course."

"Yep, and they all returned to their midwestern homes happy. I always wondered what it was like, this place Aunt Tess came from, and so, when I was discharged from the navy, I decided to come here and find out."

"Disappointed?"

"A little, at first. It wasn't the way we'd imagined it would be, my brother and I. But I stayed through the first autumn— I'd never seen leaves turn color until I came here—and after that I was hooked."

"Is your aunt Tess still alive?"

"Oh, yes! I just talked to her just yesterday, in fact, on

the phone. She's got my father's car. She's had it in her garage for about thirty years, and I guess she's tired of keeping it. She wants me to take it off her hands.''

I explained that my father had grown up here and practiced law for a few years in the town where Aunt Tess still lives. One day, saying he'd only be gone a week, he took a plane to California and never came back, for reasons nobody would ever explain to me. He left everything behind, including his new car that he stored in Aunt Tess's garage. Aunt Tess, who doesn't drive, just kept it there, waiting for her brother to make up his mind what he wanted to do with it. He died without ever doing that, and the car, less than a year old at the time he left, had been sitting up on blocks for nearly thirty years.

Ginny said, ''By now it's probably an antique, don't you think? What kind of care is it?''

''A Chevrolet sports car,'' I replied, watching her, keeping my voice neutral, ''a Corvette.''

Ginny set her iced-tea glass down with a bang that ought to have broken it. ''You're kidding!''

''No,'' I said, ''I'm not.''

''A nearly new Corvette, thirty years old? You know what year?''

I said I thought it was a '57, but I hadn't taken the trouble to try to find out. But my father had gone out to California in 1958, so that was probably the car's year, too. He'd married my mother and then I'd been born—or vice versa—the following year. And after that he'd been too busy trying to support us, trying to get rich quick, and finally, trying to drink and not fall down.

''It's red,'' I said to Ginny, who was staring at me in disbelief. I'd stunned her this badly just recently, when I told her I'd invited Lee Pierce into my apartment.

''I know people who'd kill for a car like that,'' she said. ''Is it yours?''

''Aunt Tess says it is.'' She just didn't want my mother to have it, or the money she'd get for selling it. Aunt Tess thought my mother had ruined my father—driven him to drink, as they say.

"For God's sake, Peggy," Ginny said, "take it! It'll make you the envy of the whole town. Have you seen it?"

"Yeah. Aunt Tess showed it to me on one of my first visits, four years ago. It was a strange experience. The car sat there in that little garage, taking up most of the room. It glowed a dull red beneath the light bulb in the ceiling we had to turn on because no light came from the windows. They were up too high and thick with dust and spiderwebs. Aunt Tess had washed the outside of the car, because she'd known I was coming to see it." I stopped, thinking back to that time.

"And then?"

"It was creepy," I said, looking across the low table at Ginny. She was in the wooden swing that hangs from chains from the porch ceiling, rocking slightly, using her toes to push. "I slid into the driver's seat, knowing my father had been the last person there before me—thirty years ago—and I looked out the windshield. I wanted to see what he'd seen when he sat there, after he'd backed the car in, turned off the engine."

Ginny waited for me to go on. When I didn't, she said, "Well?" accompanied by an angry creaking of the swing chains.

"I just saw the old, unpainted garage door in front of me," I told her, suddenly annoyed, I didn't know why, "that had closed behind the car thirty years before, and a rake and a snow shovel leaning up against the door that probably hadn't been touched in thirty years either."

"But how'd it feel, being behind the wheel of a Corvette?"

I thought about it, flipped through a list of possible adjectives as if they were on flash cards. "Silly, I guess," I tried, "or trapped—or both, like Brer Rabbit stuck on the tar baby. Like something big and heavy had been strapped to my waist and was making it hard for me to move. And it was holding me down—too close to the ground."

"What kind of car do you have?" Ginny asked, grinning.

"A VW. A Rabbit."

She burst out laughing, and broke the spell I'd caught myself in. "That explains that!" she said, and then added, "Your dad must have been quite a guy."

I laughed back at her and got up and went to get more ice for our glasses. It was a really nice evening. Neither of us mentioned the murder of Adam Warren, and I didn't think about it much, either.

Twelve

I behaved myself until Friday, two weeks after Warren had been murdered, two weeks during which the police seemed to be making no progress at all, at least none they were willing to share with the public, which seemed to include the campus cops. Since I didn't see any need to practice my new hobby, gourmet cooking, day in and day out, I killed a day and a day's pay shopping for a new pair of shoes, wasted an afternoon having lunch with a married friend and her sociopathic preschool twins, and lost my place on my racquetball ladder to a woman I can usually beat with my eyes shut.

Work went along pretty routinely. The summers were a slow time for campus crime, I'd been told, and except for Adam Warren's murder, this one didn't seem any different. There were the usual number of bikes stolen from racks and purses from desks, a slightly higher incidence of flashers than we get in the depths of winter, and some expensive equipment, including one computer, stolen from the science labs. A woman was attacked in a parking ramp, too, the first of the summer. This one got away without being raped or badly hurt physically.

The biggest excitement was Jesse James getting cut with a knife when he tried to arrest a nonstudent who'd snatched a purse from a woman waiting for an intercampus bus. He'd attempted to snag the guy without taking out his pistol. Lieutenant Bixler hit the ceiling over that, but some of us thought Jesse was a hero. He wasn't cut badly enough to go to the hospital, but Bixler made him take a sick day anyway, "to rethink your career plans," he'd told him with a sneer.

James isn't his real last name, but back when he was a rookie, he'd stood in front of a mirror late one night in the men's room of an empty building and practiced quick draws. His pistol went off. His real name's Jesse Porter and he's a gentle guy.

I finally got tired of being good and decided to look up Susan Carpenter. Although she hadn't known it, of course, she'd gotten me into hot water—or at least her rumored lust for Professor Warren had—and now I was going to give her the chance to get me into some more if she wanted to. It seemed only fair.

I hadn't told Bixler about her. After all, he'd only ordered me to tell him what I'd found out from Doris Parker that could be useful to Lieutenant Hansen, and I didn't see how Susan Carpenter's address could be useful—not without the knowledge that she'd once been seen in Adam Warren's arms.

She wasn't listed in the phone book, so I biked over to the University library and looked for her name in the student directory. She wasn't there either, which meant she hadn't returned to the University after dropping out of the English department. I got the directory for the year I'd taken Warren's course and found her name and address in there but no telephone number.

The address was an easy bike ride from the library, so I rode over and found it in a neighborhood of winding streets and old family homes. It was a new apartment building built by greed alone. Thin young trees strained to hide it, without success. An old car was parked in front of it, with a half-filled U-Haul trailer hitched to the rear, not an uncommon sight at this time of year in a university town.

The main door of the apartment building was propped open with a brick. I looked at the directory tacked to the stucco wall and found the number of the apartment that had once been Susan Carpenter's. It was somebody else's now. I climbed the stairs to the second floor, found the apartment, and rang the bell. No answer. Two young men wearing muscles and shirts without sleeves passed me carrying a mattress. A young woman followed them down the hall, stopped when she saw me.

"He's not home," she told me. "He's at work."

I said thanks, that I was trying to find somebody who'd once lived there, Susan Carpenter.

"Oh, yeah? Sue? She hasn't lived here for almost a year." She turned and watched the two men bend the mattress around a corner and disappear with it down the stairs, grunting and muttering advice to one another. "She owe you money?" she asked, turning back to me. She was wearing a sweaty T-shirt with a quotation on it from Emma Goldman, about revolution and dancing. She didn't wait for my answer, just walked back into her apartment. I followed her.

Her living room was nearly empty except for a dozen plants scattered around on the floor. "How'd you like to adopt one?" she asked, gesturing at them. I thanked her, said I had enough.

I told her I'd been in a class with Susan Carpenter once and we'd become friends, sort of. I wondered what had happened to her.

The woman looked me up and down slowly, as if trying to discover where I'd hidden my badge. "She left the U," she said.

"I know," I told her. "She had a problem with one of her teachers. She told me a little about it. I wasn't too interested at the time, but now I'm writing an article on sexual harassment at the University, and I thought of her. It might even become a book," I added.

I watched the disbelief spread over her face, and then I watched some more as her face told me that she'd decided to play along, humor me.

" 'An article,' " she repeated, " 'maybe a book.' Why make it hard on yourself, chasing down rumors. Why not just run an ad in the student newspaper—'wanted: horror stories of sexual harassment'—and then stand back so you don't get trampled? Or assassinated by the administration."

She was having fun with me. I should have paid more attention to the T-shirt, the laughing eyes, the stubborn chin.

"That bad, huh?" I said, playing it straight. "You sound like you've had some experience." She didn't sound that way at all, in fact.

"Uh-uh," she replied, "not me. I only like boys strong enough to move mattresses." I wanted her to be my friend, for a few minutes at least, so I grinned to indicate that I appreciated the humor there. "I suppose," she went on, "being an expert on sexual harassment and all, you've heard the story of Horizontal Sally, the coed who graduated with a perfect C average but never attended a class?"

I said I'd missed that one.

"She either got an A for a course or an F, depending on whether she scored with the professor or not. You know where I heard that story?"

I shook my head.

"In class, from a professor. Male, naturally, one with a wonderful smile, if you like them wet."

"Well," I said, "they're going to have to be more careful from now on."

"The new regulations against sexual harassment, you mean? Sure. More *careful.*"

"Is that how Susan got through school?" I asked her.

She grinned. Now she knew exactly who I was and what I wanted. Or she thought she did.

"Sue didn't *get* through school," she answered. "And no, Sue didn't need to do anything like that. She was a good student. She just fell in love with the son of a' bitch, that's all. End of story."

"Do you know where she's living now?" I tried, knowing it was a waste of my time.

"No." Her eyes didn't bother trying not to lie. They met mine without flinching. Then she shrugged and said, "Sorry." She turned to her two helpers, who'd come back into the room and were standing there waiting for orders, arms dangling out from their sides. "I'm in a hurry," she said, glancing back at me over her shoulder. "I've got to be in Chicago tomorrow morning. I'm never going to get out of here." She stared around at the cluttered floor, seemed to have forgotten me. "How'd I collect so much *shit?*"

"I'm probably gonna have to do most of the driving," one of the men said, to nobody in particular.

"Sure," the woman replied, giving him a bright smile. "Fine." She took both men by the biceps and urged them toward the kitchen. "Sorry I couldn't be of any help," she called back over her shoulder. "And good luck with your article, or book, or whatever,'' she added from the kitchen. She didn't seem to want to quit.

"Thanks," I called back.

There was a phone on the floor against a wall and a beat-up address book beside it. I'd managed not to stare at it while the woman was in the room. Now I walked over and picked up the book and turned around and walked out. In the hall I found an address for Susan Carpenter, memorized it as I went down the stairs. I dropped the book on the front seat of the old car as I passed it, got on my bike, and headed back toward the University.

I still had a couple of hours before I had to be at work. Lots of time to get into more trouble, lose my job.

Thirteen

It was a hot, breezy afternoon, the kind you want to spend at the lake. I biked back to the University, passed police headquarters and then Frye Hall, and turned into the Old Campus on the bike path that winds alongside the pedestrian walk through the big, old trees.

I had to pedal slowly to avoid the crowds of summer students strolling in the general direction of their classrooms, other things floating on their minds, as other bikers whizzed past me, ignoring the pedestrians who ignored the bike paths. I passed a biker who had narrowly missed clipping me a few moments before. Dazed, he was trying to untangle parts of himself from his spokes and from a kid wearing headphones with a skateboard. The kid didn't look hurt at all.

I pedaled over the bridge that connects the Old Campus to the new. There were whitecaps on the river below and I could look over the guardrail from my bike and see swimmers crawling slowly upstream followed by tiny boats whose occupants shouted tinny encouragement. On the other side of the bridge, grass and ivy gave way to concrete and the tall, new buildings that provide what little shade there is.

I felt strangely contented. I hadn't made up my mind to disobey orders and risk losing my job. Not really. I was just out reconnoitering, just going for a look, killing time before I had to be at work. And getting some exercise, too.

A part of me—the worried, not the ethical part—was sorry I'd lied to Bixler about not getting anything of importance out of Doris Parker, but it was too late to do anything about it now, I told myself. Besides, there was nothing important

about Susan Carpenter's address. The only thing of importance about Susan Carpenter was something that may or may
not have happened over a year and a half ago. I'd just get
myself into trouble if I went to Bixler about it at this late
date. Also, I'd been expressly ordered not to call or otherwise
contact Lieutenant Hansen. So the only thing I could do now
was check out Susan Carpenter on my own. I lie to myself
sometimes, not just to others.

As I biked to where she lived on one of the maze of streets
crouched in the shadows of the New Campus buildings, I
pointed out to myself that Susan Carpenter no longer worked
for the English department. She had no connection with the
University, and so it was unlikely that she would complain
to anybody about me if I talked to her.

She lived in a two-story frame house, surrounded by something that had once been a white picket fence. It wasn't white
anymore, most of the pickets were gone, and those that remained leaned this way and that. The fence went well with
the house.

A sign hanging from a post in the yard said, RIVERSIDE
SCHOOL OF PIANO, CHILDREN WELCOME. Somebody inside the
house was playing the piano, but it didn't sound like a child.
The doorbell lacked a button, so I knocked on the screen
door, but it wasn't loud enough to be heard over the music.
I opened the door and looked in.

A grand piano dominated the room, seemed to bully all the
dark, shabby furniture away, back it against the walls. Everything but the piano must have come straight from the Sal-
vation Army, and the piano knew it. Its white grin stretched
away from the hands of the woman playing it.

Susan Carpenter's hair was still long and straight. It fell
down her back almost to the piano bench she was sitting on.
Light from the windows flooded the room and glowed on the
rugless hardwood floor. I stepped into the house.

A man was half-sitting, half-lying on a couch by the front
windows. A cat lounged next to him. The man straightened
into an upright position when he saw me. The cat stayed
motionless, which suited me fine. I'm allergic to cats and
they know it. We all listened to the end of the piece together.
It was something modern I'd never heard before, but I liked

it and thought she was playing it well. She had long, thin arms and fingers to match, but they must have been very strong. When she finished, the man applauded, slow, heavy clapping, and I applauded, too. She didn't acknowledge either of us, just opened a book of music on the piano and thumbed through it.

"Are you still here?" she asked, not turning her head.

"Company, Suzie," the man said.

She turned to me as if she hadn't known I was there, said "Oh," and got up.

Her face was a perfect oval, just as I remembered it from Professor Warren's class, with high cheekbones and a small heart-shaped mouth. Her thick hair was parted down the middle and pulled back at the sides, held at the temples with barrettes. She was more beautiful than I remembered, and taller, too, close to six feet.

"Can I help you?" she asked.

"I hope so," I said. I was suddenly embarrassed, and uncertain about how to begin. For a quick second I thought of making some excuse and then getting out of there, giving what I knew to homicide or forgetting it altogether. "My name's Peggy O'Neill," I said. "Are you Susan Carpenter?" I knew she was, but I didn't want to explain to her how I knew.

She did something then that made it a little easier. She started to sing a snatch of the song I'd been named after, half-turning to the piano and accompanying herself with one finger, ending with a flip " '. . . and *that's* Peggy O'Neill!' " She sang it better than Arthur Fletcher had, but only marginally. When my father had cronies, drinking buddies over, he'd sometimes make me play that song on our old upright piano and he'd sing the words in what was left of his tenor voice. Childhood memories!

I stood there patiently, a smile pasted on my face, the one I'd developed for the occasion at about age seven, and the room became what it was, a student house filled with clutter and a cat, and Susan Carpenter became a former English graduate student and teaching assistant who might have had an affair with her professor and, for all I knew, might have killed him, too.

"Sorry," she said, seeing she hadn't really sold me on taking piano lessons with that approach, "I suppose you've had to put up with a lot of that. Are you here about piano lessons? I'll get my schedule. I've got openings most days."

"No," I said, glancing at the man on the couch. I took a deep breath, aware as I exhaled it that I might be blowing my brief career with the campus police out with it. "I'm with the University police," I told her. "I'm helping with the investigation of Professor Adam Warren's murder."

Susan Carpenter sat down abruptly on the piano bench, an elbow hitting keys behind her. Behind me I heard the man get up off the couch. He walked halfway to the piano and then stopped.

"I'd like to talk to you alone, if that's all right," I said.

"Let's see some identification," the man said.

Susan Carpenter ignored him. "Why me?" she asked. "Are you interviewing all of his old students? That's going to keep you busy."

The man came closer to me and I turned to him, got my ID out of my shirt pocket, and extended it. He took it, looked at it, turned it over, then handed it back without saying anything. He went over and stood next to the piano, but I noticed he didn't go all the way over to Susan.

"You were his TA," I said to her. "I'm interviewing some of them."

"A long time ago," she replied. "He had other assistants, didn't he, after me?"

"You quit in the middle of the school year," I said. "I'd like to know why."

"I decided I'd rather teach piano, do something honest." Her large brown eyes watched me without blinking.

"It wasn't all that long ago either," I said. "It was a year and a half ago."

"So? I haven't exactly been counting the months on my fingers."

"I'd like to talk to you about it," I repeated, "alone."

The man took a step toward me, pushing off abruptly from the piano. He was about twenty-five, muscular and blond, with the leathery, burned skin of men who worked outdoors, not as tall as Susan Carpenter, an inch or so taller than I.

"It's okay," he said angrily. "There's not much Suzie can tell you about her affair with that creep that I don't already know."

"Tim!"

"She knows something already, Sue," he said, still looking at me, "so let's get it over with."

"Who are you?" I asked.

"I'm Suzie's fiancé. My name's Tim Hale."

"Were. You were my fiancé."

"I'm still your fiancé, Sue," he said, his voice rising. "It doesn't bother me that that son of a bitch—"

"Goddamn you, Tim, shut up!" Susan's Botticelli face self-destructed. She grabbed the book of music off the piano and threw it at him. She wasn't kidding, she meant to hit him with it, hurt him, but he ducked in time and the book sailed over his head, its pages fluttering like a fat, frightened chicken. The cat disappeared over the back of the couch.

Tim Hale straightened up, a surprised look on his face. "All right, Suzie. You tell it, then. I guess it's your story." He didn't sound as if he really believed that.

"Thanks," she said, her voice sarcastic. She turned to me. Not surprisingly, she didn't look as if she liked me a lot. "Where'd you learn that I had an affair with Adam Warren?"

I shrugged. "Gossip. Things like that get around."

Her face said she didn't believe me but it also said there wasn't anything much she could do about it. "All right," she said, "I had an affair with Adam Warren. So what? It happens all the time. If every woman who had an affair with her adviser killed the sucker, there'd be more faculty openings for women at universities, I can tell you that. I didn't kill him."

"She wasn't the only graduate student who had an affair with the creep," Tim Hale put in.

"Shut up, Tim, okay?"

"How'd you get involved with him?" I asked her.

"How should I know? Looking back, I think I must have been crazy. But at the time it seemed like a good idea, at least for the first couple of weeks. Adam—Warren had always been interested in my work, and helpful. Or pretended to be. That's the hell of it: once he made a pass at me, I no longer knew if he liked my work or not, or if he just said he did as a part of hustling me.

"I'd heard the rumors about him, of course. Warren and his women students—he was known for it. So I confronted him with the stories, when I saw it coming. He laughed them off, said they were just stories, admitted he'd been a little wild—those were his words, 'a little wild'—at times, but not anymore, all that was over now. Or rather, he *wanted it* to be over. Shit! I bought it. I wanted to believe it, I guess. And why not? He wasn't *really* old and he kept himself in pretty good shape—"

"And he was such a *distinguished* man," Tim Hale added, anger mixed with mockery in his voice.

"Yes, Tim, he was a distinguished man. That, too," Susan replied, not letting it bother her. "He was at home with power and, quite frankly, that was a turn-on. We liked the same kind of music and art, too. We started going to concerts together, and to art shows, and after one of the shows we went to bed together and I fell in love with the son of a bitch."

"Did you know Tim at this time?" I asked.

She said no and he said yes simultaneously.

I waited for them to make up their minds.

"Yeah, she knew me at the time," Hale said, looking at her defiantly. "We were engaged at the time. We got engaged the spring before Suzie was hired as Warren's teaching assistant. Then I guess I got scared or something, or maybe I wasn't ready to settle down yet, I don't know. I'm a bricklayer. I tried college a couple of times, but I never liked it. I like to read, I read Suzie's books, some of them, but I like to read about history best, and about foreign cities. . . ." He gestured helplessly with his big hands.

"So I told her I wanted to take off for a while, just for the summer," he went on. "Go out to California—I've got contacts out there, friends. I used to spend time out there before I met Suzie. She didn't want me to go, but I went anyway. I didn't think it was such a big deal. She had her studies and her job in the English department, with Warren. Shit, we'd been living together for a couple of years, that's a long time.

I thought a little time off would be good for us. Good for me, is what I meant. I was just kidding myself.

"I didn't come back at the end of summer, I stayed out there. I had a job that paid good, I figured we could use the money. I didn't spend much, I saved a lot. For *us!*" The anger flared in his voice.

"When I got back," he continued, more quietly, "she was involved with him, they were having an affair. She says she wrote to me about it, but I didn't get the letter. Well, I didn't stay in one place the whole time either, I moved around. So she probably did." He looked at me, his eyes appealing to me for support. "So you see, it was partly my fault. Shit, I don't think Suzie's mad at herself, I don't even think she's all that mad at Warren. I think she's mad at me!"

"Mad at you!" Susan laughed bitterly. "God, I'm so stupid."

I stood there and looked from one to the other of them as they talked across the piano. They seemed almost to have forgotten me.

There was something wrong somewhere. I didn't think Susan Carpenter and Tim Hale were talking about her affair with Warren.

"You must have been pretty mad at Tim," I said, poking at the only loose thread I could see at the moment, "to break off the engagement even though he doesn't seem to want it that way. Shouldn't it be the other way around?"

They both turned to me. Tim started to say something but Susan beat him to it.

"Why are you talking to us here, instead of having us come downtown, or arresting us or something? Do the police usually go door-to-door interviewing suspects, like the Avon lady?"

"I'm not with the city police," I said. "As I told you, I'm with the campus police."

"What's the difference?"

"We work a little differently," I said, not lying at all with that one. "If I get anything I think's important, I'll report it to homicide and they'll decide what to do with it."

"And you've found a couple of fresh suspects in us, right?"

"Yes, I have," I said. "I don't think you're telling me all

there is. I don't know what you're holding back, I just know it's there.''

"I'm not holding anything back," Susan said, looking at me steadily. "What about you, Tim?" she asked, without turning her head to him.

"No," he said.

"So you were mad at Tim for staying in California," I said, "and went to bed with Warren."

"Fell in love with him," Tim corrected me.

Susan ignored him, something she was pretty good at. "I was a real jerk," she said. "A self-deceiver. I was older than the average graduate student, and I thought that would make a difference."

She didn't know where it would end, where she wanted it to end. She'd written to Tim about it, tried to break off their engagement, but he hadn't answered.

"Just an old-fashioned love story," she added.

"What ended it?" I asked.

"I got smart. I knew I'd made a mistake practically from the beginning. I tried to kid myself for a while. Pride, or something. Or disgust with myself. I'd already written to Tim, breaking the engagement. I wanted to make it work with Warren, so I wouldn't look stupid—as stupid—to myself. I tried. I just made myself look more stupid. Then I got smart.''

"What made you smart, all of a sudden?" When she was slow to answer, I added, "Come on, if you don't tell me, I'll bet you'll tell a homicide cop I know."

"There wasn't anything specific," Susan said, her voice rising. "He drank a lot. I didn't like that."

"Tell her about the water troll," Tim Hale cut in suddenly.

I wasn't sure I'd heard him correctly. "That's enough, Tim," Susan said, and gave him a long look. She got up from the piano bench and walked over to a window. She put her back to it.

"The what?" I asked. I looked at Tim, since it was hard to look at her, framed in the afternoon sunlight coming through the window.

"Tim," Susan said.

"The water troll," he said, ignoring the note of warning in her voice. "That's what I call Jack Becker, the criminologist who lives in the woods. Either you tell her, Sue, or I'm going to."

The name Jack Becker was familiar to me, but I couldn't place it.

Susan remained standing in the window, her hands at her sides as if pinned there. I couldn't see her face, just her hair. Glowing like a halo. She still wouldn't speak.

"Jack Becker's a professor of criminology at the U," Tim told me. "A very famous man. Very important, too, as he'd be the first to tell you. Right, Sue?" Susan didn't answer, so he went on. "He serves on lots of crime commissions, stuff like that. He was a friend of Adam Warren's." He turned suddenly to Susan. "You sleep with him, too?" he demanded harshly.

I thought there wasn't anything she could tell me he didn't know.

"No," she answered, in a very soft voice that floated, like a curtain in the breeze, from the window.

"Then what've you got to be ashamed of?" Tim asked. "Tell her."

She stared at him steadily for a few seconds, as if wondering where she'd seen him before, and then turned to me. Still speaking very softly, she told me about Jack Becker. Becker and his wife had parties, on Sundays, usually, and holidays. They were sex parties, although the Beckers pretended they were something else. They called them gatherings of friends to celebrate their freedom from conventional restraints. They just happened to end up going to bed with partners other than the ones they came with.

"I thought it was a joke," Susan said. "Nobody ever ended up with the person they'd come with. Except me," she added. "I usually went home alone, or spent the night in one of the guest bedrooms with the door locked."

"What about Warren?" I asked.

"At first he was 'disappointed' in me. Because I wouldn't join in the fun. Later it pissed him off. But I didn't wreck his fun, because there were always unaccompanied women there, waiting for me to go home or go to bed alone. Wild cards, I called them.''

"Who came to these parties?"

"All kinds of people. University people, people Jack Becker knew professionally. He gets around a lot, you know, gives seminars and workshops on crime, crime prevention.''

That's where I'd heard his name, I thought.

"There were lawyers there, too," Susan went on. "I recognized some of them from the newspapers. Criminal lawyers, the kind who take on hopeless cases—if the defendant has enough money or the headlines are big enough. A couple of judges, too.''

"What about Professor Fletcher?" I asked. I remembered Lee Pierce's surprise when he thought it was Fletcher who'd told me that Adam Warren chased women.

"Fletcher, the English department's straight arrow? No, I don't think so. A place like the Beckers' would scare him to death.''

"Lee Pierce?"

"Of course. He and Adam—Warren were great friends. I think he was the one who brought Warren into the group. Lee never came with the same woman twice, I think. His 'poetesses,' he called them.''

"It seems a little odd to me," I said, "that you wouldn't participate in the parties and yet you stayed with Warren for so long.''

"You think she's lying?" Tim flared at me.

"Probably," I answered him.

"Oh, shut up, Tim," Susan said, without much feeling. "It wasn't a very long affair, actually, just long enough. It started in October. He took me out to the Beckers' for the first time about three weeks later. The first time I was fooled. Everybody got high, so I thought that was why the party ended the way it did. But there wasn't anything accidental or spontaneous about it, they'd been doing it like that for years. I guess I was there maybe five, six times. I don't remember exactly. After all, it was a year and a half ago. God, they were a laugh.''

"And that's all that happened out there," I asked. "You drive out, get high, exchange partners, and go to bed?''

"Isn't that enough for one day?" she asked. "If you know of anything more, you ought to tell them."

"Maybe you *should* go out there someday," Tim Hale put in, his voice nasty. "Put your body on the line as a detective, find out what kind of people ol' Adam hung out with. Tell her about the hot tub, Sue. The water troll and his hot tub."

"I've told her enough."

"Go out there some Sunday," Tim said. "You won't need a swimsuit. The water troll doesn't allow them in his hot tub."

I changed the subject. "You haven't seen Adam Warren since you broke up? When was that?"

"Not since December. He called a few times after that, but I think it was just to see if I was going to try to get him for sexual harassment. But it *wasn't* sexual harassment! I was old enough to know what I was doing. He didn't promise me anything for it, and if he had, I'd have told him to go to hell!"

"And you haven't seen or heard from him since," I persisted.

"No. I quit as his teaching assistant just before school started in January last year—quit school, too. And I haven't been back. I wasn't anywhere near campus the afternoon he was killed, either. I was right here."

"Giving piano lessons?" It's only a ten-minute bike ride to Frye Hall.

"I was with her that afternoon," Tim stuck in. "We heard about it on the news that night. Come to think of it, it was you that found Warren's body, wasn't it? I thought I'd seen your face before."

"You've got good alibis," I said. "Each other. You still haven't told me why you broke off your engagement with Tim."

"It's none of your business," Susan replied.

"Maybe," I said. I headed for the door. My eyes were drawn to the piano again. It stuck out in the shabby room like an Angus bull in a pet shop. The keys were as white as teeth in a denture ad.

"Do you make a living at it?" I asked Susan. "Piano lessons?"

"Not yet, I just started. Summers are slow. I teach part-time at one of the community colleges, too, during the school year."

"It's beautiful."

"Yes, it is," she said. She came and stood between it and me, as if to protect it. "It was my mother's," she added when I kept looking at it. "She taught piano, too, before she got married."

"I heard Steinways increase in value with the years," I said. "Like Rolls-Royces and good houses. How old is it?"

"Oh, I don't know," Susan said. "Thirty, thirty-five years."

"It looks newer than that," I said.

"It's not."

"Her parents shipped it to her," Tim said. "For her birthday. You should've seen the clunker she had before."

Tim followed me to the door, held it open. Susan was standing by her piano, one hand on it, watching me. When she saw me looking back at her, she sat down and opened a music book. I looked at Tim and said, "It doesn't make a whole lot of sense."

"What doesn't?"

"While she was engaged to you, she had an affair with another man that ended badly. And you say you're still engaged, and she says you're not. Shouldn't it be the other way around? Shouldn't you be the one who broke it off?"

"Maybe so," he said, his eyes skidding all over my face in an effort not to meet mine. It's odd how eyes want to meet eyes, but sometimes they don't dare and then they don't know what to do with themselves. Good liars learn to overcome that.

It was too late to do anything except go to work, so I biked over to headquarters, back across the bridge. I had two more suspects than Lieutenant Hansen did, and maybe lots more. I didn't know yet what I wanted to do with all I had in the way of suspects and liars. I suppose it would have been smarter to wonder what they might want to do with me.

Fourteen

The University held a memorial service for Adam Warren the next day, Saturday, in the chapel of Valhalla Cemetery, and I decided I wouldn't be jeopardizing my career if I attended. After all, the body was mine in a sense, since I'd found it.

The chapel wasn't large and it was nearly full by the time I arrived. I recognized some of the English department faculty and a couple of students I'd seen the afternoon of Warren's murder, and a few of them recognized me, too, even without my uniform. Arthur Fletcher arrived late and, as he passed me in the aisle, tossed me a brace of raised eyebrows and an ironic smile. He was wearing a suit even darker than the one he'd worn the day of Warren's murder. As before, it went well with his dark hair and pale complexion.

I assumed the woman next to him was his wife. I could imagine how beautiful she'd been once, before the sun had aged her fair skin. She still looked good, although I thought she'd look better if she had the courage to let her hair turn gray. She was about forty-five, I guessed, Fletcher's age, but he looked younger and less lived. They found seats near the front and then she turned to smile and wave to someone in the aisle behind her. I followed her glance to the woman who waved back.

I was pretty sure it was the same woman I'd passed on the stairs in Frye Hall when I was on my way to discover the body of Adam Warren. She had the same small head and short, dark hair, and she was wearing glasses. She leaned forward and said something to Fletcher's wife, and smiled. It was the same smile she'd given me two weeks before.

Fletcher looked back at her without curiosity and then turned to the front again.

I looked around for Lee Pierce, but didn't see him anywhere. He'd told me he was leaving for Ireland after the service.

Doris Parker was there, though, off to one side in the front row, among the flower arrangements, almost a part of them in a pink dress and matching barrettes. I couldn't see what she had on her feet, but tennis shoes wouldn't have surprised me. She sat straight, radiated attentiveness and good behavior, as if she'd been assigned to take dictation.

I sat in one of the back rows and was just starting to feel grateful that Lieutenant Hansen wasn't there when he walked in, trailing two men who looked a lot more like homicide detectives than he did. They were wearing the same cheap suits they'd worn when they were snooping around Frye Hall the afternoon of Warren's murder and the same faces that absorbed light rather than reflected it. Ginny Raines insists she can spot a detective from thirty feet away in a crowded bar. Hansen was wearing a well-tailored dark suit that he looked comfortable in. When he saw me, he gave me a long look, like a resigned sigh. I stared back bravely.

A string quartet played quietly in the balcony over our heads until the service began, a quiet, restrained service filled with humanist pieties far from office jealousies, sexual harassment, and murder.

After a time, the pastor yielded the pulpit to the University president, who, as he often does, had trouble concealing his wolfish grin. For anybody who'd listened to the television news the night of Warren's death, the president said nothing new, but today it took considerably longer.

The dean of the College of Arts came next. His suit was stained here and there and unpressed, too, but stretched so tightly on his enormous body that you could hardly tell. Obesity must save him bundles on pressing bills, I thought. He spoke of Adam Warren's absolute integrity, as a scholar, as a teacher, as a man, and yes, as a friend. I'd heard most of this before, too, but it meant more to me now, or something different. I thought of Susan Carpenter and the young women who had gone before and come after her. Insisting all the way to bed that it wasn't sexual harassment, because they were smart enough to get good grades anyway.

The speeches annoyed and bored me, so I looked around the gloomy chapel. Standing in the rear, lounging against the closed door, was Lee Pierce. A thin shaft of light from a stained-glass window fell across his face. He wasn't paying any more attention to the Dean's eulogy than I was, his eyes were staring at something in one of the front rows. I couldn't tell who or what it was, and I didn't want him to spot me watching him, so I turned back to the front.

The ceremony lasted about an hour. Warren's ashes had been mailed home to Michigan, where the funeral had been held a week or so ago. Otherwise they might have been scattered on the dense, green water of the pond in the middle of Valhalla Cemetery, and on the ducks who seem to swim there with special grace. I tried to remember the word they use now for the ashes of human beings. Cremains. I shuddered.

There was coffee to drink and sweet things to eat after the service. I followed the crowd into the brightly lit room, glanced around, but didn't see the woman I was looking for, so I went back to the chapel.

She was standing there in the aisle near where she'd been sitting, talking to Lee Pierce. I watched them from just outside the chapel door. She seemed to be arguing with him, except that it was more like pleading. Her hands, moving in and out of the thin shafts of light coming from the windows, were needy and her glasses made her upturned face look more vulnerable. Pierce looked as if he were trying to calm her down. She turned abruptly and came up the aisle fast.

Too fast for me to duck away. She came past me as quickly as she had once before, only this time she didn't see me. I turned to follow her and bumped into Fletcher, standing right behind me. He hurried after the woman, calling "Lynn!"

I followed them, blinking in the sunlight. Fletcher had stopped halfway down the walk leading to the cemetery's gates, a dejected shadow in the midst of all the tombstones, like a ghost caught outside in the middle of the day. The woman was passing through the gates. Fletcher turned and came back.

I didn't bother trying to hide, just stood there and waited for him.

"What do you make of it, Miss O'Neill?" he asked, enraged, his face close to mine.

"Not a whole lot," I said. "Who is she?"

"You don't know?" he asked, surprised, then added, "Well, that's too bad," and walked past me into the chapel again, heading toward the coffee and cookies.

I went on down the chapel steps, out into the sunshine and heat, and found a monument to perch on, a substantial one planted in the midst of about a dozen smaller stones marking the comings and goings of a family long gone. And waited. After a while Lieutenant Hansen came out, alone, squinting in the sunlight but finding me quite easily, as if he knew exactly where to look.

"Hello," he said. "Looking for clues?"

"No. Just came out of respect. I've been warned to keep out of it, mind my own business."

"Me, too," he said mildly.

"What?"

"It was computer thieves," he continued, in the same voice. "Probably a ring. You campus cops had better keep your eyes open—more open, I mean—from now on. You never know when one of them'll strike again. And God help you if you're in the way. See what happened to Adam Warren."

"You don't believe that," I said.

"The University president does, and some other truth makers do too—the kind who decide whether or not I keep my job." He shrugged. "So naturally I do, too. It'll go unsolved, unless you guys catch a thief on campus and he confesses."

"Or she," I amended, again sticking up for my sex. "You remember that woman I told you about, the one who passed me as I was starting up the stairs in Frye Hall?"

"What about her?" He tried to sound uninterested.

"She just left," I said, nodding in the direction of the gate. "You barely missed her. Art Fletcher and his wife seem to know her. Lee Pierce does, too. She was pleading with Pierce about something. And then she stalked off, not looking back.

Fletcher followed her, wringing his hands. He called her Lynn.''

"Interesting. I'll ask around, see if I can find out who she is.''

"I thought you were staying away from it," I said, teasing him. "You came here looking for a computer thief—with two detectives in tow?"

"You never know," he said. He looked as if he were about to walk away, then said, "I hear you've been snooping around, tormenting people like Doris Parker. You have any particular reason?"

"No," I said.

"You get anything useful out of her?"

"No."

"No." He looked at me, gave me a quizzical grin. "If you ever happen to talk to her again," he said, stooping to read the inscription on the headstone on which I was standing, "ask her what the fuss was about between her and Adam Warren, the day before Warren got himself killed. In her office."

"What kind of fuss?"

"She was hollering at him apparently. Told him to get out of her office. A student coming to see about a grade overheard them, decided to come back later. The door was closed, although it wasn't one of Doris's normal breaks."

"What'd she tell you it was?"

"She denied it, pure and simple. Said the student must have been mistaken. But the student makes a good witness. Says Warren came out of the Parker's office with tears in his eyes. As if he'd been crying."

I couldn't imagine Warren crying. I asked, "Did the autopsy find drugs in Warren's body?"

Hansen laughed. "No, why?"

"Just wondered." I was thinking of something Susan Carpenter had told me, about the Sunday parties at the water troll's.

"You think a man has to be high on something to cry?"

I didn't want to tell Hansen about Susan Carpenter or about the water troll yet, so I replied, "Something like that."

I don't know if he believed me. He said, "Well, take care

of yourself, Officer O'Neill. I don't know what you're doing, but be careful." He gave me a worried look and his beautiful smile. His hair was almost pure silver in the bright sunlight. He walked on past me, down the path and out the cemetery gates.

I stayed on my headstone, a vulture waiting. A lot of people came out, academic-looking people, mostly—professors, with their wives—but I wasn't waiting for one of them. They gave me disinterested glances, if they noticed me at all, and strolled out of the cemetery. After a while Doris Parker, blinking in the light, came out and saw me there. She seemed surprised to find me at the service and shocked to see me sitting on a gravestone.

I got up and, on an impulse, told her I wanted to talk to her some more about Professor Warren.

"I don't really see . . ." she began, looking around for help. There wasn't any, just gravestones. "I thought you'd been . . ."

"I have been," I replied, "but as you can see, it didn't stop me. Even though I might lose my job."

"Well," she said matter-of-factly, "if you don't follow orders . . . We all hope, certainly, the police get to the bottom of this tragedy, find whoever did it. But it's just not our business, is it? That's why we have the police."

"Well," I replied, "I'm police, too, remember? And I really do think it's my business. And maybe it's yours, too. I'd really appreciate it if you'd give me a few minutes. It's a hot day. Too hot to stand out here."

"But what can I do to help?" she asked. "Everybody says it was a thief, out to steal a computer."

"It probably was," I said, and led the way down the path to the parking lot.

"I just don't want to get into any trouble," Doris Parker said, looking over her shoulder at the people coming out of the chapel behind us.

"I don't either," I told her. I offered her a ride home but she said she had her own car. I said I'd follow her and she said all right.

Fifteen

Doris Parker's small, white stucco house was set back on a street of old, well-kept-up homes. Tree roses lined both sides of her walk, but it was too early in the summer for roses to be in bloom. "They're white and pink," she told me. The house was trimmed in pink and there were tiny beds of newly planted flowers along the front. "The neighbors call it the Hansel and Gretel house," she said as she unlocked her front door. "If all the flowers were in bloom, you'd understand why."

The living room looked like the scene inside a toy Easter Egg. The walls were papered in small pink roses against a white background, the couch and chairs were pink with white antimacassars. The furniture repeated the white and pink motif everywhere. It must have taken years of patient work to create something so mindlessly sweet. I told Doris it was overwhelming. It was a weak response but the best I could do, and it seemed to satisfy her. She went out into the kitchen to get iced tea from the refrigerator. At least it wasn't pink lemonade.

I drifted to the mantel over a fireplace that had never been used. A cluster of small figurines—of children jumping rope, holding hands, petting animals, carrying parasols—were arranged neatly around a photograph of Doris's daughter Marilyn, the same photograph I'd seen in Doris's office.

Doris came back with a tray of glasses and a pitcher and caught me with the photograph in my hands.

"She's very pretty," I said. "She looks just like you." That was almost true, too. Marilyn looked the way her mother must have looked at that age, with dark-set eyes in a small, round face.

"Why thank you!" Doris said, giving me the bright smile that never reached her eyes, and gently took the picture from me. She gave it the same smile and then replaced it where it had been. She sat down and watched me until I took the hint and sat down, too.

"You look so nice in navy," she said, handing me a glass of iced tea and a coaster. In her living room I stuck out like a bruise. "Girls look so nice in dresses, I'm glad they're coming back. But I do think you should let your hair grow."

"I like the shape of my ears," I said. I haven't always. The right one is slightly larger than the left and when I was a kid that bothered me a lot. It also made me tilt my head so people couldn't see both ears at one time. I'm still working to overcome that tilt by looking people straight in the eye. That disconcerts some of them.

"I have to apologize to you," I said. "When you told me in your office the other day that your daughter had died, I assumed it was a long time ago. I'm sorry."

"That's very kind of you to say, Miss O'Neill. However, it *was* a long time ago."

"I think you said it happened last Christmas," I said.

"Did I tell you that?" She hadn't, actually. Arthur Fletcher had. "It was such a sad time for me, but it really is true that time heals all wounds."

There are dolls that when you turn them on, say things like that.

"It must have been a terrible loss," I persisted.

"Of course it was. But Marilyn no longer lived at home, you know. You know how children are. She made up her mind that she wanted to live by herself. Still . . ." She let whatever else she was going to say remain unsaid.

"How old was she?"

"Marilyn was eighteen. She had just started at the University in the fall. She was interested in art, she was going to major in it. I don't think that's wise, do you? So little security for a girl."

"If she had talent," I said.

"Oh, she did. For my last birthday she gave me that drawing over there. It's one of hers."

I looked where she gestured, then got up to look more closely at the framed picture on the wall. It was a child's face, sketched in pink. At first I thought it was a child's work, a crude copy of the face from a package of toilet paper. But Marilyn had put extra work into the eyes. They were her eyes, and her mother's, staring out of the pink, pastel drawing just as, behind me on the edge of the couch, her mother's were staring at me from the pink and white living room.

I felt goose pimples popping out on my arms. I was sure it was a joke of some sort, a joke Marilyn Parker had played on her mother. With her talent, or with her lack of talent.

Appalled, I said, "It matches the living room. That was thoughtful." Doris continued to stare at me for a long time, her eyes glittering but without any kind of expression I could label. Unless, somewhere deep inside, she was laughing at me. I shook off the thought. Ice tinkled against the inside of her glass.

Then she put the glass down, put her hands in her lap, and said, "You didn't come here to talk to me about my daughter, Miss O'Neill, did you?"

No, I hadn't. But it took me a moment to try to remember why I *had* come there. I moved back to my chair, tried to keep my eyes from straying to the eyes watching me from the wall. The pair on the couch were enough.

I said that since she'd been in the English department so long—twenty years?—she ought to be able to tell me something about Professor Warren that would be helpful in solving his murder. Anything she could tell me about Warren's character, his relationships with other members of the faculty, might be important.

She said she'd already answered questions like that from the city police, from that homicide man, Lieutenant Hansen, who'd investigated Professor Warren's murder. He'd even come out to her house to interview her and had gone over it with her again. She asked me if anything new had developed that made the police think it wasn't just a murder committed because Warren had surprised a thief.

It surprised me that Hansen had come out to her house

himself to talk to her, but I didn't let her know that. I told her there'd been no new developments and that was why we were retracing our steps, hoping to find something we'd missed the first time. "I'd like to hear it from you myself," I said, looking around the room with new eyes and wondering what Hansen had made of it.

She sounded annoyed. "All right," she said. "Professor Warren was a lovely man, a gentleman. He got on well with everybody as far as I could see. I can't believe that anybody would set out to deliberately harm him. That's exactly what I told that lieutenant."

I believed her. Word for word, too, probably. I said, "Arthur Fletcher didn't like Adam Warren much. I'm sure you know that. And you heard how Lee Pierce spoke of him when he saw him lying there dead, because you were there, too."

"Those two! Of course there was resentment against Professor Warren, and especially from Professor Fletcher. There is always resentment from the weak against the strong. Professor Warren could be hard sometimes, very determined to have his way. Not everybody agreed with his decisions. Professor Fletcher did not agree with Adam Warren on *any-thing*. It was jealousy, in my opinion."

"What happened between Pierce and Warren seemed to be more personal than professional."

"Frankly, Miss O'Neill, I never understood what Professor Warren saw in Lee Pierce in the first place. Lee Pierce was a bad influence on Adam Warren."

I asked her what she meant by that and she replied, "It's just a feeling I have—had, I mean. I wanted to warn Professor Warren against Pierce. I wanted to . . . but I couldn't. I didn't have that kind of relationship with him. With Professor Warren. Professor Warren's troubles started when he became friends with Lee Pierce."

"What kind of troubles?" I asked.

She looked at me and then quickly away. "Neglecting his duties as chairman, his writing, his teaching," she said.

"Neglecting them for what?" I persisted.

Doris's mouth pursed up like a raisin and she didn't answer me.

"He chased students," I said. "Women students."

"What makes you say that?" she asked, her eyes darting to me and then away.

"I've heard it from various people," I said.

"When I said Lee Pierce was a bad influence on Adam Warren," she said, "I meant that when he was with Pierce, he drank too much. That's what I meant."

"How do you know that?" I asked.

"Because I could see it," she replied, "from my desk. I know when men drink, Miss O'Neill! I saw them coming into the office some mornings, arm in arm, after a night on the town. Professor Warren and Pierce." She almost spat Pierce's name out. "Professor Warren would hardly say a word to me, and I didn't like it when he did. He scared me sometimes. His eyes were bloodshot and angry. I wanted to warn him. And I tried, in little ways. But he wouldn't listen. I knew that sooner or later, the way he was living was going to kill him. And I was right!"

She said it fiercely, almost triumphantly.

"It sounds as if you cared about the man."

"Oh, I cared about Adam Warren, Miss O'Neill. We were in the English department the same length of time. We started there the same year. For as long as I've been in the department, Adam Warren remembered me at Secretary's Week, with flowers. And even at his worst, he could be kind. He was so sympathetic, and such a comfort, when Ralph, my husband, went away. It was a time of heartache for me, and Professor Warren saw it. He came to the house with flowers."

"That was kind," I agreed, and asked her when her husband went away.

"Almost two years ago," she replied reluctantly.

"You're *divorced*," I said, wanting to be sure.

"Yes." She gave me a hurt look, because I'd used a real word.

"Then you and Marilyn lived here alone, and then Marilyn left, too."

"Yes," she said.

"And Professor Warren—was he kind to you when Marilyn died?"

If possible, Doris Parker sat up even straighter. "What do you mean?"

"You said he brought you flowers when your husband left you. I was just wondering what he did when he'd learned that your daughter had died."

"He brought me flowers," she answered, "of course he did. He brought me flowers then, too."

"This past Christmas," I said.

"This—yes." She had grown very still, like her daughter in the drawing on the wall behind her. She got up suddenly from the couch. "Is there anything more you want? It's so hot, and I'm tired. It was such a nice service, didn't you think?"

"Her death was never cleared up," I said.

She didn't answer, as if she hadn't heard me. "It was a hit-and-run accident," I said, more loudly, "that was never cleared up."

"You know it was! You know the police haven't found out who did it. And does it matter anyway? Will it bring my Marilyn back to me if they ever find who did it? I don't want to know who did it. I don't want it brought up again. It's too painful."

Her hands were trembling and she said the words as if she were about to cry. But her large, dark eyes were dry as she stared at me. She went to the mantel, stood a moment with her back to me, and then picked up one of the figurines there, put it down again, and then knocked it off with a hand that jerked suddenly. It shattered at her feet on the tile in front of the fireplace. She fell down onto her hands and knees as if, if she hurried, she might be able to save it. She stared down at the broken figure, a child's head next to a shattered body. She turned her face up to me.

"You made me do that!" she cried out, and scrambled to her feet. "These belong to Marilyn. I give her one every year on her birthday. They come from Germany, and they're very expensive."

I got up and started toward her, to help her pick up the pieces.

"No," she yelled. "Stay away. I'll take care of it, after you're gone. Don't you understand that I want you to go?"

"I will," I said. I felt dirty and mean, but I didn't think I'd feel less dirty and mean if I left, so I stayed. "Adam Warren hustled students."

"What?"

Maybe she didn't know the word.

"Dated students, went out with students, used his prestige, his power, to have affairs with students. You know what I mean, you've been at the University a long time. It's called hustling."

"I told you I don't know anything about that. Gossip! Lieutenant Hansen didn't ask anything about that. And you don't know anything either. You've been talking to that girl, Susan Carpenter, the one you asked me about when you lied and told me you were helping the police. *She'll* know all about Adam Warren and women students! Did she tell you how *she* tried to get him—and how it ended?"

"You tell me," I said. "You seem to know."

"Yes, I do. I see things from my desk. I know what goes on in that department. Adam Warren *dumped* her!" A brutal word for Doris. "And she deserved it. Don't come to me with talk of sexual harassment! She was old enough to know better. That's all I know about Adam Warren's private life."

"You mean, that's all you're going to tell me. A lot seems to have happened in the English department around Christmas vacation. Unusual things. Your daughter was killed in a hit-and-run accident. Something suddenly went wrong with Warren and Pierce's friendship. Warren resigned, unexpectedly, as chairman of the department." And then I asked her, "Was Adam Warren having an affair with your daughter, too, Mrs. Parker?"

I had no idea what kind of response I'd get to that one, so I guess I wasn't really surprised when she took a sudden step toward me, her face twisted in rage, and raised one hand as if to hit me. I stepped back.

"I think you're crazy," she said, still coming, her voice low and steady, almost a whisper. "You shouldn't have thoughts like that." Then an idea occurred to her, one that stopped her in her tracks. Her dark eyes lit up. "You're trying to—to *frame* me," she said, "to blame Professor Warren's murder on me; you've been sent by the University to try to find some reason why *I* might have killed him, they're afraid one of their professors did it! Well, it's not going to work. My daughter wasn't that kind of girl! She wasn't! Now get out of here, get out of my home!''

She came at me again. She wasn't the same person I'd come into the house with, the Hansel and Gretel house. She wasn't the same person at all. Hansel and Gretel must have made a similar discovery. I backed to the door. I caught the eye of Marilyn—the picture of Marilyn on the wall—and it seemed as if she were watching me, but I didn't have much time to consider it—I just wanted to get out of there.

Sixteen

The next day was Sunday. Tim Hale, Susan Carpenter's fiancé—or ex-fiancé, depending upon whom you wanted to believe—had told me that if I really wanted to play detective I should go see Jack Becker, a professor of criminology who lived in the woods. The water troll, Tim called him. Go out on a Sunday, he'd sneered, get to know the kind of people Adam Warren hung out with. He didn't think I would.

I didn't think I would either, even as I turned onto the freeway and headed south. I told myself that I'd never have a better opportunity to do it than now, when Lee Pierce wouldn't be there. He ought to be in Ireland right now. And the only risk I'd be taking, I thought, would be the risk of getting fired and/or making a fool of myself.

Jack Becker lived in one of the newer, expensive developments, in what was once an area of rolling, wooded hills without a name. The freeway had homed in on the area, and now the hills don't roll as much as they use to, the woods have been manicured like poodles, and much of the fauna native to the area has been replaced by upper-middle-class professionals. They named it Arcadia.

Becker's was a large, new home built of unpainted cedar siding in a grove of trees at the end of a cul-de-sac. It was quiet there, and cool, especially after the noisy and sunscorched freeway. I parked my Rabbit on the street and walked up to the house. The driveway was filled with new and casually expensive cars, not at all what I would have expected for a university professor's friends. But then, I didn't expect a university professor to own a house like this one either.

I rang Becker's doorbell and listened to the opening bars of "Greensleeves" from the other side of the door. I thought I heard a shout from someplace deep in the house, but I wasn't sure, so I rang the bell again and had to listen to the same snatch of "Greensleeves" all over again, as if a child had lost its place and started from the beginning. This time I heard a muffled chorus of "Come in!" so I tried the door, pushed it open, and went in.

The living room was air-conditioned and empty. A large picture on the wall in front of me was constructed of maroon jeans material stretched on a frame, its seams making a minimalist statement diagonally across it. The picture served as a backdrop for a clay pot on the floor that held a weed.

The furniture seemed to have been chosen to underscore the bleakness of the wall-to-wall carpeting. Everything in the room but the weed looked as if it were one in a limited series of identical such objects. I liked the weed a lot.

Laughter, the buzz of conversation, and the splash of water was coming up from a flight of stairs in the wall on my right. I followed the sounds down the steep, narrow stairs and into a large recreation room that opened onto a sunken patio with sliding glass doors. Sunlight flooded the patio and I had to squint to see into it.

A naked man was bustling in my direction, a welcoming grin splitting his face. He had short legs and a whiskey vat for a torso and he was covered with dark curly hair from top to toe. He was about fifty. He stopped in front of me and shook himself like a friendly St. Bernard, apparently as a form of greeting. "You're not what I expected, and you're nobody I know, but I don't mind if you don't," he said. "Take off your clothes and join us in the tub. The water's terrific! You won't believe it."

I stared over his shoulder at the big redwood tub that stood half in, half out of the patio doors. A few heads and the tops of heads, of men and women, stuck up above the rim. A woman was just climbing out of the tub on the patio side, her hair dark and so short that, wet, it looked plastered to her head. I couldn't see her face, but I wanted to. It didn't have to be the woman I'd seen in Frye Hall when Adam Warren was murdered, the woman Fletcher had called Lynn the day before at the memorial service.

Other people were out in the patio, some of them splashing in a swimming pool, some just standing around and talking or sprawled in lawn chairs, their bodies glistening with oil. There were between fifteen and twenty people there, about evenly divided between men and women. "You won't need a swimsuit," Tim Hale had told me. He'd been right about that.

"Are you Professor Becker?" I asked. It was an unnecessary question. Although I'd never met a water troll, he looked the way I imagined one would look.

"Jack!" he bellowed. "Call me Jack. Unless you're one of those Seventh Day Adventists, or Mormons, we get here on Sundays sometimes. But hell, what if you are? Come baptize us in the blood of Abraham!" He laughed and shook some more. I was getting soaked.

"I'm here because of Adam Warren," I said. "Professor Warren."

The fun seemed to leave Jack Becker's eyes, close-set and as round as marbles. "Adam?" He looked confused. It might have been my imagination, but the level of noise coming from the hot tub seemed to diminish considerably. I could hear the splash of water from the patio, and the voices of the people out there. "What about Adam?"

"I'm his sister," I said.

"His sister." Becker said the words as if stalling for time, to give his brain a chance to deal with a concept so stupendous. Then he seemed to get it. "Adam's sister," he said, on track once again, "Adam's sister! Of course you are! Here for the memorial service the University threw for him." He was pleased to have figured it out, and I was pleased for him. "That was yesterday, wasn't it? Jerry and I couldn't make it." He looked at me. "You look just like Adam," he said, and threw a fat, wet arm around my shoulder, stretching a bit to reach. "We can't begin to tell you how sorry we were about Adam. Insane, it's just *insane!* Who'd want to . . . ? And for what? A measly computer! A computer!" He changed the subject abruptly. "How'd you find us, way out here in the woods?"

I followed the shopping malls, I wanted to say, but said instead, "Adam mentioned you in his letters sometimes. He didn't make friends easily, as I'm sure you know—didn't really *need* lots of friends—but his Sundays out here with you must have been precious to him. I couldn't find your phone number in the book, but the University gave me your address. Your phone's unlisted."

"Of course," he agreed, "of course it is. Adam wrote about us—about our Sundays—in his letters home, did he? You can't know how that moves me—us. Jerry, did you hear that?" he called over his shoulder.

One of the women in the tub behind him replied that she'd heard it. She didn't sound moved.

"And so, here you are. Out looking up Adam's friends."

"I've got a few extra days on my plane ticket," I told him, "and I had some vacation time coming, so I thought I'd spend a little time in Adam's town. I've never been here before, you know, and there's so much to do and see. We're small town, you know." I wondered if I dared risk saying I owned the Sears catalog store, but decided against it.

"Good idea! Maybe we'll have the honor of showing you some of the sights. But for now, come join us in the tub. You'll learn more about Adam's life just by sharing with us than by standing here talking. You ever been in a hot tub before, on a day like this? You won't believe how great it feels—especially when you get out!" He chuckled fatuously. "But I have to warn you: no bathing suits, in the event you brought one. They're against our religion. But maybe Adam told you all about it, in one of those letters of his?"

"No," I said, and laughed the sort of nervous laugh I imagined Adam's sister, from some small town in Michigan, would laugh. It wasn't hard to do either, because I was nervous. The idea of being naked among strangers—even naked strangers—wasn't appealing to me at the best of times, and that's not what these times were.

But I did it anyway. As soon as I stepped out of my underpants, I ran to the hot tub. Without pausing, and ignoring the ladder, I vaulted over the side and into the water with a splash and a grim face. The people already in there applauded.

The water was about as hot as the day, and the bubbles, mercifully, pretty much clothed us all. My feet slid off a body concealed beneath the surface. As I moved back against the wall, the body shot straight up out of the water and then fell down again, water running from deep-set eyes that looked at me steadily. "Hi," he said, "I'm Fred." Without waiting to hear from me, he ducked back under and, after a long time, shot out again. "Polaris missile!" he sputtered, at the apex of his flight. The other people in the tub stayed near the sides, tried to pretend Fred and his splashing weren't there at all. Fred didn't seem to mind. He was tall, thin and bare-assed white all over.

"No woman thinks she's got a good body," Jack Becker announced as he levered his bulk over the side of the tub and into the water from the ladder. He had buttocks like fallen wedding cakes. "But I'm here to tell you that every woman has." He gave me a stern stare, as if I were a longtime advocate of the opposing viewpoint. "*Every* woman has!"

I managed a smile of sorts, to assure him I was in his corner.

A woman standing next to me turned and smiled. "I'm Jerry," she said. "Jack's wife. You haven't told us your name."

"Joanne," I said. As I was driving out to the Beckers' I'd thought a lot about what Adam Warren's sister's name would be, if he had a sister in Michigan. Joanne felt right. I've always had an instinct for details like that, one of the few things I inherited from my father, the con artist, liar.

"Joanne," Jerry Becker said, tasting it. "Warren?"

"Yes."

Jerry Becker smiled. Smiling was apparently not something she did on a regular basis or with much pleasure. She had short gray hair and no expression on her face above the mouth. Her eyes were large and matched her hair in color. She was probably the same age as her husband, but she kept in much better shape. She gestured at the other people in the tub. "Friends," she said. "You can meet them later, if you want."

There were four other people in the tub, in addition to the Beckers, Fred, and me. I recognized one of them easily enough, a municipal court judge who'd recently been reprimanded for making sexist remarks from the bench to a woman lawyer. The reprimand, if I remembered correctly, had been for poor judgment. He'd kept his glasses on in the tub and they were streaked with steam, but he twisted and turned his head so that he could watch me through the clear spots.

Jack Becker butted in, standing too close to me. "You must be twenty-five years Adam's junior, at least. Quite a family, having two litters like that so many years apart."

"What peculiar planning," another woman said, on Becker's other side, leaning across him to get a better look at me. "My name's Merle, by the way."

"Twenty-eight," I said. "We didn't have the same mother, of course."

"We'll tell you all you want to know about Adam," Becker said. "We'll hold our own little service, a wake for Adam, right here in the water. He'd have liked that. Much better than that solemn thing the U threw for him, with the faculty getting up to mouth their pious platitudes. Hypocrites! Sorry if I hurt your feelings, dear," he said as an afterthought. He studied the bubbles I was wearing.

I asked innocent questions and got answers, mostly from Jack Becker. But everybody seemed eager to give me what they thought I wanted to hear, and to make me feel at home. Everybody, that is, except Fred. The Polaris missile just kept bouncing up and down in the middle of the pool, like a mechanical water sculpture. His eyes stayed open when he went under, were open and streaming water when he shot up, and they never left me. They were curiously alive, as if some kind of fire were burning behind them, behind his weak, pale face.

It all seemed innocent enough, if somewhat strange, and I almost began to feel ashamed, a tendency I have, for having sneaked into their lives in such a mean way. But I remembered Susan Carpenter and what she'd told me about this place and some of the things that went on here, and decided I didn't have to feel ashamed just yet. Maybe later—if I decided that these were just fairly ordinary people with too much money and time, who'd grown tired of all the traditional ways of spending both.

The pool out in the patio looked cool and I envied the swimmers. The woman with short dark hair, Lynn, was fixing herself a drink at a portable bar on the other side of the pool. She was wearing her glasses now.

"We were a second family to Adam," Jack Becker told me. "I told the police that, too."

"The police were here?"

"Here?" Becker gave his barking laugh, and some of the others thought that was funny, too. The judge had left the tub and was standing next to a young woman in a lounge chair, drying off. "No, not here! But they're good men, the police, and you can rest assured they'll catch whoever did Adam in. After all," he added, "every man jack of them is Jack's man!" Seeing the puzzled look on my face, he explained, "I teach criminology at the University, you know. The cops take my course—they have to. But some things I don't teach them," he added, looking around happily at his domain. "No sense overloading their minds."

"Jack," his wife said to him.

"Even the governor's attended some of Jack's seminars, hasn't he, Jack?" the woman who'd introduced herself to me as Merle put in.

"When was my brother here last?" I asked.

Becker appeared to think about that. The other people in the tub appeared to wait expectantly for his answer. "Not in several months, I think," Becker replied finally. "When was it, Jerry? Merle?" Neither answered. "It's been a while," he went on. "Adam was very busy toward the end, you know. He'd resigned as chairman of his department and was trying to catch up on his real work, research and writing. We missed him, we missed him. But now we have you, Adam's sister—Joanne. For a time at least, a brief time, to make up in some measure for our tragic loss."

"What else do you do," I asked, "besides stand around in a hot tub in the buff?" It came out more crudely than I'd intended it. "I mean," I tried again, "is this a nudist club?"

"Adam's dead?" Fred asked suddenly, no longer bouncing up and down. He looked from Becker to me.

"Yes," I said, surprised at the question. Where'd he been for the past couple of weeks?

"I didn't know that," he said. "When?"

"Two weeks ago," I told him, "two weeks ago Friday."

"Taking off our clothes," Becker said, "is only the preliminary act in our struggle to attain real freedom in this modern, overcultured world. It brings us closer, breaks down the artificial barriers civilization has imposed upon us."

"What comes next?" I asked, watching Fred, who had crouched down in the water so that his eyes, fixed on me, were just above the bubbling surface.

"What comes next?" Jack Becker asked. "Why don't you stay, Joanne, and find out for yourself? What comes next is what you want to come next."

"That takes in a lot of territory," I said. "It sounds like 'Fantasy Island.' "

"How did he die?" Fred asked, his voice almost a wail as he stood up suddenly. He didn't wait for an answer, just subsided back under the water.

"It's *better* than 'Fantasy Island,' " Jack Becker said, "because this is real! It's no accident we gather on Sundays. This is, perhaps, a kind of halfway house between the conventional life we were born to and the freedom we are seeking—and which some of us may already have found. We're all—"

"You talk too much, Jack," his wife interrupted.

"No, go one, Jack," Merle said, "it's really nothing to keep secret."

"There's not much more to tell, Jerry," Becker said, giving his wife a reproachful look.

Something moved in Jerry Becker's light blue eyes. I preferred them expressionless. I wondered if Jack Becker had a preference.

"I'd really like to hear it," I said.

"Of course you would," Becker said. He grabbed Merle and dragged her through the water to his wife, and draped his fat, short arms around both of them, or as much of them as he could reach. "Jerry and I have been involved in an

open-ended relationship for nearly nine years,'' he announced to me. ''Open-ended in every sense of the word.''
He gestured at the people still in the tub, who seemed to
enjoy hearing him talk. ''We lock ourselves into nothing in
our quest for higher levels of integration.''

''Integration into what?'' I asked.

''Not since Christmas Eve,'' Fred said, suddenly shooting
up in front of me in a plume of water.

''What?'' I asked. My mind tried to relate Fred's statement
with Becker's quest for higher levels of integration.

''Adam hasn't been here since Christmas Eve,'' he said.
He stared at me for a long moment. The water streaming
from his face made him look extremely mournful, but his
eyes were still on fire. He disappeared below the surface of
the water again and stayed there, the top of his head just at
my navel.

I tried to keep my face expressionless, felt everybody's
eyes on me. ''What does that mean exactly?'' I asked Jack
Becker, as if Fred hadn't interrupted. ''That you have an
open marriage?'' I'd thought open marriages had gone out
with the sixties.

''Oh, more than that,'' Becker answered, ''much more than
that.'' But his heart didn't seem to be in his words anymore.
He looked deflated, no longer sounded interested.

''The term *open marriage* doesn't begin to describe it,''
Merle put in, as if really anxious for me to understand. ''No
more than *marriage* conveys anything about the situation of
the couples involved in them.''

''It's barbecue time, Jack,'' Jerry Becker told her husband,
speaking over Merle's tidy, golden head. ''I'm sure everybody's getting quite hungry. I know I am.''

Fred shot up, spattered water in my face.

''Indeed it is,'' Jack Becker agreed, some of his enthusiasm back. ''It's time to cook something that *bleeds*. Men are
good at that,'' he added, giving me a wink. He bustled toward the ladder.

''I've been hoping to meet Adam's friend Lee Pierce out
here with you,'' I said to his back. ''The poet, you know?
Adam spoke of him often.''

Becker kept going, started to pull himself out of the water.

"Did he?" he asked. "We don't see much of Pierce out here. We know him, of course, but who doesn't? He's not a regular member of our little band."

"The poet, you know!" cried Fred, spitting more water and trying to imitate the way I said it. "The poet, you know! Where is the poet, you know, anyway?" He looked around at all the faces. Nobody seemed interested in the question. Getting no answer, he turned back to me. "I write poetry, too. Listen! 'Hope, the actor, must the whole play memorize, but doesn't know the end until—he speaks the lines and dies!' What do you think of it?"

"Why don't you help Jack with the charcoal, Fred?" Jerry Becker said to him. It was an order, one even Fred could understand.

"Yes," he agreed, and pulled his long body out of the water. At the top of the ladder he turned back to me. He said, "Lee was here Christmas Eve, too, but he left early, I think. He doesn't like my poetry, and I don't like his."

Seventeen

I wanted to talk to Fred and also learn more about the woman with short hair, but I didn't see how I could do either, stuck there in the hot tub. The few people remaining in the tub were starting to follow Fred up the ladder. I started after them.

"Stay here a minute," Jerry said to me.

I turned around reluctantly. I didn't like the sound of her voice. "I'm getting poached," I told her, and I kept going, up the ladder.

"You're the campus policewoman who found Adam's body," she said. She stared at me levelly with her cold eyes. "I saw you on the news."

There wasn't anything I could say to that, so I just waited for what would come next.

"This isn't very nice of you," she went on, "abusing our hospitality like this. You're going around asking questions about Adam's murder. On your own."

"Who told you that?" I asked her.

"It's a small world, the University, no matter how big it sometimes seems."

"Not that small."

She ignored that, asked, "How'd you find out about us?"

I considered answering that it's a small world, the University, no matter how big it sometimes seems, but said instead, "Doris Parker, Marilyn Parker's mother," and watched her face closely.

"Those aren't names I know," she replied.

"The English department secretary," I said. "I don't suppose Adam Warren ever mentioned her either. She was very upset by his death, perhaps because she'd recently had a tragedy of her own. Her daughter was killed, too. Marilyn Parker. She was killed on Christmas Eve.''

''That's too bad,'' Jerry Becker said. It sounded as if she were going to say something else on that subject, but instead she said, ''You've done good work, to get this far. I don't know your name.''

''Peggy,'' I replied. ''Beginner's luck.''

''I wonder if you've shared your luck with the police, Peggy,'' she said. ''The real police, I mean. I suppose I could call and find out. Tell them a campus policewoman's barged into our Sunday gathering, playing detective.''

''Why don't you?'' I asked.

''You haven't begun to annoy me enough. Not yet, anyway. But when you do, I will. There's nothing here for you.''

''You want Warren's murderer found, don't you?'' I asked her.

''Oh, he will be, I'm sure. A thief, caught stealing the English department's Macintosh or IBM, or whatever they're called! What a waste of a beautiful man's life.'' She paused, as if thinking about that waste, then went on, ''Catching Adam's killer won't bring him back, so I really don't care if he's caught or not. I do care about my own peace of mind. I don't want my husband upset. I don't want our friends''— she gestured out at the patio—''upset either. You came out here for a reason. I'd like to know what you thought you'd find.''

There was no real threat in her voice, just the potential for it. Jerry Becker was as tall as I and obviously in good condition.

''I need a swim,'' I told her, ''and then I'll get out of here.'' I went past her, giving her a fairly wide berth, and out to the pool. Jack Becker, wearing nothing but a short apron, was down at the other end of the patio pouring kerosene into a grill, talking to Merle and Fred, both of whom were wearing shirts and shorts. Fred turned and watched me as I walked to the pool, but nobody else seemed to pay any attention. Lynn, the woman I was interested in talking to, wasn't out there. She hadn't come past the hot tub while I was in it, so she must have gone into the house through the sliding glass doors down by Jack Becker.

I dived into the pool and swam a couple of laps, figuring I might as well enjoy some of the pleasures of the idle rich while I had the chance. The water was cold and felt wonderful after the hot tub.

I noticed that Jerry Becker and I were the only two still not wearing clothes—if you count Jack Becker's absurd apron and hair as clothes. I was glad he was too far away to stare. He had eyes like slugs.

Jerry Becker followed me into the pool, and was waiting for me when I came over to the side at the shallow end.

"What else do you do besides mill around in the buff while seeking higher levels of integration?" I asked her.

She gave me a faint smile. "We're innocent enough," she replied. "Jack's told you most of it already. We're all professionals of one sort or another, or living with them, or married to them. A lot of those women have careers, as I do."

I asked her what she did and she told me she was a therapist who specialized in marital problems. "I'm a good one, too," she added.

"You save a lot of marriages?"

"I didn't say that. I save lives. But I saved my own marriage, Peggy."

She explained that when her husband reached the top in his field, he began to feel that he had no place to go except around and around, and so he started having affairs. Nothing new in that, but it took her by surprise anyway, she said, when she finally caught him at it.

He promised he wouldn't do it again—and did it again. Then she realized that he wanted her to catch him. He wanted a freer life or a younger wife, but he didn't have the guts to break out of the marriage by himself. He wanted her to throw him out.

"Why didn't you?" I asked her.

"Because I didn't want to do his dirty work for him," she replied, "and besides, that wouldn't have been a very creative response, would it?" Jerry Becker would have been quite beautiful, I thought, if the lines around her mouth weren't so deep and if she'd had any emotion in her eyes. "So," she went on, "I started a little group—Jack's little band of freedom-seeking individualists."

"You did?"

"Yes, I did." She laughed at my astonishment. She created, she said, their open marriage and the group of people who served as Jack's congregation, too. "You've met Merle," she said, nodding in the direction of her husband and Merle at the other end of the patio, "our 'open-ended marriage partner.' I met her when I went back to school, seven years ago. Jack made a pass at her then, she responded—you may have noticed that she's not very bright—I caught them at it, and that's when I got my idea. They both liked it. Obviously," she added dryly.

I waited for her to continue, but she didn't. She just sat there on the edge of the pool, her feet in the water, staring in the general direction of her "creation."

"Didn't you just trade one evil for another?" I asked. "Instead of occasional affairs, now you've got weekly sex parties to deal with?"

"Sex parties?" she repeated, as if she'd forgotten I was still there. "Is that what you've heard—from whom? The secretary—Doris Parker, was it? Dear me! What else, Peggy?" She'd turned and was looking at me. Her voice sounded as if she hadn't heard a funnier story in years. Her eyes had gained some life and seemed almost alive with interest.

"Nobody told me anything," I said. "I just assumed—"

"A little nudity—no doubt shocking to you—swimming in the summer, drinks, dinner, and that's it. Jack gets to stare at all the naked women, show off his harem—Merle and me—and everybody's happy. What the rest of them do after they go home is their business. Jack and I just turn off the tub and go to bed."

"With Merle."

"Oh, no," she said, "I draw the line at that. Merle's bedroom is down the hall, way down the hall. They have their nights, we have ours."

Wonderful. It sounded almost true. If I hadn't heard Susan Carpenter's story first, I'd probably have believed it.

I couldn't help it, I blurted out, "It sounds tacky!" I didn't wait for her reply, climbed out of the pool, and headed in the direction of my clothes.

She didn't get mad. She laughed, strolled after me. "You're young," she said. "Maybe someday you'll be more tolerant of the things people have to do to get from the cradle to the grave without falling into the area marked 'Fuss.' "

"You make it sound like Monopoly," I said.

"Life is, in a way," she replied. "You'd be surprised to learn what a therapist has to invent for people sometimes to keep them on the path."

"Drugs?" I asked.

"I don't practice medicine," she said evenly, "if that's what you mean."

"I don't suppose Adam Warren came here alone on Sundays," I said.

"I wondered when you'd get around to Adam. He joined us about three years ago, right after he came back from Washington. He was exhausted—burned out, really—and needed to learn how to relax and play again. And he was just what we wanted, too—a new face, an interesting man, and he brought new people with him, the women he dated. They changed rather frequently and frankly I don't remember all their names."

"Students?"

"We don't ask for IDs."

"Christmas Eve," I said. "That was the last time Warren was here, according to Fred."

"Maybe it was. I'm not sure. Adam was so busy—"

"I know," I said impatiently. "You said you didn't know who Doris Parker was, and then you launched into the story of your marriage. Doris Parker had a daughter, Marilyn. Marilyn died on Christmas Eve."

"I'm sorry to hear that. That's the second time you've mentioned her name," Jerry Becker said, "and I still don't know it."

"It's also the second time you haven't asked me how Marilyn Parker died."

She blinked. That was the first time I'd surprised her, or the first time I'd surprised her enough that she couldn't conceal it.

"Well, how did she die, then?" she asked, trying a smile.

"Hit-and-run," I told her. I was dressed by then, except for my socks and tennis shoes. Jack Becker hollered something at us and waved a barbecue fork. Fred stared in our direction. "You can't keep all those people out there quiet," I said. "If Marilyn Parker was ever here, the police are going to find out about it."

"So what?" Jerry Becker asked. "What's she got to do with us—with Adam?"

She'd moved close to me. I wanted to get out of there, but with her standing so close I didn't want to stoop down to get my shoes. She was still naked, but she didn't look defenseless. I took a step back, and bumped into someone behind me.

I spun around and found myself staring into Arthur Fletcher's startled face. "What the hell are you doing here?" he demanded.

"How about you?" I said, and stepped aside. I didn't like having Jerry Becker so close behind me, Fletcher so close in front of me. Call me claustrophobic. "Looking for Lynn?"

He stared at me for another long moment, then raised his head and looked into the patio.

"Art!" a happy voice shouted, and Fred appeared from the patio. "Art Fletcher! Long time no see. Now, who could you be looking for, out here in the woods? Eh? Do I get three guesses?"

Fred came at Art Fletcher with both arms outstretched, as if expecting Fletcher to catch him. Instead, Fletcher did the last thing I'd have expected from him. He threw a punch that Fred's face rushed to meet. Fred didn't even yell. His head, still grinning happily, just rocked backward as his legs sagged beneath him. He fell into a kneeling position and then keeled over onto his side, bleeding from his mouth and nose.

Jack Becker came around the tub and stood there amazed, his long barbecue fork in one hand. The words on his short apron said "Come and get it."

"Where is she," Art Fletcher said, to nobody in particular, "where's Lynn?" He said it the first time in a nearly normal voice. The second time he shouted it.

"Who's Lynn?" I asked him innocently. "Your wife?"

He remembered I was there then, looked at me. "You get out of here," he said. But he wasn't giving me room to move.

Jack Becker asked Fletcher, "You know her? You know Adam's sister?"

"Adam's—"

I decided I'd outstayed my welcome here. I scooped up my shoes, ducked under Fletcher, and ran up the stairs behind him, taking them two at a time. He didn't follow me. Nobody did. Behind me I heard Jack Becker say, in a pleading voice, "Will somebody please help me understand?"

Eighteen

As I stood by my car putting on my shoes, I looked back up at the house. Jack Becker was standing outside, on the porch. It should have been comic—a short, fat man with lots of hair covering his body and wearing only an apron that said, "Come and get it." But there wasn't anything funny in the sight of him there, staring after me, unmoving, his arms at his sides. It was late afternoon, still sunny and warm, but with those eyes watching me I felt the kind of chill you get when a cloud passes unexpectedly in front of the sun. There's not much to a summer cloud, you can remind yourself, but the sun's gone anyway.

I started my engine and made a tight U-turn and felt better when I'd driven out of the water troll's sight.

Instead of following the main road back to the freeway, I turned down one of the little winding lanes that fed into Arcadia from the main road and turned around and parked.

Something told me Art Fletcher wasn't going to stay to enjoy the Beckers' hospitality, so I decided to wait to see if he got who he'd come for and would take her away with him. I intended to follow them, try to find out who she was.

I only had to sit there a few minutes before a car came around a curve in the road, heading for the freeway. Fletcher was alone in it, unless he had the woman tied up on the floor. That wouldn't have surprised me much.

I waited until he was far down the street and then turned out behind him and followed him onto the freeway. I'd never tried to tail anybody before but it was easy, since Fletcher didn't seem to be paying any attention to anything or anyone.

He drove fast and angrily and got off the freeway at an exit that took him into one of the older suburbs, not far out of town. He drove into a neighborhood of nice but unspectacular homes, most of them just one story. Halfway down the block, Fletcher turned into a driveway and disappeared into the gloom of a garage.

I pulled over and watched and waited.

He came out of the garage, hit a switch on the way, and the garage door flowed down behind him like a curtain. He started across his lawn to his front door.

I got out of my car and slammed the door noisily behind me. He turned at the sound. Almost without pausing, he changed direction and came over to me.

"What do you want?" he demanded, speaking softly, angrily.

I stood my ground. I remembered the suddenness and the violence with which he'd decked Fred back at the Beckers' place. Art Fletcher looked a lot different from the way he'd looked at our previous encounters. No dark three-piece suit today. He was wearing well-used tennis shoes, light summer slacks, and a white polo shirt, and looked as if he'd spent the afternoon on a tennis court. His nearly black hair was a mess, as if he'd run his fingers through it a lot, and his dark eyes were blazing with anger that didn't hide the fear.

"I want to know who that woman is you came for at the Beckers'," I said, "and why you just about took Fred's head off. I want to know what's going on out there."

"I don't have to answer questions from you," he said. "You're not any part of the investigation into Adam's murder, you're just a nosy b—"

"Dad!"

Before Fletcher could lay the noun—*bitch? busybody?*—to the adjective, a girl about ten or twelve years old sped down the street on a bike and screeched to a stop next to us. Fletcher turned to her, startled, the look of anger still on his face. The girl's grin faded and she turned to me, giving me an accusing look. She knew it was my fault. It's always somebody else's fault, never your dad's. She had freckles, a sweet face.

I gave her a hi and a smile and waited for Fletcher's next move.

"Go inside and tell your mother I'm home and she can start dinner, will you, Chrissy?" he said, the pleasantness forced.

"Sure, Dad," his daughter said, not fooled. She gave me another quick look, swung her bike around, and pedaled up the driveway.

"Aren't you going to invite me in?" I asked Fletcher. "From what I've seen so far, yours seems like such a nice family."

I kept my voice neutral, but it wasn't easy. Was Fletcher another of Jack Becker's groupies, one of the people Jerry Becker worked to keep on the straight and narrow path from cradle to grave? And, if so, how far in the area marked "Fuss" had he fallen?

"You've got no right to come here, goddamn you!" he said, but now he was trapped, and his voice was pleading. "This is where I live, goddamn it, this is my *home.*"

"Yes, I know," I said, "I recognize it. Now let me guess: I'll bet Lynn's your sister! Your wife seems to know and like her. I saw how happily they were chatting at the memorial service yesterday. And you went out to the Beckers' today to try to rescue her from the water troll."

"Water troll . . . ?"

"Jack Becker," I said. "You know, the squat, hairy fellow with the hot tub. That *was* you out there, wasn't it? I didn't just dream it?"

"Why are you doing this? What do you want?"

"I want to find out who killed Adam Warren," I said, my voice rising, and for some reason shaking, too, "and I'm not going to quit until I do."

"Or until you're dead," Fletcher replied, looking at me as if I were crazy. "You don't know what you're doing. Don't fool around with those people out there. 'Water troll!' Don't laugh at the Beckers, or you'll be sorry you did."

"I'm not laughing at them, but they don't scare me either," I lied. "What's her problem, Lynn's—aside from the fact that she's having an affair with you?"

Fletcher swore and reached for me, then remembered where he was and caught himself and let his arms drop. I brushed past him, heading for his front door. I'd had it with the jerk.

"For God's sake," he said, running to catch up, "where the hell are you going?"

"You won't tell me what I want to know," I said, "so I'm going to ask your wife. She'll know." I wasn't bluffing.

"Stop! My wife doesn't know anything about this!"

"Come with me," I said, not stopping, "and we'll both learn something."

"Please! We can't talk here."

"Then where can we talk?" I asked, stopped and looked at him. His face couldn't get any paler than it was naturally, but it did my heart good to see how he was sweating.

"Tomorrow," he said, thinking fast. "Call me at my office. I'll be through with my summer classes by eleven. Call me then."

"I'll *be* at your office at eleven tomorrow," I said.

He agreed to that because he had no choice. I went back to my car and drove away from there. I looked at all the nice houses in Arthur Fletcher's neighborhood. The late-afternoon sun was glinting in the windows on Fletcher's side of the street, so it was impossible to tell how many of his neighbors had been watching us, there in the street. It would depend on how many of them were at home.

His wife wouldn't be at a window watching us, of course. She'd be in the kitchen, fixing dinner for her family.

I biked over to Frye Hall the next day, arriving just at eleven when Fletcher's last class was due to end, expecting to catch him as he left his classroom. The classroom was empty. There wasn't even a stray student in it to indicate that Fletcher had dismissed class a few minutes early. It looked as if there hadn't been a class that morning.

I continued on down to Fletcher's office and knocked. Behind the frosted glass, his office was dark. The door was locked. I saw Doris Parker in her office at the end of the hall, sitting in a sunbeam. She was wearing red. I tried to remember if that's what Fletcher had told me she always wore on Mondays.

I walked down there. I was sure she'd seen me coming, but she ignored me and continued to type. Her fingernails, stained as bright a red as when I'd first seen her lying on the floor in Warren's office, were flying on the keys of her large electronic typewriter, looking like a bloody mist. I knocked on the doorframe to get her attention. She looked up, pretended to be surprised at seeing me there. She asked me what I wanted, her voice not very friendly, and I asked her where I could find Professor Fletcher. We had an appointment, I told her.

Professor Fletcher had called in sick, she replied, and had told her to cancel his classes that morning. She continued to stare at me, tried to stare me down. I didn't feel like getting into it with Doris Parker again, so I thanked her and left.

I went to the phone booth across the street from Frye and looked up Fletcher's number in the mutilated but still partially usable phone book, invested a quarter, and dialed. A woman answered. I asked for Professor Fletcher and she told me he wasn't available. I gave her my name and told her I was with the campus police, and she replied that her husband was sick. She sounded worried.

"Has something new happened in the English department?" she asked.

I told her no. I started to do what I'd promised I'd do, both to Fletcher and to myself: tell his wife why I was calling. But it's one thing to think you know everything, another to act on that assumption and maybe hurt someone. Maybe Fletcher's wife didn't know about the other woman. It wasn't my business to tell her.

So instead I said that I was calling to ask her husband if he knew the last name of a woman the campus police were trying to get hold of, a woman whose first name was Lynn.

There was a silence for a long moment, and then she said, her voice absolutely colorless, "Arthur is asleep now. He told me, however, that he plans to meet his classes tomorrow. You can try to get him at his office then and perhaps he'll help you. I'll tell him you called."

She waited until I said thank you to hang up.

Nineteen

We patrol alone, men and women alike. At least there's no discrimination there. The campus police used to patrol in pairs, but that was before I joined the force, back when the University had more money than it does now, and more cops. There was a lot of resistance at first from the men—not the women, who had something to prove—but now it's taken for granted. "You carry guns, don't you?" Lieutenant Bixler had asked at the time. The rhetorical question was one of his specialties. Bixler's days of working outside were long over. Besides, he might have added, the city cops patrol alone, don't they? And their world is a lot dirtier and more violent than ours. Or was, until the murder of Adam Warren.

It had only been a matter of time, some of the campus cops were saying, before a cornered thief killed somebody. The stealing of computers had become epidemic, no question about that, and most of us were sure that one of the motives for it was to get money for drugs. Bixler liked the computer-thief theory, too. According to scuttlebutt, he'd been told to like it by his superiors, who weren't enthusiastic about cops rummaging for murderers among the faculty.

It didn't make patrolling any easier, expecting at any time to come across somebody desperate enough to kill to support a drug habit. I was glad I had the middle watch. It didn't get pitch dark until toward the end of it, and there were more people around than on the dog watch.

By Monday morning, the hot spell had ended and it was cold. Monday night I walked my beat in my summer uniform, shivering.

I hadn't ridden my bike to work that afternoon, the way I usually do. I'd driven and parked in the lot outside headquarters where we keep the squad cars. It's well lighted there now. Strong overhead lights were installed in the lot during the Vietnam War, when a police car had been booby-trapped by antiwar protestors.

We walk our assigned beats in a random way, enter buildings at random, just to let people know we're there. As it gets later the buildings, the campus, grow more deserted. *But we carry guns, don't we?* You can get a real pain in the neck, looking over your shoulder every few seconds, and it looks stupid, too. For the first time in my brief career as a police officer, I'd have liked to patrol the west side of the University, the New Campus. It's much better lighted there, perhaps because that's where the sciences are located.

Even the streetlights are old on the Old Campus, and far apart, and they cast light that colors the darkness but doesn't drive it away. My imagination worked overtime and I tensed at any sound that came from behind me. I remembered how much I enjoyed walking around in this part of campus before Adam Warren had been murdered.

You can't patrol with a gun in your hands, not even when a murderer is loose in the neighborhood.

Two young women, coming out of a building, asked me to escort them to their car. One of them wore a T-shirt that said "Take back the night." They were parked too far away, so I used my portable to call the student escort service, something the University started several years ago after the number of incidents of rape and assault against women had risen sufficiently high to justify the expense as good public relations.

I stayed with them the ten minutes it took for the escort to arrive and then continued on my patrol, feeling lonelier than before.

I'm more frightened of the random, the aimless, than I am of the premeditated. I'm not afraid of sitting in the window of a lighted room, but I'd never sit there in the dark.

Blaming Adam Warren's murder on a computer thief didn't satisfy me for a similar reason—and also perhaps because I'd learned too much about the man to want his death to be senseless. I think people should earn their deaths, especially if they die unexpectedly, violently.

I thought Warren had earned his death. And I was beginning to get a scary feeling that I knew how.

I'd spent the rest of Sunday and all day Monday waiting for the phone to ring, to tell me I was wanted in Lieutenant Hansen's office downtown or in Lieutenant Bixler's on campus. To learn that I was suspended, or out of a job. But nobody from the Beckers' had complained, as far as I knew, either to the campus or to the city police, and Fletcher hadn't either, even though I'd behaved obnoxiously to all of them. That just made me more certain that I was on the right track. Some or all of those people knew something they didn't want brought to light. It had to be more than just their little sex parties—or sex and drug parties, if what Susan Carpenter had told me was true. None of that could be proved against them.

And Doris Parker, who'd almost certainly reported my meddling the first time, apparently hadn't done it again, even though the second time I'd talked to her she'd really been upset.

What were they all waiting for?

I had too many suspects. Tim Hale and Susan Carpenter, of course. I should have turned them over to homicide, let Hansen try to trace their movements the afternoon Warren was killed. There was something wrong about the story they'd told me, something left out. Would a woman as strong as Susan Carpenter seemed to be break off her engagement to a man who loved her just because she'd done something stupid? There should be more to it than that.

Someone was coming toward me along the path between the architecture building and the library. His head was huddled down in his raincoat, his hands deep in his pockets—on account of the cold, I hoped. I fought off the temptation to put my hand on my pistol.

"Good evening," he said, shooting a glance up at me as he passed.

I repeated his words and continued on a few more steps before turning to stare after him. He didn't look back, wasn't anybody I knew.

So much seemed to have happened around Christmas, and

that's where I was beginning to suspect that it had all begun—the story that ended, at least so far, with Warren's murder. That seemed a long time ago, a distant, white dream, cold the way an early summer night can never be cold. "It feels like fall," one of the women I'd called the escort service for had said. Maybe, but not like winter, when the cold gets into your blood.

Warren's friendship with Lee Pierce had broken up then. That's when Warren had stopped going to the Beckers', too. And soon after Christmas he'd resigned as chairman of the English department and started to try to catch up on work he'd been neglecting for a long time, ever since he returned from Washington. He'd been going out to the Beckers' since returning from Washington, too.

Marilyn Parker had been killed on Christmas Eve, a hit-and-run killing that had never been solved. Just a coincidence? Lots of people get killed on Christmas Eve. Jerry Becker denied knowing Marilyn's name, but Jerry Becker denied that anything other than a little nudity went on out at their place on Sundays, too, and I doubted she was telling the truth there. I didn't think it was a coincidence that last Christmas had been so busy for some of the people in the English department.

None of the people at the Beckers' wanted me to know that the last time Adam Warren had been out at their place had been Christmas Eve. None of them except Fred.

In spite of what I'd said to Jerry Becker, it would probably be impossible to get any of the people at the Beckers' to admit that Marilyn Parker had ever been there with Warren. "Every man jack of them is Jack's man," Becker had crowed. Becker was an internationally known expert in criminology, he'd written some of the most influential books in his field, and the police would treat him very gently, the way you treat your old teachers—especially if your old teachers have powerful friends.

Lieutenant Hansen had been warned off the case, just as Bixler had been, but I didn't think Hansen was following orders. And I wondered if my suspicion that he'd been urging me on at the memorial service on Saturday was just my overheated imagination.

Peggy O'Neill: Hansen's proxy. I wondered what his first name was. I wondered if he'd hire me if the University fired me for trying to do his dirty work.

Doris Parker. The cops would be happy to have her as their murderer. Nobody important, just a secretary, as serviceable as a computer thief. Under the pressure of interrogation or a trial, she'd probably go nuts, if she wasn't already.

I thought of her, of her bright, expressionless eyes shining out of their dark sockets, fading into and out of her pink and white fairy-tale world, and I shuddered at the thought of her being taken to police headquarters and forced to answer their questions. She'd sit there neatly, as if waiting for orders, and they would maul her like a maniac with a wedding cake.

I didn't like her. She was a child eater; I could see that easily enough. I saw her daughter's eyes staring at me out of that dreadful drawing she'd made for her mother, and I knew that she'd tried to talk to her mother, reached for her, and found nothing there. A long time ago, before she was old enough to know what it was she was trying to get, and before she knew she'd never get it. Her mother didn't want to hear anything upsetting. There's no sense in dwelling on our sorrows, she'd told me the first time I'd talked to her. We have to wipe out and pass on.

The drawing on the wall wasn't some last-ditch effort on the part of Marilyn Parker to communicate with her mother, it was a desperate taunt. I knew Marilyn Parker, I knew her temptations. I just didn't know how some people were able to avoid succumbing to them. Luck, maybe.

Doris Parker had had the opportunity to murder Warren, the murder weapon had been in her file cabinet, and now, if my guess was correct, she had a motive, too.

What if Doris had discovered—or suspected—that Adam Warren was the hit-and-run driver who'd killed Marilyn, maybe even deliberately? But how could she have found out? Unless it had something to do with the quarrel they'd had in her office, the day before Warren was killed.

But then again, it didn't have to be Doris Parker. There were other suspects. Tim Hale, for one. He'd come back from California just before Warren was killed. What'd he been doing out there? Smoking dope and brooding on Susan and Warren? And Susan had a new, expensive piano, one she told me had belonged to her mother. I knew that wasn't true.

And Art Fletcher and the woman he came out to the Beckers' to look for—Lynn. What was that all about?

And the Beckers themselves. In spite of Jerry Becker's efforts, somebody had fallen off the path and into the area marked "Fuss": Adam Warren, lying in his own blood, his white hair stained with it.

I walked my beat and kidded myself that I could play detective just a little longer—until I'd found out more about Fletcher and the woman he was involved with, and Lee Pierce and Fred, the Polaris missile—but I knew it was just that: kidding myself. I needed someone to find Warren's car and I needed someone to test it for evidence of having killed Marilyn Parker, and I knew only Lieutenant Hansen could help me with that. And the longer I waited, the greater the chance that the evidence would be lost. For all I knew, the car had been taken to the wreckers, and had been crushed into a small square or cannibalized into parts for other cars, scattered, lost forever.

I could, of course, just drop the whole thing and let the crime go unsolved. What if I did? Was Adam Warren such a great loss?

I worked it, as I usually did that month, so that I ended my patrol at Frye Hall, the building nearest to police headquarters. Across the street the fraternity houses were dark and silent, like abandoned wasp nests. I didn't have to go inside, it wouldn't have mattered at all if I skipped Frye. But I don't like to run from my fears, I don't like being afraid.

I used my passkey to let myself in and walked down the hall to the stairs, looking into all the open classroom doors as I did. The unoccupied chairs stared blankly at blackboards from which the custodians had erased all meaning. There's nothing much emptier than a classroom in the middle of the night.

On the second floor I went down the hall toward the English department. I noticed that I was making no noise, decided to keep it that way. I walked past Lee Pierce's office door and then Warren's and the computer room's. I stopped at Arthur Fletcher's door on the other side of the hall, remembering the night of Warren's murder and how Fletcher had come up behind me and scared me. There'd been somebody in his office then, somebody he didn't want me to meet. It didn't seem like such a big mystery to me now.

I continued on down to the English department office, Doris Parker's office, and then retraced my steps to the stairs and climbed to the third floor. I paused at a bulletin board and scanned the posters stapled there. Lee Pierce, I noticed, was giving a reading of new poems on Saturday night, at the University Arts Center. He hadn't stayed long in Ireland, then—less than a week. I wondered if he'd finished the poem he'd been working on at the time Adam Warren had been killed, and if he would read it. I tried to recall the lines Hansen had quoted: something about finding the flame again, somewhere in the alphabet. Dumb, I thought, but it fit with what Art Fletcher'd said about Pierce's latest poetry: poetry about poetry about poetry, masturbating in the hall of mirrors. I liked the image. Maybe Fletcher should have been a poet.

A sudden noise cut into the silence. A high, thin complaint that came up the stairs from the second floor. It sounded like the sharp whine of a cicada, except that we don't get those until early fall. I stood in the half darkness and listened, trying to figure out what it was.

Then it registered. A printer, like those attached to the computers in the English department's computer room.

All the offices down there had been dark and silent when I'd walked past them a few minutes before. Now someone was using one of the printers, even though it was close to midnight. I went down the stairs to the second floor and back to the computer room next to Warren's office.

It was still dark behind the frosted glass, but the keening of the printer was coming from there.

I took out my pistol and held it ready, then tried the door. It was locked. I got out my keys and opened the door, reached for the light switch, and turned it on.

The printer was louder now, paper flowing slowly out of it and dropping into a pile on the floor. I took several steps into the room when suddenly the room went dark and the printer stopped.

There was just silence for a few moments. I reached for my flashlight and then heard a loud thud that sounded like something hitting the building's front door on the first floor. I spun out into the hall and into pitch darkness. All the lights in the building were off. I didn't stop, just flicked on the flashlight as I grabbed the banister post with my pistol hand, swung around it and started down the stairs. I'd taken three steps when something grabbed at my right ankle and tripped me and I fell into the darkness.

Twenty

I hurt too much to move, just lay there, half on my side, sprawled head down on the stairs. At first I couldn't tell where the pain was coming from. My body was a single throbbing ache, the pain stabbing through it like knives. Then I tasted blood. Dazed, I touched my lips with my fingers, felt the deep slit in my lower lip and the warm blood pulsing from it.

I shifted slightly to reach in my pocket for a Kleenex, and almost passed out from the pain in my knees. I lay there listening only to my own whimpering until the pain receded, and then I heard a soft footstep coming up the stairs from the first floor. I held my breath.

My eyes had grown accustomed to the dark now and I could make out the banister and the curve of it as it continued down into the darkness to the first floor. I tried to change my position so that I'd have a better chance to defend myself, but the pain was too great and I'd fallen too awkwardly: I couldn't move my body around to get my legs under me and I couldn't reach the banister with my hands.

I stayed sprawled in the middle of the stairs, head down, and listened until I heard another soft step, closer this time. And when I heard the next one, I pushed myself up off my hands and stared into the gloom and screamed straight at the darker, human figure coming around the corner, and then I fainted.

When I opened my eyes, Doris Parker's face was brooding down at me. She was sitting on the stairs and holding my head in her lap. I realized that not much time could have

129

passed since I'd screamed and fainted, because she was still looking frightened and confused, as if she'd just arrived.

"Don't move," she said. "I'll call an ambulance."

"How can you," I asked, "if you're sitting here with my head in your lap?" I tried to laugh at my wonderful sense of humor under such adverse circumstances and then winced at the pain of stretching my mouth. From the look on her face, I realized she hadn't understood a word I'd said. I'd mumbled it through a mouthful of blood and a swollen lower lip. It was just as well, I thought. She'd probably consider humor inappropriate on such an occasion. She handed me a little handkerchief that smelled of perfume.

"I'll go now," she said, "I just wanted to be sure you were all right."

"No," I said, very carefully, "help me sit up."

She made a number of objections to that, but I didn't want to lie there the way I was, so she finally helped me. We were both clumsy about it, and it hurt a lot, but after what seemed a long time I was able to sit up, propped against the banister.

She got to her feet then and started up the stairs and then stumbled. "Look at this," she said.

I turned to look, moving as little as I could. In the light that seeped through the window high up under the building's roof, I saw a cord stretched across the stairs, secured to the banister on either side. I'd tripped over that in the darkness.

"Who could have done a thing like that?" she asked, staring at me. I noticed she had blood on her blouse where my head and hands had touched her. Surprisingly, she was wearing fitted jeans, not one of her colorful costumes.

I stared back at her, but it hurt too much to talk, so I didn't answer.

"It wasn't me!" she said, guessing my thoughts. "I wouldn't have stayed here to help you, if it had been me, would I? Besides, I'm here because that Lieutenant Hansen told me to come. He said it was urgent."

My mouth wanted to fall open, but didn't dare, so I just stared at her in astonishment. It still hurt too much to talk, or even shrug, so I just nodded to humor her, relaxed back against the banister, and tried to will myself not to hurt so much. If she wanted to kill me, it was okay with me. She went away, presumably to call an ambulance, leaving me alone to nurse another defeat at the hands of Frye Hall. I wondered where my pistol was. My flashlight was on the landing below me, dead.

They X-rayed my knees and arms, couldn't find anything broken, put two stitches on the inside of my lower lip, and made me stay in the hospital overnight for observation. They put me in a roomful of other women, all of them either asleep or dead. I couldn't tell which, and I asked the nurse for the phone. She thought I was going to call a concerned person.

I called information and managed to make myself understood well enough to get homicide's number and told the duty officer to give me Lieutenant Hansen's home phone number. She tried to get my phone number instead, no doubt thinking I wouldn't last long enough to get through to Hansen for his personal attention, but I got extremely agitated at that and, finally, got his number.

The body in the bed next to mine had come alive by then and was glaring at me as the nurse came back and tried to take away the phone. I threatened to grimace horribly, rip the stitches out of my lip, and bleed all over everything if she didn't let me make one more call. I called Hansen at home and woke him up and mumbled what had happened to me. Then I told him to try to find Adam Warren's car and check it for evidence that it had hit Marilyn Parker and killed her.

Twenty-one

I couldn't sleep very well and talked my way out of the hospital a little before noon the next day. I took a cab home and spent the rest of the day—it was Tuesday, my day off—either in bed or in a hot bath. I was waiting for the sky to cave in on me, but nothing happened. My phone squatted there on the table in the living room, growing more and more inscrutable and full of menace, like a terrorist's bomb with a timer bought at a garage sale. I was stiff all over from the fall I'd taken, but the only damage, aside from the deep cut on my lower lip, was to my knees and forearms. When I'd tripped, I'd made a four-point landing—five-point, if you count my mouth, and I had bruises like pools of ink to show for it, aching teeth, and scraped aching knees.

When the phone finally did ring, it was Aunt Tess, demanding to know when I was going to make up my mind what to do about my father's Corvette. The mortician, she complained, was calling her nearly every day, urging her to sell it to him.

I asked her, speaking very slowly, what an undertaker—especially a blind undertaker—wanted with a Corvette, and she said it was for a rich client who wanted to be buried in it. "I'd just hate to see your father's beautiful car end up like that," she said.

I told her I'd try to get some vacation time in a couple of weeks and come up there and look at the car again and make up my mind. Ginny Raines's folks' summer place wasn't far from where Aunt Tess lived, and Ginny had invited me to spend a long weekend up there sometime when we could both get off work.

Tess asked me why I mumbled when I talked and I said I'd been punched in the mouth while trying to arrest a flasher. Flasher wasn't a term she knew. "You know," I told her, "a creep who spreads his raincoat like bat wings in front of startled maidens and doesn't have anything on underneath."

She was appalled. "You mean they allow women police officers to handle things like that?"

I said that was why I got punched in the mouth, because I wouldn't, and she told me not to talk that way and to take care of myself. She hung up, as usual without saying good-bye.

The article with the biggest headline on the front page of Wednesday's paper reported how traces of paint found in the wounds on Marilyn Parker's body matched the paint on Adam Warren's car. Work done on the front of the car shortly after Marilyn was killed convinced the police that it was the vehicle that had struck her. Professor Warren, the paper reminded its readers, had himself been murdered on June 7, nearly three weeks ago, and his murder was still unsolved. The police, the newspaper reported sadly, wouldn't comment on whether they believed there might be a link between the two violent deaths.

The article also reported that Marilyn Parker hadn't died from the injuries caused by Warren's car—Adam Warren had presumably left her in the road to freeze to death.

With morbid curiosity, I watched the morning television news and learned that the university president was unavailable for comment. A university spokesperson, speaking for President Wolf, said through tight lips that the University did not condone hit-and-run on the part of its faculty any more than it condoned murder, but would wait for more information before issuing a formal statement that would make everything better again.

The dean of the College of Arts issued a statement through a secretary close to tears that said the dean's heart went out to everybody involved.

I wasn't mentioned. The police had been acting on an anonymous tip.

A television camera crew had trapped Doris Parker in her office and tried to interview her. They captured the startled look on her face at their appearance, and then her face as it shut down when she realized what they were after. The assistant chairman of the English department, Art Fletcher, appeared then and shooed them away. All that was run as news.

A lot of my soreness was gone by the time I drove to work that afternoon, and some of the stiffness, and I could talk almost clearly and almost without pain, although the two stitches on the inside of my lower lip were annoying. If the flesh hadn't been so sensitive, I would probably have chewed them off. I changed into my uniform and went down the backstairs more slowly than usual to the squad room for roll call. I didn't know what I'd find there. I glared defiantly at my image in the mirror on the landing as I gave my belt an angry tug and was given a childish pout in return, although it was mostly just the swollen lip.

Bixler and Hansen were standing in Bixler's office, waiting for me. We all went in and sat down.

"You first," Bixler growled to Hansen, "and then me." But he couldn't wait. His eyes darted to me and he blurted out, "You're suspended, O'Neill."

I just nodded. It felt almost good. I turned to Hansen.

His face was its usual bland mask, his blue eyes guarded by their hooded lids and wrinkles at the corners. He told me to give it to him in detail, everything I knew and how I knew it. He didn't look friendly, or as if we were partners. He didn't doodle quiet things on his pad of paper either, as he'd done the last time I'd told him a story.

When I'd finished, I said, "You know the rest."

"You have any idea who it was in Frye?" he asked. "You think it was Parker?"

I didn't know. Whoever had arranged the trap for me must have followed me into the building, waited until I was on the third floor, and then tied the cord across the stairs and started up the printer. What I couldn't figure out was how the person who'd done it had gotten from the computer room to the building's main light switch, which was in the basement, so quickly. Once I'd heard the printer start up, it couldn't have taken me more than twenty seconds to get downstairs to the computer room.

"That one's not so hard," Hansen said. "I asked somebody who knows computers. Whoever did it instructed the computer to start printing the document at page fifty. We timed it and it takes forty-six seconds for that computer to get to page fifty and start printing. It's as if it has to thumb through the manuscript to the right page first. That's plenty of time for somebody to get down to the basement—somebody who knows the building."

"Whose manuscript was it?" I asked.

"Art Fletcher's. A book he'd just finished writing. It was already printed, he told us. The floppy disks were in a box in the computer room, available to anybody to reuse."

"But somebody had to know there were fifty-some pages on it, didn't they? The trick wouldn't have worked if the printer had started up right away because I would have come downstairs too soon. Whoever did it has to be somebody who knew a disk like that would be in the computer room, and knew how to use it."

"That thought occurred to me, too," Hansen said dryly. "Fletcher typed his manuscript onto the disks himself, but Doris Parker proofed it for him and printed it out. So she knew about the disks and where they were. But anybody in the English department could have known about them, and how to work the printer."

"All the evidence points to one person," Bixler said. "Doris Parker. Unless you buy her story that somebody tricked her into going over to Frye."

According to Doris, Hansen had called her and said that he'd found something about her daughter among the papers in Warren's office. He'd suggested that he might not have to let the media know about it if she came over to Frye and explained what it meant.

"No," Hansen said, "I don't buy that story, but I can't disprove it either."

"You need to?" Bixler asked. "There's a lot more against her than trying to kill O'Neill."

"She claims," Hansen said, "that it never occurred to her that Adam Warren might be responsible for her daughter's death. She also claims she doesn't care, that finding the killer won't bring her daughter back.''

"And you believe that?" Bixler said. "Did you ask her what she was quarreling with Warren about in her office the day before he was killed? She's got motive and she's got opportunity.'' He used two thick fingers to tick off these two facts so he wouldn't lose track of them.

If it wasn't going to be a computer thief, I realized, then Doris Parker would be the next best thing, at least for Bixler. Especially now that one of the University's most distinguished professors had been exposed as a hit-and-run killer.

That was my doing, of course. But not only was I not going to get a medal for it, I was going to lose my job. "What about the Beckers?" I asked Hansen. "Aren't you going to talk to them?"

"We have," Hansen told me. "They were pretty upset by it all. They readily admit that Warren had been drinking Christmas Eve, but they didn't think he'd drunk so much that he couldn't drive. They say he didn't appear drunk when he left the party.''

"*They* say," I interrupted.

"O'Neill," Bixler warned.

"We showed them a photo of Marilyn Parker, and the Beckers identified her as the woman who was there with Warren on Christmas Eve. They said they hadn't seen the newspaper report on her death. They said they didn't even know her last name.''

Hansen looked at me steadily as he told me all this. He didn't look particularly happy about it. Bixler stirred restlessly in his chair.

I didn't let Hansen off the hook. "Sure, and if they'd seen anything in their newspaper or on television about Marilyn, they'd have come running to the police with what they knew, wouldn't they? Because they're all such responsible citizens. And Adam Warren was just out there sipping a little sherry along with the rest of them—such a distinguished man—with his pants down around his ankles! Bullshit!''

"Get off your high horse, O'Neill," Bixler said. "This isn't your show anymore and it never was." To Hansen he said, "Let's wind this thing up.''

"Did you search the Beckers' house?" I asked Hansen, ignoring the jerk. "And what about that weirdo who was out there? Fred, the guy Art Fletcher punched?"

"Of course we didn't search their house," Hansen replied patiently. "On what grounds, Peggy? They're not suspects in Warren's murder, and none of their friends are either. The most we could get them for would be letting Warren drive with too much booze in him. But it was a long time ago. How could we prove it?"

I'd been thinking of drugs, but of course the Beckers and their friends must have done a pretty thorough housecleaning after I left there on Sunday. Toilets flushing all over Arcadia, I thought. I hoped that whatever it was, it was good and expensive stuff going down the drain.

"Then what about their sex parties?" I demanded, getting dumber by the minute. "I don't believe for a second that they just prance around bare-assed naked like sun-worshippers at a barbecue."

Even Bixler laughed at that one. " 'She doesn't believe for a second,' " he said, trying to mimic me and, in my opinion, doing a crummy job of it. Then he got serious and said, "You're just repeating what you heard from that Carpenter woman. Or her boyfriend. They're just pissed."

I started to say something I'd almost immediately regret, but Hansen jumped in to save me. "Peggy," he said, "we don't arrest people for what they do in the privacy of their homes. Besides, how could we prove it? You want us to stake out the Beckers' home and wait until they start shooting up, cooking up, or snorting? It's going to be very quiet out there for a long time, you know. Maybe there's laws on the books against some of the things they do—I wouldn't know, I've never looked—but as long as they don't do them in public places, they're safe from the police. Remember, Jack Becker's an important man. *I've* taken his seminars, sat in on his workshops, even read one of his books. More significantly, so have my superiors."

"Me, too," Bixler put in, not to be upstaged.

"Becker's peckers," I mumbled.

"What, O'Neill?" Bixler asked.

"Maybe Jack Becker is next in line for a University Scholarship,'' I said. "Maybe he killed Warren to create a vacancy.'' I was only half kidding. "I've spent some time with the man, I wouldn't put it past him.''

Hansen laughed. "Or his wife. What'd you think of her?''

"No,'' I said. "Jerry Becker wouldn't kill for something as flimsy as a title. I don't know what her murder price is.''

"But she's got one?''

"Oh yes,'' I replied. "And it's not so high that it prices her out of the market, either. But even if they're as innocent of any wrongdoing as they say they are, they aren't going to lift a finger to save Doris Parker. That's for sure. And I'm not sure you will, either,'' I added to Hansen.

"Funny, Peggy,'' Hansen said. "You've done more to hang Warren's murder on Parker than anybody, and now you don't like it.''

"She's just letting herself be led by the nose, emotionally,'' Bixler said. Both Hansen and I looked at him expectantly, to see if he planned to elaborate on that one. "Women!'' he added, as if that were elaboration enough.

"I don't care one way or the other who gets stuck with Warren's murder,'' I said to Hansen, "as long as it's the person who did it.''

Then Hansen dropped what he thought was a bombshell. "We may not need to prove that Doris Parker knew Adam Warren killed her daughter,'' he said.

"Why not?''

"In April, Adam Warren withdrew over fourteen thousand dollars from a retirement account. We only just found out about that. If we can find evidence that Doris Parker got that money . . .'' He left the sentence unfinished, shrugged.

"In April?'' I asked.

"Yes.'' Hansen looked as if he'd just swallowed a canary, and found it very good.

"You think Doris was blackmailing Warren, is that it? Then why'd she kill him?''

He shrugged again. "Maybe it wasn't enough. Maybe he told her that was the end, he wasn't going to pay any more. Or maybe Doris Parker's conscience told her, somewhat late, that she was a bad person for taking money from her daughter's killer. The point is, if we can tie the money to Parker, our case against her will be even stronger. Don't forget, we have a witness who's willing to testify that Warren and Parker were quarreling in her office the day before he was killed and that Warren came out looking as if he'd been crying.''

"Meaning he'd begged her to let him off the hook and she said no.''

"Something like that. And then killed him when he wouldn't pay any more. Or enough.''

"I don't think you're going to be able to prove that,'' I said, and was immediately sorry.

"Why, O'Neill?'' Bixler demanded, quick off the mark for once. "You know something we don't?''

"No,'' I answered.

"Then what did you mean, Peggy?'' Hansen asked mildly.

"Nothing,'' I lied. "I just mean it sounds to me as if you're spending too much time on Doris Parker and ignoring other possibilities, just because she's an easy answer to your problems. Remember,'' I reminded him, "somebody out there tried to kill me. If it wasn't Doris, then—''

"You're no longer a part of this, O'Neill,'' Bixler interrupted me, "and nobody's out there trying to kill you anymore. If you've been honest with us for a change, there's no longer any reason for anybody to want you dead.'' His logic made him feel good about himself. He turned to Hansen. "If you're through,'' he said, barely concealing his impatience.

Then Hansen did something that surprised me. He turned to Bixler and said, "Peggy—O'Neill—did a good job, Mel, even though she made some mistakes. I wonder if we'd ever have cleared up Marilyn Parker's death without her meddling. What threw us off at the time was that she'd obviously been partying heavily—there was a lot of alcohol and cocaine in her body—but she wasn't dressed to be outdoors. It was damned cold Christmas Eve, you'll remember, and snowing, too, so we assumed she'd been at a party somewhere in the neighborhood where we found her body, not way the hell out in Arcadia.'' He paused, took a breath. I was finding all this fascinating stuff, of course, and hanging on his every word.

"We interviewed Jack Becker,'' he continued, "after Warren was murdered. Lots of people knew of their friendship. But the subject of Marilyn Parker never came up. Why should it? We had no idea there might be a connection between the two deaths." He turned to me. "We do our job according to the book, but sometimes things fall between the cracks."

"She ought to have told you about Susan Carpenter," Bixler said, his voice surly, "let you deal with it. That would have put you onto Jack Becker."

Hansen laughed. "Maybe. But I guess I'm glad she did it on her own, Mel. Frankly I wouldn't have liked to go out there, to the Beckers', and have to take all my clothes off and get into that hot tub with all those strange people. I'm sure I don't look nearly as good bare-assed naked as Officer O'Neill does, all pink and wrinkled."

You bastard, I thought. I turned red and apparently let my thoughts show. The sight of that and the vision of me all pink and wrinkled must have appealed to something soft and moist in Bixler's brain. He grinned in spite of himself and then he was laughing, too. It sounded like bowling pins exploding for a strike.

"You can see," Hansen said, observing my reactions, "that she's suffered enough. Not to speak of those stitches in her lip and the bruises on her arms and legs. I think she's learned her lesson this time. When she called me Tuesday morning, Mel, it sounded to me as though she'd learned her lesson the hard way. I think she knows when to quit."

I hoped he did.

There was a pause when Hansen stopped talking. Bixler looked from me to Hansen and back again. He looked like a rooster being reasoned out of a worm. He started to say something.

His phone rang. "Bixler," he said absently into the receiver, his attention still on Hansen and me. All of a sudden his angry little eyes sharpened and his dull face lit up. "Yeah," he said, and shot a glance at Hansen and then stared hard at the mouthpiece. "Hiller's office," he said. "Hold him there, I'll be down in a minute. And be careful!"

He hung up, tried to paste a poker face over his own.

"All right," he said, "all right. We're short of cops at the moment. But hear this, O'Neill, hear this. You're working for *me*, not Lieutenant Hansen here. And the next time you step out of line, he won't be able to get you off the hook.

Nobody'll be able to get you off the hook. Now scram." As I got up and turned my back on him, he couldn't resist adding: "Your *gun,* O'Neill, was found in the basement of Frye Hall. It needs servicing before it can be used again. Go find another, and try not to break it."

I left, too wrung out and too sore in other places to feel the knife he'd tossed throbbing dully between my shoulder blades. I went down to Ginny's office, but she wasn't there. A note told me to meet her at the McDonald's down the street, whether I was fired or not. I checked out a new pistol and left the building.

Hansen was just driving out of the parking lot as, moving gingerly, I started down the street. He stopped in the driveway and I walked over. I thanked him for speaking up for me to Bixler.

He glanced over my shoulder, as if Bixler might be tailing me. "I wonder how much good it would've done," he said, "without that phone call. What do you suppose it was?"

I said I had no idea.

"You hurting?" he asked me.

Only when I tried to make faces or sudden angry movements, I told him.

"That's good," he said, squinting up at me. "Maybe that'll encourage you to back off now. You've done enough— more than enough. You're lucky to be alive."

"I wonder," I said ambiguously, and waved, and hobbled on my way.

Twenty-two

Ginny was wiping salt and grease off her face when I came in. She hollered to me to get her a cup of coffee, black, so I got that and a carton of chocolate milk for me. I would rather have had coffee, too, but it was too painful for my mouth.

I sat down across from Ginny at one of those things that function as a table at fast-food restaurants, in the same way what they serve functions as nourishment. She was appropriately horrified at my wounds and close call in Frye Hall, nonjudgmental about my behavior for a change, and surprised to learn I hadn't been suspended. She said Bixler had made no secret of what he intended to do to me, and it must have taken quite a lot to make him change his mind.

I was telling her about Hansen's efforts to save me and Bixler's mysterious phone call when Lawrence, a big, curly-headed cop who thinks he's remarkably good-looking—and he is, when he's not trying—stopped at our table and asked us if we'd heard the news: Jesse James had caught a computer thief.

I asked him when and he said, "About half an hour ago. And you ought to see the Rooster! He's down there now, fastening electrodes to the poor sucker's gonads. Gonna make him confess he murdered what's-his-name, Professor Warren."

Ginny said to me, "That explains the mysterious phone call."

"Where'd Jesse catch him?" I asked Lawrence.

"In the language-arts building. Spanish department. I'm in a rush." He headed for the door, trying to work a lid down

142

on his cup of coffee. His squad car was double-parked on the street outside, trapping an enraged little man in a big new car who was leaning on his horn.

"I've got to see this," I told Ginny.

"Why?" she asked. "Not even Bixler can still believe a thief killed Warren, not after what you've done, and especially after somebody tried to kill you."

"Are you claiming you know what Bixler's capable of thinking?" I asked her as I painfully squeezed up and away from the table. "You've been working for him too long."

It took me less than three minutes to run back to headquarters, ignoring my aches and pains. Before I even got to Bixler's door, I heard a voice with some kind of foreign accent shout, "You are being absurd!"

Almost instantly there was a loud noise, like a pistol going off. I swung into Bixler's office in time to see him lift his metal yardstick. He'd apparently swatted his desk with it, not liking to be accused of being absurd. If he'd intended to make some impression on the suspect in that way, he'd failed miserably. But perhaps he was just swatting a fly.

Bixler looked up and the rage on his face moderated into irritation when he saw it was me. "What're you doing back, O'Neill? Can't get enough? Somebody tell you Porter here caught your computer thief?"

He was never my computer thief, but I ignored that and gave Bixler a weak, phony smile. Jesse James was standing against the wall next to the door, presumably to back up Bixler, since Bixler couldn't have handled this one by himself.

The suspect was sitting in the chair I'd just recently vacated. He was tall, lean, and very blond, and his eyes, when he turned to stare at me, were so pale a blue that I almost thought he didn't have irises at all. He looked me up and down, fast, impersonally, professionally. I learned later that he was only twenty, but he looked much older.

"Have you seen this man before, O'Neill?" Bixler asked me. "Take your time before answering."

"Who is this?" the suspect asked, still looking at me over his shoulder.

"No," I said, without needing to spend any time on it at all. "I've never seen him before. Who is he?"

"I can talk for myself. It seems I am in trouble, I know that. But it is not as bad as this man says. I have killed nobody. My name is Stein-Eric Wallin and I am here at this university to play tennis."

"We caught him in the act, O'Neill," Bixler crowed. "Porter there did," he added, gesturing with his fat chin at Jesse behind me. "Carrying the Spanish department's Macintosh down the hall, bold as brass. Bold as brass! So maybe, just maybe, we've caught ourselves a killer tonight."

"That is nonsense," Wallin said, more accurately than he knew. "I do not even know who it is who has been killed."

I turned to Jesse. "How'd it happen?"

"I was just finishing my patrol," he said, "and decided to swing by the Spanish department—just to see if a girl I know was still there. It was on my way," he added, glancing quickly at Bixler. "So I was walking down the hall, even though I could see the office was closed and she was probably gone. And suddenly the door opens in my face and this guy here walks out and right into my arms. Practically knocked me down with the computer he's carrying. I figured I'd better ask him what he was doing with it."

"What'd he do?" I was thinking of the last time Jesse'd tried to make an arrest.

"He tried to bluff me. Just kept going, saying the Macintosh was heavy and the service truck was double-parked outside. Well, I knew there wasn't any service truck outside 'cause I'd just come in. So I told him he had to take the computer back inside and show me some identification. He turned right around and took the computer back into the room where it belongs, me right behind him."

"He just put the thing down and did what you told him to, got out some identification?"

"Well, no," Jesse said, and turned red and looked down at his feet.

"He took a swing at Jesse," Bixler cut in impatiently, "and Jesse ducked and kneed him in the nuts. Some of you women could take a lesson—"

I grinned at Jesse over Bixler's gush of words, and then

Sergeant Hiller came in and told Bixler they'd discovered how Wallin entered the Spanish department's office: one of the windows was broken.

"That's doing it the hard way," Jesse said. He was right. The Spanish department's on the third floor, which meant Wallin had to climb the side of the building. "The human fly," Jesse added, admiration in his voice. "And in broad daylight, too."

There wasn't much risk of getting caught. It was late afternoon in the summer, the campus was almost empty, and the Spanish department's windows face the windowless back wall of the auditorium. All it would take would be good nerves, and maybe a certain desperation.

I studied Stein-Eric Wallin with morbid curiosity. He looked to me as if he wouldn't hesitate to hurt anyone who stood between him and a piece of raw meat, or its equivalent in the world of sports, if he believed he could get away with it and it was feeding time. He had the makings, in other words, of a folk hero. If he got himself a good lawyer, I was convinced, the theft charge would be dismissed as a high-spirited prank, and someday we'd see his face on a box of cereal. His arms were long, lean, and muscular. Good tennis arms. What a waste, I thought, that such a gorgeous body should hang from such a mean spirit.

"Note this, O'Neill," Bixler said. "He *struck* at the same time of day that Warren was killed—almost to the minute."

I just stared at Bixler, wondering why he was doing this. Self-delusion, or just taking his rage at me out on Wallin? For I knew that Wallin hadn't killed Adam Warren.

"Who is this man?" Wallin demanded. "Why did I wish to kill him?"

"You're saying you haven't heard of the murder of Professor Warren?" Bixler said. "You expect me to believe that?"

"I wish to see a lawyer," he said. "Is that permitted in this country?"

"You haven't been charged yet," Bixler said. "You can phone a lawyer when you've been charged."

Jesse cleared his throat very loudly. Bixler looked up at him, started to say something, looked over at me, changed his mind. Once a suspect asks for a lawyer, the interrogation has to come to a screeching halt.

"Let him call a lawyer," Bixler said finally, "but get him out of here first. Take him back to Hiller's office." He slumped back into his chair, looked around for something to destroy.

I said to Wallin: "Do you happen to remember where you were three weeks ago—on the seventh?"

Bixler exploded: "O'Neill, what the hell do you think you're doing?"

Wallin looked up at me, as if he'd forgotten his English. "The seventh," he repeated slowly. And then suddenly remembering, "Of course I remember where I was on the seventh. Why?"

"I just wondered," I said in my sweetest voice.

"I was in Sweden on the seventh," he answered. "I can prove that. My passport will prove that. This Professor Warren, was he killed then?"

There was a brief silence as total defeat settled over Bixler, and then he reached for his phone. I waited until he was on the line asking to talk to somebody in the city's robbery division and then I ducked quietly out of there. I gave Jesse's arm a squeeze as I passed him.

When I came in from my patrol that night, I asked the dispatcher if there'd been anything new in the Wallin case. Ron looked up from his *Reader's Digest* and said that Wallin's apartment had been searched and his passport found, and it supported his alibi for when Warren was murdered.

"However," he added, "on the bright side, Bixler's hemorrhoids would appear to be terminally inflamed, to judge by the gingerly way he settles into a chair, and the city robbery-division girls and boys found scads of little baggies of cocaine in Mr. Wallin's dresser. So the lad probably won't be playing tennis for the venerable alma mater again."

"No," I agreed, "he won't. He'll get off with a slap on one of those strong, tanned wrists and turn pro."

Twenty-three

I wanted to do one more thing before giving up on solving Adam Warren's murder, and I thought I could do it without risking either my life or my job. The next morning I drove over to Susan Carpenter's house. Standing on the porch, I listened to the piano music coming from inside, a child playing something very earnestly. I looked through the screen door, saw a little girl sitting up straight at the big, new piano. Susan was sitting next to her. I let myself in quietly and stood inside the door. A cat's head rose from the couch and stared at me over the armrest, blinking indifferently. I made a noise so that Susan turned and saw me. I came as an unwelcome surprise to her. She said something to the child, got up, and came over to me. The child played on.

"The police were here," she whispered, an angry hiss. "They said you weren't any part of the investigation. You had no business coming here, getting Tim and me in trouble."

Thanks, Hansen, I thought. But maybe it wasn't Hansen.

I pointed out to her that it was because I'd talked to her and Tim that the police had learned how Marilyn Parker died. That was worth something, wasn't it?

"No," she said. "Thanks to you, I've helped you point the finger at Doris Parker for Warren's murder. That makes me sick!"

"You don't think she did it?"

·"I don't *care* if she did it!" she replied, still hissing. "Adam Warren *deserved* to die! Do you care who did it? Really?"

Her rage made my skin crawl. It upset the cat, too. It dived over the armrest of the couch and strolled rapidly out of the room.

"Yes," I replied, "I care. I want to know who killed Warren. I want to find who did it! I'd hate to see Doris Parker go to jail for a crime she didn't commit. Worse, though, I'd hate to see the person who killed Warren—and who tried to kill me—go free."

"You?" She sounded surprised. "Is that what happened to your mouth?"

"Miss Carpenter?" We'd forgotten about the little girl.

"I can't talk now," Susan said to me. "Give me five more minutes." She didn't wait for my answer, just went back to the piano. I sat down on the couch and watched and listened. She was a very good piano teacher. She made the little girl feel that her practicing had been worth it and that she had talent. When the lesson was over, the child carefully gathered together her music books and thanked Susan for the lesson. Without having glanced at me once, she walked out.

Susan came back to me and said, as if we'd never been interrupted, "Somebody tried to kill you? You don't think it was Doris Parker? I mean, she's got the most obvious motive, doesn't she, for killing Adam—for killing Warren. *I'd* kill a bastard like that, if he killed my daughter."

The screen door opened and the little girl stood in it, not knowing if she should come back in. "Miss Carpenter?" she said. "I forgot to give you your check."

"Oh, thanks, honey," Susan said, and went over and took it and the child disappeared. Susan tossed the check on the old coffee table between us. It was for six dollars.

"We don't know that Doris knew he'd killed Marilyn," I told her. Then I said, "But they've got another motive that might make her a strong suspect. Blackmail."

"Blackmail!" She stared at me with her large eyes. The cat, who had returned and was now sitting in her lap, did, too, but the cat had less trouble with it.

"Yes," I said. "The police have found a chunk of money missing from Adam Warren's savings. Fourteen thousand dollars. They think Doris Parker got it."

"Can they—can they prove it?" Her voice had started the

question too high, so she was forced to start over from the beginning, the way you do with "The Star Spangled Banner."

"Will they have to?" I asked. "You know how blackmailers operate. They don't keep bank accounts, the way the rest of us do. They're too cunning for that—especially if their plans include murdering their victims. The police might get suspicious, might notice how a few thousand dollars went out of the victim's account one day, the same amount showed up in the blackmailer's account the next. Who knows what kind of ideas that might put in a cop's head! Doris Parker probably has the money hidden in a safe-deposit box somewhere. Or buried in one of her flower beds."

"You believe that?"

"A jury might."

"But there's no evidence linking the fourteen thousand to Doris Parker?"

"Nope. And there's not going to be, either."

"How do you know?"

"Because she didn't get it, you did."

"You can't prove that," she said. She'd seen it coming.

"You'd stand by and let an innocent woman be tormented, charged with murder, maybe convicted because of you?"

"Oh," she replied, "she's guilty. She's guilty *enough!* Have you seen her? Have you *met* her? A tiny little thing with a fake smile too big for her face! I remember seeing her once, at her desk, waiting for someone. It was lunchtime. I asked her who she was waiting for, because usually she was out of there as soon as the big hand hit the little hand at the top of the clock. 'My daughter,' she said. 'We're going to have lunch together.' Her daughter never showed up. 'That's too bad,' I said to Doris later. 'Oh,' Doris replied, giving me that smile, 'something must have come up, something more important than her mother.' What a phony! Doris Parker's a daughter-killer, if there ever was one. I know the type."

That was a long speech. "How could you?" I asked. "Your mother couldn't have been anything like that. You told me she sent you that piano"—I nodded in the direction of the grand—"as a birthday present."

She started to say something, thought better of it, looked confused.

"It's funny," I went on, "what a person'll do to pass the time when she's bored. I was in the navy for four years, did I tell you that? I was stationed in the Azores for part of the time. Pretty boring, unless you find the Atlantic Ocean, all around you, fascinating. I had time to read, plenty of time to read. They've got lots of odd books in base libraries. I probably read most of them at the library in the Azores."

Susan said, "This is fascinating."

"One of the books I read was on the history of the piano. It *was* fascinating. One of the things that stuck in my memory, and popped loose when I saw your piano the first time I was here, was that the world started to run short of ivory about twenty years ago. A shortage of elephant tusks, due to a crackdown on the indiscriminate slaughter of elephants. Good for elephants, not so good for the great white hunters. Or concert pianists." I went over and stood by Susan's piano, stroked a key, looked at Susan as I did. She watched me, half turned. It was a very smooth key, as I had seen it would be. And it was very white, not the way ivory ever is, even when it's fresh off the elephant. "The author of the book, a concert pianist himself, was quite upset about it. Steinway switched to plastic for its keys, and plastic is greasy—a lot more slippery than ivory. Now the serious pianists have to use more rosin than they used to. Maybe keep rosin bags at their feet, like baseball pitchers. Didn't you tell me this was your mother's piano before you got it, that it's pretty old?"

"I bought it myself," she said. "I paid for it with—"

"Sure," I interrupted her. "With a sackful of grubby little six-dollar checks like that one over there."

I looked down at the piano keys. It wouldn't be hard to find out where the piano came from, even if Susan had tried to file off the serial number at the same time she'd scratched and dented the wood.

I was so busy playing detective, and Susan was so busy playing suspect, that neither of us noticed that Tim Hale had come into the room from the porch behind me. He must have been outside listening for some time. He grabbed me, his fingers digging into my arms close to the bruises, and pulled me back against his body. The pain was so stunning I couldn't move.

"Tim!" Susan screamed, jumping up. "Don't be stupid!"

"What's she talking about, Suzie? And what'd you mean, you paid for the piano with your own money? You told me—"

"Let her go, you sap!" Susan said again loudly, but not yelling. "For God's sake, don't make it worse than it is. It can't get worse than it is." She ran out of gas, sat down on the piano bench, and put her face in her hands. Tim Hale held on to me for a second or two longer and then relaxed his grip. I pulled loose carefully and stepped away, touching my forearms gently with my fingers. They felt like they were on fire. I made my face into as bland a mask as I could to hide my rage. I couldn't even kick him to death, my legs were still too stiff and sore.

"It wasn't blackmail," Susan said, bringing me back to that reality. "He just gave it to me."

Then I lost my temper with her. "You can tell that to the police," I almost shouted. "You can also tell them where you got the money to buy a new Steinway back in April, at the same time Warren withdrew enough money to buy one. I'm sure they'll believe you. God, you're stupid, Susan!"

"Cut that out!" Tim flared at me and started toward me again.

"Shut up, you little shit!" I fired back, and too pissed to feel pain, or too numb, or both, I started toward him, too, which gave him just two choices: keep coming and try to hurt me, or back away.

"Go sit down!" Susan commanded him. Since he was backing up anyway, he must have found that an attractive thing to do. So he did, pouting. Undoubtedly he would have called it scowling.

"I'm not lying," Susan said, watching me. "He just showed up at my door a couple of months ago, told me he wanted to do something for me—*atone.*"

" 'Atone,' " I said. "For what? For *not* sexually harassing you?"

"He thought he had," she replied, looking away.

"When was this, exactly?" I asked, not believing any of it.

"A few days before my birthday. Late April. I don't remember the exact day. He said he wanted to talk to me. I listened to what he had to say. I was curious, because he looked so *changed*. He no longer looked like he owned the world, like he had some kind of in with Shakespeare and T.S. Eliot. He looked sick. But I didn't trust him, didn't believe him just like you don't believe me, so I wouldn't let him in. He just stood out there on the porch. He looked inside, through the screen, saw the old piano I'd always had. I'd had it when he and I were together, an ancient upright. I'd played it for him sometimes. Then he asked me if I'd let him buy me a better one, as a kind of atonement. Atonement! I just laughed at him, you know, and asked him what sort of piano that would be. It would have to be some piano, wouldn't it? I didn't think he was serious, I told him to scram. Well, there's the answer! The movers just showed up at the door one day with it. I stood and stared, couldn't believe it. It was the most beautiful thing I'd ever seen, I'd never owned anything like it before. 'Where do you want it?' they asked me. 'There,' I told them. And I told them to take the old one away with them, they could just have it, and they did."

"And you told Tim it was your old childhood piano, it belonged to your mother."

"I was afraid he'd try to make me send it back, or something." She was standing next to the piano now, where I'd been standing before, and touched it, ran her fingers gently over the scars she'd put in it herself. "I wasn't going to do that," she added softly. And then, even more softly, "I hated having to beat it up."

I stood there in the middle of the floor. My forearms were still sore from Tim's grip. I looked at him, sitting on the couch, his face troubled. He was having problems with Susan's story, too, but they weren't the same as mine. I looked back at Susan, at her tall figure at the piano, at her long hair falling down her back.

"No," I said.

She didn't move for a few seconds, and then slowly she

turned to me. "You don't believe me?" she asked, surprised. "You still think I was blackmailing Adam?"

"I don't know about that," I said. "I think I'm still going to have to let Hansen and homicide find out about that. What I don't believe," I said, "is that Adam Warren gave you a Steinway grand piano just because he had an affair with you. And another thing: you hate him too much. Remember, you've told me, over and over again, that you didn't think that what Adam Warren did to you was sexual harassment. You said you were too old for that. I don't happen to believe that, but I think you do. So why do you hate him so much? Another thing: you broke off your engagement to Tim. Why? Tim's forgiven you for your affair with Warren. Hell, he even blames himself! But you were the one who broke it off. Why?"

"Either you tell her, Sue," Tim Hale said suddenly, "or I'm going to."

"You asshole!" she said, but her voice was tired and it didn't sound as if she meant it. "Don't you see. It'll just give her a better motive for one of us having killed Warren."

"So what? We didn't kill him." Then Tim looked up at her, and there was something in his voice I hadn't heard before: despair. "At least, " he said, "I didn't."

She stared back at him for just a moment and then turned to me. "Adam Warren gave me herpes," she said.

Twenty-four

"That wasn't very nice of him, was it? He didn't tell me he had herpes, he didn't give me any choice in whether or not I wanted to risk getting it for the pleasure of his deadly dull lovemaking. He never did tell me, until it was too late, until the doctor told me I had herpes and I asked Adam about it. He denied it at first, lied about it, said I must have gotten it from somebody else. From Tim."

She started to cry, but apparently she didn't know it because she continued to stare straight ahead, at where I was standing. But the tears were streaking her face. "But Tim doesn't have herpes, and there wasn't anybody else."

"That wasn't Warren's fault," Tim Hale muttered.

"No, it wasn't Adam's fault there wasn't anybody else. I told you before, the last time you were here, how he was always trying to get me to go to bed with his friends. If I'd done it, I'd have no idea where I got the herpes. But I didn't. I told you the truth about that. I asked him why, you know? After I'd found out what it was I had. Why he didn't tell me he had herpes, give me a chance. You know what his answer was?"

No, I replied, I didn't.

"It wasn't any of my business. He said he'd always been very careful, that he'd never infected anybody before, that I must be unusually sensitive to diseases like that. And he said he didn't hold any grudge against the woman who'd given it to him." She started to laugh through her crying. "Wasn't that nice of him? And he said I mustn't hold any grudge against him."

154

The cat jumped suddenly into my lap. It had been watching me for some time, waiting for its chance. I tossed it off and it hit the floor strolling, as if I'd given it a lift to just where it wanted to be.

I sat there, trying to feel what it was Susan Carpenter was telling me, but all I felt was confused. I'd known there had to be something that she, and Tim Hale, too, had been holding back. But I'd thought only of pregnancy and abortion. For some reason venereal disease hadn't entered my mind in connection with Adam Warren.

Tim got up and went over to her, put his hands on her shoulder. She stiffened and stayed that way.

"You sure know how to make it hard for yourself," he said. "You're not a child. But Jesus, you can act like one sometimes."

"Surely you could have sued him for that," I said. "It seems to me I read of a case somewhere—"

"I didn't want to sue him!" she shouted, jerking away from Tim. "I just wanted to get the hell out of there, go hide somewhere. Die."

"But you didn't die," I said.

No, she said, she didn't die. She didn't have the guts. Tim took hold of her arms from behind, the way he'd done with me.

"He sounds like a complete bastard," I said.

"He *was* a complete bastard," Susan agreed, not shaking Tim off.

"Then what brought about the change? You said he looked changed, sick, and that he came here in April to tell you he wanted to atone."

"No—not atone," Susan said hesitantly. "He used another expression. He wanted to make amends—that's what he called it. 'Make amends.' I asked him where he got that from, and he laughed, as if he were ashamed, and told me he'd become a member of—are you ready for this?—AA!"

"AA," I repeated and then stupidly, "You mean Alcoholics Anonymous?"

"Yes, Alcoholics Anonymous! Can you see Adam Warren down there on skid row, or wherever it is they gather, singing hymns and dunking donuts with the winos? It was hard to believe. But he convinced me. Every Friday night he said he went. Every Friday night. Will miracles never cease.'' She shook her head as if she'd only just heard the news.

''What's the matter,'' Tim Hale said, looking at me, ''you look like you've just seen a ghost. You okay?''

Yes, I told him, I was fine. It was just hard to believe, Adam Warren and Alcoholics Anonymous.

''Fine for him,'' Susan said. ''He had a place to go. Where do I go?''

I couldn't answer that. Instead I said, ''By the way, I took your advice and went to the Beckers', last Sunday.''

''You're kidding!'' she exclaimed. She looked me up and down. ''The whole trip?''

''The hot tub. No swimsuit.''

''God, aren't they creepy! Why couldn't one of them have killed Adam? Jerry Becker's my choice!''

''Any of them would be fine for me,'' I said, ''but it's not going to be easy to pin it on one of them. Jack Becker's a friend of the police. Oh, and Art Fletcher was there, too. He was looking for his girlfriend, a woman named Lynn. Do you know anything about that?''

''That's a new development,'' Susan said, shaking her head. ''Is Fletcher divorced or something? I never saw him out there.''

''How about a tall guy named Fred? Acted a little screwy.''

''I remember him. Very weird. I couldn't figure out what he was doing out there, why they kept him around. Nobody seemed to like him much. He stuck pretty close to Lee Pierce, so I assumed he was one of Pierce's poet pals. He didn't seem to have any women out there, either, but he sure liked to look!''

I asked her if she thought Warren used more than just alcohol. She said everybody out there, at one time or another, tried whatever was passed around, but Warren preferred Scotch. He often drank too much of that.

''I doubt that he was very good in bed at those parties,'' she added. ''He wasn't very good at the best of times, and when he'd been drinking he was lousy—if he could do anything at all.'' She said this straight at Tim. Tim went white around the lips, but pulled out a smile from somewhere and offered it to her.

I got up, headed for the door. "You going to the cops with"—Tim called after me—"with this thing about Suzie?"

"I will if she doesn't. It'll help Doris Parker's case a little; at least take away the blackmail motive. But it's going to make you two look pretty attractive to homicide, that's for sure. Maybe if you go in and tell them about it yourselves, it'll be easier for you—if one of you didn't kill Warren. I don't have to tell them I was here and neither do you."

"We'll have to think about it," Susan said.

"Don't wait too long," I replied, from the door. I wished her luck. Then I wished him luck, too, and left.

Twenty-five

When Susan Carpenter told me Adam Warren had joined Alcoholics Anonymous, it felt like getting a pie in the face. My father had tried AA, too, but it didn't work for him. My mother wouldn't believe that alcoholism could be a disease. That would somehow have let him off the hook, or made all that she'd suffered from him less tragic, or both—I never really understood it: Besides *alcoholism* was a shameful word. It was better to go on being abused by a drunk than live with an alcoholic who didn't drink anymore.

She wouldn't let him talk about it, even made him keep his AA books in his study. I remember seeing them there. I remember my eyes going toward them and darting away quickly, not wanting to see them. My brother and I were ashamed, too, and lived during that period in fear that our friends would find out our dad was an alcoholic. It was bad enough him being a drunk.

After a time he started hiding his liquor behind his AA books. He knew we'd never find it there.

The day after I talked to Susan and Tim, Friday, I looked up Alcoholics Anonymous in the phone book and called the central number. I told the woman who answered that I was looking for a group that met in my neighborhood on Friday nights. I gave her Warren's address. She went away for a minute and came back to tell me there were several groups that met in places in or near that neighborhood on Fridays and asked me if I wanted the list of addresses sent to me. I said I'd come over and get it.

I drove over to the central office and felt the same sense

of shame I'd felt as a child when I saw my father's AA books. I went in and told a man at the desk what I wanted.

He handed me a booklet. "You might call before you go," he said. "Some groups meet in the same place year in and year out, but others change their meeting place for one reason or another and some even vanish without a trace."

"Thanks," I said. I turned away and looked up the part of the city that included Warren's neighborhood. There were two AA groups that met on Friday nights not far from where he lived. I went back to the desk and asked the man if he had membership lists.

He gave me a shocked look. "You've got to be kidding!" He looked at me as if I were a very slow learner. "It's anonymous, right?"

"I'm looking for the group a man belonged to who's dead now," I told him. "I'm a police officer and I'm investigating his death. He was murdered."

"That's too bad. We don't have lists. Each group keeps its own list, but only of members who want to be on it. You're out of luck," he added, satisfaction in his voice.

I called in sick that afternoon. That night I drove to the church nearest Warren's address, a beautiful old church of granite and ivy. There was an eight o'clock AA meeting. I hoped Warren had found what he wanted there, close to home. If he'd gone farther afield, I'd never find it.

I stood outside and watched people go in. They were a mixture of men and women. Some of them looked as if they'd spent a lot of years in dark, crowded bars, trying to talk above the blare of television sets and the laughter of drunks, but others didn't look the way I'd imagined alcoholics look at all. None of them looked ashamed of being where they were.

Some of them were smoking as they came in, but they crushed out their cigarettes in a bowl of sand by the door before they disappeared into the room. I wondered how often Warren had put out a cigarette in that thing, and remembered him coming to class, taking a last drag before walking in, grinding out his cigarette in the ashtray on the wall next to the door, still exhaling a little smoke as he approached his desk. It was the only unpleasant thing I knew about him, then.

I wondered what these people were like when they returned to their homes. Maybe they had their AA books in their studies, too, fronting for their booze.

I followed the last one in. Someone asked me to close the door.

They stood in a circle with their arms around each other. I tried to stay outside, but they made room for me and waited until I joined them. My being there didn't seem to surprise them at all.

Strangers touching me always gives me goose pimples, so I avoid it whenever I can. But at least these people didn't look as if they planned to take off their clothes. They recited a prayer, their heads bowed. I'd seen it before, on posters and plaques of the kind you can buy in gift shops, but I didn't remember the words, so I just stared at the floor, at shoes, tennis shoes, boots, sandals.

I wondered if I was seeing what my father had seen when he'd been a member of AA.

We found chairs along the walls and sat down and they began introducing themselves. They gave just their first names and always said what sort of addiction they had. The rest of the group responded with a greeting. A tall black man about my age chewing gum blew a bubble and, just before it was his turn to introduce himself, inhaled it. "I'm Edward," he said, "and I'm chemically dependent."

"Hi, Edward," the group responded, and he looked around at everybody with big, amused eyes.

I didn't know if "chemically dependent" meant alcohol or drugs. Somebody who'd introduced herself earlier had called herself a drug addict.

My dad hated drug addicts. I wondered if he'd have been in a group with them.

Before my turn came, I got up and went out.

I left the church, intending to walk around and kill time until the meeting was over and the people came out. I went out into the sunlight and bumped into a man coming up the steps toward the door.

"Excuse me," I said. And then, even though my eyes

were still startled by the brightness of the low evening sun, I recognized him: it was Fred, the Polaris missile. He turned and started quickly down the steps.

"Wait a minute!" I hollered, running to catch up with him. He walked very fast. He was tall and thin and his legs were long like a basketball player's. He went around the front of a car and opened the door.

"What're you doing?" I yelled from the curb. "You followed me here. Why?"

"I don't know what you're talking about," he said. There was an ugly bruise on his jaw where Fletcher had hit him. We could have made a beautiful couple, an advertisement for the same gym.

He folded his long body into the small car and pulled the door shut. The window on the passenger side was down. As he started his engine I stuck my head in and said, "You asked me a question, out there at the Beckers'. How did Adam Warren die? I never got a chance to answer it, remember? He was murdered."

Twenty-six

I killed an hour walking through the neighborhood, even strolled past Adam Warren's home. He'd owned a home, although he lived alone. It was fairly new, modern, not like the rest of the neighborhood, which was full of the kinds of houses you expect to see on elm-shaded streets here in the Midwest. There was a FOR SALE sign on the lawn and, attached to that, a smaller sign that said SOLD. The lawn was yellow and ratty from lack of water. "Weep for Adam Warren, he is dead." I mouthed the words, forgetting where I'd heard them before. Then I remembered: Lee Pierce had spoken them, standing over Warren's body. I shuddered in the evening heat, moved on.

I returned to the church before the hour was up, just in case the meeting broke up early, but I had to wait another fifteen minutes in the dim entryway. I looked into the growing darkness outside every once in a while, but I couldn't see anything that looked like Fred or his car.

At last people started coming out of the meeting room, singly and in small groups, laughing, talking, looking relaxed. I didn't know how to approach any of them, and suddenly I didn't want to. But then a man about my age came over to me. He stuck out his hand and I took it. "Hi, I'm John," he said. "I just wanted to say you're welcome to come back." His grin said the same thing.

I thanked him and told him I wasn't an alcoholic, I was a police officer.

His eyes and his grin both got a little warier, but he said, "I've known people who were both."

"I mean I'm not here because I'm an alcoholic," I explained, not making it a lot better. "I'm here to get some information. I'm investigating a murder."

"Oh," he said, and then his face went blank. "Then I guess you've come to the wrong place." He smiled, maybe to indicate there were no hard feelings, and then turned and walked away.

I started after him and then saw the black man, Edward, standing with a woman in her sixties with gray hair and a new permanent. Helen, she'd said her name was. They were pretending not to see me. When I changed directions and headed their way, Edward popped a bubble and turned away. Helen started talking to him.

"Please," I said, "I'm sorry I came here the way I did, but I didn't know what else to do."

Edward turned, chewed slowly, and looked me up and down.

"We don't inform on our members," Helen said.

"Professor Warren—Adam Warren—didn't have any family, not anybody here anyway. The only person who's going to get hurt is whoever killed him. Adam Warren," I repeated. "He might have ben a member of this group."

"Never heard of him," Edward said.

"We once had an Abel," Helen offered. "Might have been Adam's son. Would that help? He got killed, too."

"Oh, that's clever, Helen," Edward said. "You're swift, you know that?"

"You bet I am, sonny," she replied.

"I want to know who killed him," I said, starting to feel really helpless.

"Was it you, Helen?" Edward glared at her.

"It was Cain, you dummy. Didn't you ever go to Sunday school?"

"Listen to me," I said loudly. "I'm already in a lot of trouble. I've been told to stay away from Adam Warren's murder or I'll lose my job. Somebody tried to kill me. I was followed here tonight." I was fighting back tears, not very successfully.

"Oh, yeah?" Edward was suddenly interested. "Who followed you here tonight?"

"I don't know," I said. "I mean, I do know, I just don't know why, where he fits in."

"Huh. How come you were warned off? You're a cop, aren't you?"

"A campus cop," I told him. "The university police. It's not supposed to be any of my business. Can I tell you about it?"

He shrugged. "What do you think, Helen?"

"Not much," she responded. "But it can't hurt to listen." She looked me up and down with old, indifferent eyes. "What's your name?"

"Peggy," I said. They seemed to find first names sufficient.

I told them a little about Warren's murder, that I'd learned he attended AA meetings on Friday nights, and that he was probably going to attend one the night he got killed. I explained that I'd gotten interested in the case because I'd found the body.

"What'd he look like?" Edward asked.

I started to describe Warren, but that wasn't what he meant. So I told him that Warren's head had been beaten in with a hammer and there was a lot of blood.

Edward listened, then nodded. "Rough," he said finally. Then, "You can get in a lot of trouble, talking to us, that right? We just pick up the phone, tell your boss you're trying to hassle some recovering lushes and dope fiends, and bam! You're finished. Out of a job, right?"

I said he'd put it very well. He said he was a communications and business major at the U, so he knew he'd put it very well. "Succinctly," he added. "What'd you say this boss of yours name is?"

"Bixler," I said, "Melvin Bixler."

"That's an excellent name," he said. "It sounds like a curse. One thing, however: How do we know you're telling the truth? How do we know this guy Warren's really dead? You got a newspaper clipping or something you can show us?"

I said I could get one.

Edward thought some more. Finally he snapped a long thin finger up into the air and said he had an idea. "Let's go to

Heinz's. Helen and I usually go there to talk after meetings. They've got a phone."

We walked to a coffee shop called Dunkin' Heinz's and Edward went to the pay phone, looked up a number, dialed it, and a few seconds later, in a voice very different from his own, said, "Yes, at least I hope so. This is Kendall Sudbury—that's with two *u*'s—calling from the Red Alert Press, a small independent newspaper consortium serving the midwestern family and its sympathizers. I'm calling to learn if you have made any progress in the slaying of Professor Adam Warren—that's large *w*, small *a,r,r,e,n,* in that order. He was quite a cultural hero, as I'm sure you realize, and our readership wants to know what, if anything, you are doing to bring the guilty party, or parties, to justice." Edward's voice had grown fruitier and fruitier as he spoke. Now, mercifully, he fell silent and waited, blew a large bubble, and cocked his head to inspect it before turning it back into gum. He noticed I was watching him and said, "I can blow one inside the other, too," and to the phone, "I was not talking to you, sir," and then, "You have suspects, but no firm case against any of them? Too bad. Keep hammering away at them—it seems only fair." He hung up.

We found a booth in a corner by the window and ordered coffee. Helen ordered a plump glazed donut as well. "She's going to dunk it," Edward said. "Don't watch." I laughed, thinking of what Susan Carpenter had said about Alcoholics Anonymous and donuts on skid row. After the waitress left, Edward took his gum out of his mouth and pressed it on the underside of his saucer and then looked at me with his large eyes. "What did your Adam look like?" he asked.

I described Warren.

"Adam looked like that," Helen said. "A real professor. You knew he wasn't a cement contractor."

"Can you remember anything he ever said that might help explain why somebody might want to kill him?" I asked. "According to one witness, he was going around trying to make amends for things he'd done to people."

Helen shook her head. "You mean names, dates, secret crimes, people out to get him? Nah, nobody'd say anything like that in a meeting."

"What'd he say he was?" I asked.

Helen couldn't remember. Edward said he was pretty sure Warren had called himself an alcoholic.

"Whatever he said he was," Helen went on, "he didn't really believe it. I remember that about him. He wasn't ready for AA yet."

"Coming to meetings is just a start," Edward explained to me. "It means you've started to figure out you've maybe got a problem, but it's no quick fix. Also, you've got to go to more than one meeting a week, at first anyway. Adam just came to ours, like we were the Elks Club or something. Something you go to once a week. You think Adam was going around trying to make amends for things he'd done to hurt people? That's just the remorse that comes with a bad hangover. It can be dangerous, too, you know."

"It probably got him killed," I said.

"Yeah, but that's not what I meant. Some people new in AA start blabbing about all the dumb shit they did when they were using. They end up wrecking their marriages, the marriages of their friends, things like that. I never heard of anybody getting killed, though. At least not till now."

"I remember Adam when he first came to our group," Helen said. "He was real upset and looked sick, like he was coming off a bad, bad trip. But he was uptight, too. Like he didn't know why he'd come, thought maybe he'd made a mistake. I knew he'd never been to a meeting before. You could see that. I knew you'd never been to a meeting before, either," she said, giving me a gentle smile. "You looked just as uptight as he did."

"Well, you're a lot nicer to look at," Edward put in. "But that's how I remember Adam's first time, too. When it came his turn to talk, he just sat there and stammered. Like he was warming up to give a speech, but left his notes at home. I didn't think he'd come back, but there he was the next week. It surprised me."

I asked them if they could remember when Warren had started coming to their meetings. They argued about it, decided it was late March or early April, which fit with Susan Carpenter's story.

"He was always so evasive, like he was sitting on a

fence," Helen said. "I remember he talked a couple times about people he'd hurt, how he wanted to make it up to them—make amends, like you said—but didn't know how. I guess he thought we'd be able to help him out, but we don't give advice. Not in meetings, anyway, that's not why we're there."

"I recall thinking sometimes that he felt sorrier for himself than for whomever he'd hurt," Edward said. "But you know, I just thought of something. You remember, Helen, how, after the first four, five meetings, he sort of clammed up. Just sat there, lips tight, passed when it came his turn to talk? And then he didn't come to any meetings for a while."

Helen nodded. "When he came back, I was surprised."

"Me, too," Edward agreed. "I'd figured he'd used us up, you might say, that we didn't have anything more to offer him, but damned if he didn't show up again—must have been one of the last times he came."

"It *was* the last time he came—it was the last Friday in May, May thirty-first," Helen said. She turned to me. "You said he was killed on Friday, June seventh, didn't you? Well, he never came back again. Because he was dead."

"Was he any different," I asked, "the last time?"

"He sounded pretty depressed—about like he was when he first started coming. He said he was thinking of going into a treatment center."

"We all told him we supported him," Edward said. "That's kind of our way of saying 'right on' without actually saying it. Most of us have been in treatment programs, you know."

"But he said he had some things to clear up before he could," Helen said.

"What things?" I asked.

"I don't think he told us. Edward?"

"No."

They were probably things, some of them, that got him killed, I thought. He'd given Susan Carpenter a piano for having given her herpes. I wonder what he gave to Doris Parker, or tried to give to Doris Parker, for killing her daughter. I wondered if that was what the quarrel was about, in Doris's office.

"Hey, there!" Edward said, pretending to shout. "You still here?"

I smiled, nodded.

"See!" Edward said suddenly. "She's doing it." Helen had dunked a rim of her donut in her coffee and was now biting off the resultant mess. "There's no way to do that in a refined way," he told her.

She ignored him, said, "Well, it's too bad somebody had to kill Adam before he could go through treatment," which made Edward laugh. "He was pretty confused, but he did make a lasting contribution to the group, I'll give him that. You know what I'm talking about, Edward."

"No, what—oh, yeah, I do!" Edward replied. "It was Adam who got you guys to quit smoking in meetings, who made us turn the group into a nonsmoking one."

"Yes, bless his heart!" Helen explained that before Warren started coming, people smoked in meetings. She smoked, too. About half the members of the group were nonsmokers, but until Warren showed up, none of them objected. Warren did. He told them he'd quit smoking and couldn't stand being in the room with people who did. That had given the other nonsmokers the courage to take a stand, and the result was that they'd agreed not to smoke in meetings.

"I'd almost forgotten that," Helen finished. "That was the last straw for me, smoking-wise. I hated him for a while, but it was because of him I quit."

So Warren had done some good, toward the end of his life. I found it hard to accept, for some reason, that he'd quit smoking. Just about whenever I thought of him, I saw him with a cigarette in his hand. He'd been smoking one when I went into his office to ask him about an assignment I'd missed, when I took his class. Even though he seemed to have plenty of time for me, I'd made the discussion short because I'm allergic to cigarette smoke. And I could still see a pack of cigarettes lying in his blood when I found his body. So he must have started up again. I decided not to tell Helen and Edward that.

"Peggy," Helen said, "you haven't told us why anybody'd want Adam dead."

"We don't know yet. He killed an eighteen-year-old girl,

probably while he was drunk or high on drugs. It was hit-and-run. Last Christmas."

"How'd they figure out it was him?"

"I figured it out."

"Nice work," Edward said.

"Poor Adam," Helen said. "But how does that connect with him getting killed? Revenge? The girl's mom or dad or somebody found out he did it?"

"That's one theory," I said.

"Maybe somebody killed Adam to keep him from telling *us* about it," Edward suggested. "You know, maybe he was into drugs and told his drug connection that he was coming to AA, that he was thinking of going through treatment. And the connection was understandably nervous, thought maybe Adam wouldn't know when to quit confessing to stuff and messing up other people's lives, especially the drug dealer's. Those folks survive by limiting their risk factors as much as they can. Maybe you're up against a big drug ring."

"You watch too much television, Edward," Helen said. But she turned worried eyes on me and said, "You told us you thought somebody followed you here."

"Yes," I said.

"You'd better be careful," Edward said. "There's some mean, mean dudes out there. I know."

Helen, hearing his tone of voice, reached out and covered his young black hand with her old white one. She wore matching wedding and engagement rings with lots of small diamonds in them. They looked like they'd been on her finger a long time.

I dug into my pocket for some bills, said, "I'll pay for the coffee."

"Hope we've been worth it. You looked pretty embarrassed, coming to our meeting," Edward said.

"I was."

"That's okay," he said. "I would've been, too, when I first came, except that I'd gone through treatment first. I was embarrassed then, you know—ashamed—when I went into treatment and got in there with all those honkies who drank. I learned a lot, saved my own life. Got to know a lot of different people I never would've met if I hadn't been court-ordered to go through treatment. Doctors, actors, lawyers, old white ladies like Helen here who used to drink manhattans—would you believe it? Shit, even an airline pilot! That really spooked me at the time, but now I wouldn't even *fly* in a plane if the airline company didn't allow alcoholic pilots.'' He stopped, perhaps to catch his breath, and pulled his bubble gum off his saucer rim and poked it into his mouth.

''Why not?'' I asked, trying not to laugh at his earnestness.

He was waiting for that. ''Because you *know* there's just as many drunks and junkies flying airplanes as there are teaching school or taking out kids' tonsils or just being the general public. But if they can't get help for their illness because they'd lose their jobs if their bosses found out about it, and they can't drink or use either, then they just have to white-knuckle it. You know, sit there in their cockpits behind all those controls and be raging mad inside because they can't drink or use, and the whole world sucks, and there's eight inches of ice built up on their wings and the copilot says, 'Hey, Cap'n, sir, the second engine's out, how 'bout we abort the flight?' The captain throws the copilot a mean John Wayne dry-drunk sneer and says, 'You chicken, boy? We're gonna go for it!' And he tries to fly that froze-up tavern on wings out of there. No way!'' Edward said, getting mad, as if I'd been urging him to fly with dry-drunk pilots. ''You won't get me to fly with anybody who'd lose his job if anybody found out he was sick.''

''I'm sure this is why Peggy's here, Edward,'' Helen told him.

It was dark when I walked back to my car. I looked over my shoulder a lot on that peaceful, tree-shaded street, but I didn't see anybody who looked like Fred, and nobody else seemed to be following me either.

Twenty-seven

Al was back from his two weeks in Arizona and left a message on my answering machine asking me to meet him for brunch at Eleanor's, a new outdoor restaurant on Lake Eleanor that features food grilled over combustible materials scavenged from desert floors. I hadn't eaten there before—it's expensive—but I wondered what an omelet cooked over old prospector's bones would taste like, so I showed up at the agreed-upon time. Al was late.

I found an empty table next to the path that circles the lake and sat enjoying the warm, sunny morning. Windsurfers flickered in the breezes gusting on the water, colorful water bugs. A waiter brought me a tall glass pitcher of iced tea. A jogger on the path staggered past my table in a cloud of noisy agony. I sipped tea and watched him, the way people once watched the inmates of asylums, before television. It was a great day to be a cop who works nights.

"Hi, there." I came back to reality and to Lee Pierce, who was standing on the path, leaning on the railing that separated it from the restaurant. "I've been standing here for, oh, twenty, thirty minutes, waiting for you to notice me," he said.

I smiled. It no longer hurt much to smile, but I made it a small one anyway. I hadn't seen Pierce in a week, since the memorial service for Adam Warren, and he looked considerably better than he had then. Rested. Relaxed. He had the beginnings of a good tan and his lank hair was neatly trimmed. I still couldn't decide what color it was. Colorless, even in bright sunlight, still seemed to describe it.

He must have been thinking hair, too, because he said, "I recognized you even before I saw your face, Peggy. A woman going up in flames. May I join you?"

"I'm waiting for a friend," I replied.

"That's too bad. I'm giving a reading tonight, why don't you come? All new poems. The best I've done. Or do you still work nights?"

I recalled the poster I'd seen, advertising his reading. It wasn't a pleasant memory, since about a minute later I'd fallen down a flight of stairs. "I'm still working nights," I told him.

"Same hours?"

For some reason I didn't like that line of questioning, but I couldn't think of a polite way to tell him it wasn't any of his business, so I said yes.

"Then that's perfect! The reading starts at eight-thirty and it should be over by ten. There'll be a party afterward. Friends, writers—a few who are both. It'll go on until the wee hours, so you could come when you get off work."

"I guess not," I said.

His face darkened, as it had once before when he didn't get from me what he wanted. "You won't have to take off your clothes at *this* party," he said, still working to make it light, but not working hard enough.

I felt my face turning red. I reached for my glass and took a careful sip.

"I'm sorry I missed it," he went on, his eyes drifting quietly over what there was to see of me.

I pretended to look around for Al.

"For Christ's sake, Peggy," Pierce blurted suddenly, "can't you loosen up! What're you afraid of?"

The answer to that seemed pretty obvious to me. I turned back to him and said, "I'm afraid of whoever killed Professor Warren."

He blinked, then laughed, as if exasperated with me. "That's not exactly what I meant. Jesus, are you still stuck on that? We both know who did Adam in! Anybody who can put two and two together knows."

I asked him who he thought four was.

"Doris Parker, of course. You know that better than anyone."

"Why's that?"

"Oh, stop acting dumb, Peggy! We know you were behind the cops finding out Adam killed Marilyn Parker."

"We?"

"The Beckers, Peggy, the Beckers. *I'm* not playing dumb, at least. I know you know I'm close to them."

"And you knew from the beginning that Adam Warren killed Marilyn Parker," I said. "That's another thing I know."

Lee Pierce looked left and then looked right and then back at me. "You're not wired for sound, are you, Peggy?" he asked, his voice soft.

"No."

"I'm not sure it would make any difference if you were. Yes, I knew Adam killed Marilyn, of course I did. But would it have brought her back to life if I'd turned him in to the cops? I owed him too much to do that anyway. He was a father to me. I told you that before."

"And now he's dead," I said. "Do you still think you were doing him a favor?"

"I'm not like you, Peggy," was his answer, "I don't play God."

He must've figured that was a pretty good line to exit on, so he shoved off from the railing and went on his way down the path.

"Who was that?" Al asked, folding himself into a chair across from me. It was nice to see his big, moon-shaped face again. It was nice to see the rest of him, too. He was reasonably tanned and had lost some weight and looked good. "And what are those hideous black things on your arms?" he went on. "I'm speaking of the big ones with the yellow borders, not the others."

"That was Lee Pierce," I replied, deciding to take the questions in order.

"The poet? I didn't know you knew him—oh, he's the guy you told me about. The one who stood over that corpse you found and recited poetry—how'd it go?"

" 'Weep for Adam Warren,' " I said, " 'he is dead.' "

"Right. Extremely inappropriate. But that's not what I asked." A waiter appeared and handed us tall menus. Al opened his. "I meant, how'd the sleuthing go? You wrap it up for the cops?" Without waiting for any answer, he started scanning his menu.

I didn't realize until then how much had happened in just the two-plus weeks since he'd left and I'd begun to get involved in the murder of Warren. Al knew nothing about it at all. I looked at him sitting there, big and complaisant in the morning sunshine, nothing on his mind but a good breakfast, a walk around the lake, and getting laid.

"It went like this," I said, not being very fair, and held up my arms so he could get a better look at the bruises.

"That must have hurt a lot," he said. "How'd it happen?"

I told him. My food got cold. His didn't.

Twenty-eight

At first I thought the voice on my answering machine was suffering from stage fright. "Hello," it said. "This is Fred Lundeen." I recognized the voice, from the Beckers' and from the church the day before. He didn't mention our encounter at the church, though; he just said, "I was at Jack Becker's party last Sunday, you remember?" A pause, perhaps waiting for me to nod and say yes. "I'd like to talk to you, is all," he continued. His voice didn't become less frightened. "It's just getting way out of hand. I didn't know about Adam, about Adam Warren. That he'd died—been killed. You're working on it, right?—and I'd like to talk to somebody about it. I guess I'd like to talk to you about it, that's what I've been thinking."

Another pause. This time it was so long, I was afraid he'd hang up—hung up, I meant. "Can I come over? I need to talk to somebody soon." He'd begun jumbling words, perhaps afraid he'd run out of tape. "Call me," he said, and gave a telephone number, "I'm here. I'll be here the rest of the night. Call anytime, I know you work nights." The silence was a long and living one, although canned, but then he decided he had nothing else he wanted to say, so he hung up.

I know you work nights, he'd said. How did he know that? I sat there thinking about it until another voice came on the line.

"Peggy?" it asked, as if wondering who might be sitting there in the dark, listening. "Aunt Tess. Your mother called

175

a few minutes ago. She's upset. There's nothing new in that, of course, but I really do think—''

I decided that what Aunt Tess really thought could wait. I called the number Fred Lundeen had given me, but got no answer. I let it ring a long time before I hung up. The clock on my kitchen wall said it was 11:30.

It was another hot, humid night. I'd stayed at Al's as late as I could and then had to drive like a maniac to make it to work on time. I'd walked my beat as usual and seen and heard nothing out of the ordinary. Saturday nights are pretty dead on a university campus, at least in the summer.

At a little after nine I'd walked over to the Arts Center where Lee Pierce was reading his poetry. It wasn't that far off my beat. They'd given him a good-sized room, but I couldn't see why. There was a group of people crowded together up front, and maybe another thirty people scattered among the empty seats behind them—about fifty people in all in a room that I guessed would seat more than twice that many.

Pierce was on a raised platform, reading from something on the podium in front of him. I was surprised at that: I'd heard that he was a real showman on stage, stalking back and forth, shouting and gesturing like a television evangelist. That would go with the poetry of his I'd read, his older poetry, but maybe not with whatever it was he was trying to become now. He looked pretty tame and was even wearing a jacket and dark tie.

I watched for a few minutes from the window in the door, but I couldn't hear any of his words. I recognized Jack Becker, a squat, dark figure in one of the seats in the front row, and Merle, the woman who made his marriage work, if you believed his wife, Jerry, next to him. But I didn't see Jerry. I didn't see anybody else I recognized either.

A couple that had been sitting near the back, a young man and a woman, came out, sliding through the doors so as not to disturb Pierce, but he looked up anyway. I was glad for the darkness in the hall. He couldn't see me in it. After another minute of watching his poet's pantomime, I went back to my patrol.

Then I'd driven home and turned on my answering ma-

chine and gone out to the refrigerator to get a bottle of sparkling water. The only call before Fred had been Al, asking
me to call him when I got home. I knew what he wanted, but
I'd already told him I wasn't going to stay with him that
night.

When Al comes back from visiting the kids, he doesn't
like to be in his house alone for a couple of days.

"I'm here," Fred had told my answering machine. I looked
up here in the phone book, dialed the number again, and then
went back out to my car.

He'd be there the rest of the night, he said. What I'd heard
in his voice wasn't stage fright; it was fear.

Why didn't he answer his phone? I wondered when he'd
called me, wished I'd had one of the newer machines that
records the time. He'd probably changed his mind, or something unexpected had come up, something quite harmless.
Maybe he was home, but decided not to answer his phone,
no longer wanted to talk to me. The worst thing about speaking into somebody's answering machine is that you can't take
it back.

I should have called Hansen, of course, but Fred Lundeen
didn't want to talk to Hansen, he wanted to talk to me. He
might not talk to Hansen or to any other cop. And the police
didn't seem very interested in the Beckers and their friends
anyway.

Mine was the only voice in my head telling me I should
be doing what I was doing. The others—and there were several—were making a lot of noise, just not enough. You should
take your father's Corvette off your aunt's hands, I heard
Ginny telling me, and make it the cornerstone of a new safe
hobby, and Al wanted to know why I couldn't just come over
and spend the night with him. That afternoon, when I'd finished telling him all that I'd been involved in since he went
off on vacation, he'd turned and looked at me and asked me,
"Why? What're you getting out of this? Do you think it's
fun?"

For some odd reason I suddenly thought of a boy in high
school, somebody I hadn't thought of in years. His hormones
were driving him crazy and he thought it was love and that I
was the cause of it and the sole means of its gratification,

too, and as a consequence he drove around my house night after night in his car. He knew he'd achieve nothing that way, or any other way, but he did it anyway. I could set my clock by him. His car needed a new muffler. I couldn't imagine what he got out of it.

I seemed to have acquired some of his addiction to futility. I didn't know what I was getting out of what I was doing either and no, I didn't think it was fun.

I wondered what my mother was upset about, and why she'd called Aunt Tess instead of me.

The freeway was almost deserted, and I was able to drive fast. My radio was on—I'd forgotten to turn it off when I got home from work—and I suddenly heard it for the first time. I tried to make sense of the words, but couldn't at first. Three kinds of latex for your four kinds of exterior, someone was telling me in an excited voice, four kinds of latex for your three basic interiors. Latex and water-based paint for your exterior trim, enamel for your woodwork. New colors and old colors, antiques and pastels. It was hypnotic, stunning, and mine if I wanted it.

Then a cool woman's voice began to report heavy storms marching toward us through county after county. After the house paints, storms were a relief. The temperature was still in the eighties, the humidity was high, and the wind was gusting uncertainly in all directions.

Fred Lundeen lived in a section of Southwest that was made up of old, run-down houses and tall new condominiums that looked like grain elevators with balconies. I parked under one of the few elms that hadn't been taken either by disease or developers, and turned off the engine. The radio was suddenly silent, and so was the inside of my head. I waited a minute, took some deep breaths, and then got out and walked down the sidewalk looking for the address I wanted. It was one of the condos.

The big glass front door was locked, of course. I found Lundeen's name in a framed board beside a long row of buttons like one side of an accordion, inadequately lit by a light over the door. I pressed the button beside Lundeen's name and waited. No voice asked who I was; the door didn't buzz.

I pressed the button again, feeling more relieved than disappointed that I wouldn't be able to get in. I turned to leave.

I bumped into someone standing behind me, stepped back fast, and almost screamed. He stumbled back, a tall man, but he wasn't Fred Lundeen. He recovered his balance and started toward me again, stumbled, and dropped the keys he was holding. I realized he was drunk. We bent simultaneously to pick up the keys and our heads bumped.

"Ouch," he said, and then, slurring his words, "Let me, by God! Chivalry isn't dead, not by a long shot!" He scooped up the keys after several tries and handed them to me with a bow.

I thanked him and opened the door.

"After you," he said, and bowed again, overbalanced, and staggered headlong into the foyer.

I followed him and handed him his keys.

"Thank you," he said, regarding them as if they were holy relics, "I knew they had to be here someplace." The building was heavily air-conditioned. He looked at me closely the way drunks do, perhaps to see if there were more there than met the eye, then lurched back. "I'd invite you in for a drink," he said at last, "but at the moment I'm too lonely." I said I understood and watched as he toddled down the hall into the gloom at the other end. The hall was dimly lit, the light tinted green by the wallpaper and carpeting, like a summer night just before a storm, like the summer night I'd just left outside. And it was quiet.

I stepped into the elevator, pressed eight, and rose in silence, as if not moving at all. My heart was beating too fast. I imagined Lieutenant Hansen's stern, disapproving face. *She's learned her lesson,* he'd said in Bixler's office. Right.

The eighth floor looked like the first. Thick, green carpeting, green walls, low lighting. A gold plush chair stood beneath a mirror in a gilt frame, across from the elevator. The hall reminded me of the mausoleum where we'd stuck the copper box containing my father's ashes, behind a piece of marble bearing all the information we wanted the world to know about him. *Creamains,* the funeral director had called them. A repulsive new word to have to learn, at a time like that. My mother never stopped complaining that we'd had him cremated, but that's what he wanted and that's what he got.

I stared at myself in the mirror as I got out of the elevator. Both of us tried to shrug off what we were doing as making perfect sense, we both tried to smile, and then I turned down the hall in search of Fred Lundeen's apartment. If he didn't answer his door, would I try to break in? Was I going to use a credit card, the way I'd seen it done on television and in the movies, to open his locked door? I doubted it; I suspected that things like that don't really work.

I waited outside the door for a moment and then knocked. There was nothing but silence, on this side of the door and on that one. I started to turn away, glad to be going back home. I didn't even knock a second time. I didn't really want to be there.

I heard a small noise from inside the apartment. I turned back, waited, and listened. Nothing happened. I knocked again, louder, longer. Silence again. I figured the noise I'd heard was my imagination, or a cat, and I started to turn away again and then something fell inside the apartment, something heavy and soft.

Then something hit the door from inside and I flinched away.

"Open the door," I said, "can you? It's Peggy O'Neill."

The door opened. I pushed on it and it opened more, about six inches, and then met something solid. I leaned my weight on it and it opened enough for me to slip through into the room.

I stood in the darkness listening, willing my eyes and ears to grow accustomed to it. Green light leaked out from around the edges of drapes across the room. Then something heavy rolled onto my legs and I screamed and tried to twist away. My shoulder scraped a light switch and I groped at the wall for it, found it, and pushed it up with my palm.

Fred Lundeen was in the process of making himself comfortable on the floor at my feet. He'd settled back against the door I'd just squeezed through. He was looking up at me, as if trying to tell me something, but that wasn't possible—I could have told him that—because there was a knife in his throat.

Twenty-nine

He died as I knelt down beside him. His eyes were wide and still staring at me, just as they'd been in the Beckers' hot tub when he shot up out of the water in front of me, but nothing at all was living behind them now, and that made their intelligent glitter horrible. His blood was still running down his naked chest and into his pajama bottoms. The index finger of his right hand—the hand he'd used to pull down the handle of the door—rested on his chest, pointing at his throat, as if he were trying to explain why he wasn't able to speak.

I remembered that the doggerel he'd recited to me out at the Beckers' had been about death, but I couldn't remember how it went. Too bad. On a crazy impulse I reached out and pushed his hand, and it fell with a small thud onto the linoleum of the entryway. There! I thought. He looked better that way.

I stayed where I was, ignoring the rest of the room. It seemed to me I'd experienced this before: the body, the blood, the smell of blood. You're getting closer, O'Neill, I thought. Adam Warren had been dead several minutes when you found him. This one died as you watched. Can you get closer to it than that?

I didn't think I was going to throw up this time, but just to make sure, I stood up and went into the living room, avoided stepping into what looked like spots of still fresh blood on the beige carpeting, and sat down on the nearest chair, stayed sitting awhile. Whenever I looked up, Fred was still there, his eyes still aimed at me.

After a few minutes I made myself get up. I stood there

181

for a moment asking myself what I wanted to do, and then decided to look through the apartment. I could hear voices telling me to dial 911, tell them what I'd found, tell them to secure the building, but I ignored them. I'd done it wrong the last time, and look how far I'd got, I said to myself, and giggled out loud. Who knows where I'll end up this time. I didn't expect to find anybody in the apartment with me, or anything that would explain Lundeen's death. I was just curious, and wasn't sure what I wanted to do next.

A hall ran down to my left. I flipped the light switch and went down there, looked into a bedroom, looked under the unmade bed, nudged open a closet door, and looked in there, too. Nothing of interest, nobody lurking there. The bathroom was empty, too. The toilet seat was up; the toilet needed flushing. Great detective work, O'Neill: Fred Lundeen had been a slob. Or his killer had been, so don't flush it. I heard somebody chuckle inanely, realized it was me, didn't like the sound. I'd giggled once; now I was chuckling. I don't usually do either. At the end of the hall was another bedroom. It looked unused, not even bedclothes covering the mattress.

I went back to the living room and through it to the kitchenette. I had to step over Fred to get there, tried not to look at him, breathed shallowly so I wouldn't have to smell his blood. There were cupboards over the sink, their doors open. I looked in.

The lower one had three shelves, only the first of which had anything on it: a clutter of mismatched glasses, cups, plates.

I wondered why the doors of the cupboard above that one were open, if Fred's cupboards were so bare. I got a chair and stood on it and looked in. There were two pistols on the lower shelf and a box of ammunition. I stood on tiptoe to see onto the upper shelf, but it was empty.

In the living room the phone was on the carpet next to a dark stain. I touched it; it was sticky with blood. Maybe Fred had been at the phone when he was stabbed, or tried to get to it afterward—but for what, with a knife in his throat? I cradled the headset to bring it back to life and looked up homicide in Lundeen's phone book, dialed the number, and told the voice that answered what I'd found and where I'd found it. I gave my name and assured her that I'd still be there when they arrived. I also told her that the murder was connected with a case Lieutenant Hansen was working on, and that he should be notified, too.

I had an afterthought, one that amused me, and I said gruffly, "Send a squad to secure the entire building." I hung up before I started giggling again. Usually I giggle only when somebody is tickling me. That doesn't happen very often.

It didn't smell good in Fred Lundeen's apartment, so I made sure the door wasn't locked and then squeezed through it into the hall. It was quiet there, green and peaceful, an unexpectant stillness. It reminded me of the calm I'd noticed in Frye Hall after I'd discovered Adam Warren's body. As if a mass murderer had gone from room to room and silently murdered everybody. Eerie. I wanted to run from door to door and pound on them and shriek, "Murder!"

Instead I sank down on the deep pile of the carpeting, my back against the cold wall, and rested my head on my knees. I stayed that way until I heard the elevator stop and its doors open.

Thirty

I led the two homicide detectives I'd seen at Adam Warren's memorial service, plus some lab men, into Fred Lundeen's apartment, then went over to the chair I'd sat in before and, no longer very interested, watched them work. They ascertained that Fred was dead, photographed everything, went around taking fingerprints off every reasonable surface and a few that didn't seem reasonable to me at all. I waited to see how long it would take them to find the pistols in the kitchen. When they did find them, they wrapped them in plastic and put them in a box with other treasures they'd looted from Fred's tomb, including his garbage.

When they were through photographing Fred, they rolled him over on his side. One of the detectives reached down and picked up something on the floor that had been under the body. It was yellow, a piece of cloth.

I got up, went over, and asked if I could look at it. The door opened then, and Hansen came in. He gave me a quick nod and asked his men some questions. As they were answering I took the piece of cloth out of the detective's hand. It rubbed my fingers the wrong way, as polyester always does.

"This means today's Saturday," I announced.

"What, O'Neill?" Hansen looked at me with some interest. The two detectives looked at me with intensity, but without any interest at all.

I realized I'd leaped to a silly conclusion without explaining the steps. "Because yellow's for Friday," I said, not making things much better. "If yesterday was yellow, today's Saturday." That wasn't quite what I meant to say either.

"Doris Parker," I said, very slowly now, noticing that all three men had turned to me, not necessarily because they thought I would have anything useful to say but because they expected me to destruct noisily right before their eyes, and they wanted to be prepared, "wears yellow on Fridays. She always does, according to Arthur Fletcher. You remember Arthur Fletcher," I said to Hansen, and he nodded, perhaps to humor me. "The Friday Adam Warren was murdered, she wore yellow, too. Maybe she does all her killing on Fridays, for some obscure religious reason."

"Do you know what you're talking about?" Hansen asked me.

"Of course I do," I said, working up some heat. "You can ask Fletcher. Doris was wearing a yellow polyester blouse the afternoon Warren was murdered. This scrap probably came from the same one."

"Lots of people wear yellow," one of the detectives said, giving me a disgusted look. "Friday don't got nothing to do with it."

"I am willing to swear," I said solemnly, "that nobody connected with this case—nobody I know about, anyway— would wear anything made of yellow polyester, except Doris Parker."

Hansen went over and looked up a number in Lundeen's phone book and dialed it and waited awhile.

"She's not home," he said, hanging up. He told one of the detectives to find her and bring her in and then turned to me. "Why'd she murder this guy, do you know that, too?"

"This is Fred," I told him. I was pleased that he'd started the search for Doris before asking me my reasons. I was making progress with Hansen. I reminded him that I'd told him about Fred in Bixler's office the week before.

"All right, so this is Fred. I remember what you told me about him. Now tell me why she killed him."

"I think," I said slowly, "because she thought or knew he was partly responsible for killing her daughter. I think drugs are a part of this." I pointed to the cupboard, where I'd found the guns. "I think Fred was a drug dealer."

"A hunch, O'Neill? I thought you told me once you weren't psychic."

I didn't feel much like banter—I hadn't felt much like it the time before either, when we were going over Warren's murder in Doris Parker's office. "No," I said. "What else would he have those weapons for, if it wasn't something criminal? I don't think he was a hunter, and those pistols aren't for hunting anyway. Fred told me on the phone that things were getting out of hand—those were his words—and he sounded scared. I think Adam Warren told Doris about Fred, that time they were quarreling in her office, when he was trying to make amends."

I'd lost Hansen again. He was looking at me as if I needed to be taken somewhere for a long rest. I couldn't understand it at first, then I remembered that I'd outrun him on this investigation, maybe even lapped him. I started to try to explain but he put up a hand to stop me.

"Take it easy," he said. "We're going down to my office. You can tell me all about it there."

As we were going down in the elevator I told him my car was outside. He wanted me to go with him anyway, let somebody else drive my car home, but I said no, so he walked me to it, checked it for murderers, and let me drive off.

I rolled down my window and stuck my head out, hoping the wind would clear my head. It was still hot and humid and far to the south lightning flickered on the horizon. It was storming violently somewhere.

Ours were the only two cars on the freeway, Hansen's and mine, but he kept his distance.

Thirty-one

I parked behind an empty police car in front of the police station, Hansen pulled in behind me, and we walked up the steps and inside together. The duty officer told Hansen to call Burke at Doris Parker's house; the number was on his desk. We went down a long well-lighted hall. The sign on an office door about two-thirds of the way down said MANSELL HANSEN. In spite of how tired I was, I turned and stared at Hansen in amazement: Mansell Hansen! He refused to meet my eyes.

He went in first and sat down behind his desk. It was an old desk, oak and cluttered. As he dialed Doris Parker's number I sat down in a leather armchair against a wall and occupied my time trying to pronounce his first name. I placed the stress first on one syllable, *Man*sell, and then on the other, Man*sell*. In my confused head it wasn't a real name either way.

"She's still not home," he said to me after he'd hung up. "Where the hell could she be this time of night? We've put an all-points bulletin out on her car." I said yes to his offer of coffee and he poured it from a battered thermos into a Styrofoam cup. His own cup was a china mug that had probably once been white. "Didn't you promise to stay away from the Warren case?" he asked me.

I started to say something flip, to indicate that I knew he knew I had no intention of staying away from it. But something in his face made me change my mind: he didn't know he'd wanted me to keep poking at it.

"Lundeen called me," I told him. "I didn't even know his last name until he told me who he was. I didn't talk to him, he left a message on my answering machine. He wanted me to call him back, to arrange a time when he could come over and talk to me. When I called him, he didn't answer, so I drove over to his place." I told him how Lundeen had managed to open his door for me and then died at my feet—on them, actually.

"That wasn't too smart," Hansen said when I'd finished. "Lundeen couldn't have been stabbed much before you got there, if he was still alive. You were lucky you missed his killer."

"She was lucky she missed me," I snapped at him, tired of being called dumb. Lundeen had wanted to talk to me, I told Hansen, and if he'd wanted to talk to the police, he'd have called them. "And if you'd wanted to talk to Lundeen," I added, "you'd have gone looking for him. I told you to find out who he was last Wednesday."

"I did," Hansen replied.

"You did what?"

"Found out who Fred Lundeen was." If Hansen enjoyed my surprise, he was kind enough not to show it.

"How?"

"By asking one of the people you told me was out at the Beckers' place last Sunday."

"Who?"

"Never mind who. More than one of them's not sleeping well these nights, now that we've traced Marilyn Parker's death back to the Beckers—and not because of the humidity, either."

He rummaged around on his desk, found a file. "Lundeen had a record. Not much of one, but interesting. I think your hunch about drugs out at the Beckers' is pretty good. You want to hear about it?"

He didn't bother to wait for me to nod or say yes, just settled back and told me what he'd found out. Fred Lundeen had one conviction for selling drugs, some six years before. Nothing big, a few months' jail time, and no previous arrests. "From all indications," Hansen said, "he was the kind of little guy you could go to if you were having a party and needed a couple of eight balls or some good dope. He's a chemist, even worked for a while at the University—but got into some kind of trouble there. We're having a little difficulty finding out what that was about, but we will. My guess is he was caught brewing designer drugs for his friends and forced to resign. All very quiet.''

He looked at me with some satisfaction on his face. I'd misjudged Hansen. He'd been busy since I last saw him.

''But what was Lundeen doing out there at the Beckers'?'' I asked. ''You don't usually invite your dealer to the party, do you?''

''I don't know,'' Hansen answered. ''Right now I just want to get my hands on Doris Parker.''

I said, ''Arthur Fletcher told you who Fred was.''

''Quit guessing. Fletcher'd only gone out to the Beckers' a couple of times before last Sunday. At least that's what he told us. It scared the pants off him. Or rather, he kept his pants on, that was the problem. He didn't like the drugs, the kind of free-floating sex they did, at all. Lynn Cross—the woman he went out there to find last Sunday, the one you wanted us to find for you—was the one who introduced him to the Beckers and tried to get him into their group. They were—are—having an affair, of course. But she's also a friend of Lee Pierce's,'' Hansen added.

''And last Sunday,'' I said, ''Arthur Fletcher went out there to try to rescue her.'' From the damp clutches of the water troll. And Lee Pierce. I recalled her at the memorial service for Adam Warren, her hands moving in the chapel air as she pleaded with Lee Pierce. For what?

''That's what it amounts to,'' Hansen said.

''Arthur Fletcher,'' I said, ''the white knight. I'll bet she was grateful.'' I thought of Fletcher's wife, and his daughter, wondered who was going to come to their rescue. He'd called his daughter Chrissy.

''Lynn Cross is an assistant professor in the Psychology department,'' Hansen said. ''Young and promising and up to her neck in drugs and trouble.''

So I knew where Hansen had got Fred's last name.

''Does *she* know that?'' I asked. ''And if she does, what's she planning to do about it?''

Before he could answer me—assuming he intended to—the

phone rang and he picked it up, listened, agreed to whatever the person at the other end had in mind.

"That was Burke," he said. "One of the neighbors came over when she saw all the activity at Parker's house and told him she was on vacation. She took her vacation early this year, to get away from—all this."

"Does she know where she went?"

"She's got a cabin on a lake. It's just about a hundred miles north of here, a little over two hours on the freeway—at least, it is if you're driving under fifty-five because you've just committed a murder and don't want to get picked up for speeding."

I thought of Doris Parker driving the freeway back to town from her cabin, bent on whatever part of her revenge Fred Lundeen's killing was. She would drive conscientiously, courteously, obey the speed limit. She was a conscientious person. And now she was on her way north again, back to her cabin, her latest task completed. I recalled her eyes with the dark rings, like a raccoon, and the glint of mica in them. The memory made me shudder. The police would be there, this time, waiting for her. She wouldn't put up a struggle. Doris Parker wouldn't make a fuss.

"She had good reason to kill Warren," I said to Hansen, surprising myself, and when I saw the look on his face I added, "from her point of view, at least." I was thinking of what the newspapers had said, that Warren's car hadn't killed Marilyn Parker. Warren had left her to freeze to death.

"But not from mine," he answered. "Revenge isn't any better than any other reason for killing people—at least if you want to make a civilization work. And that's something else we're going to have to get out of her: how she found out that Adam Warren killed her daughter."

"Warren told her," I said.

"Why do you say that?"

I described Warren's efforts to become a member of Alcoholics Anonymous and what Helen and Edward had said about his clumsy efforts to make amends to people. "I think Warren went to her and confessed and that's what they had the fight about. She didn't want to hear it, didn't want to know, and didn't want whatever it was he offered her."

"Or wanted *more* than he offered her," Hansen added. "And then decided to kill him when he couldn't or wouldn't give it to her." He offered me more coffee. "It's funny," he went on, pouring some for himself, "we figured we'd find a connection between Parker and Warren through the money missing from one of Warren's retirement accounts." He screwed the top on his thermos, set it aside as he talked. "We were about to bring her in to ask her about that when two scared kids showed up and told us another story of Adam Warren trying to make amends. Susan Carpenter and her boyfriend. Want to hear about it?"

He was watching me with those very blue eyes of his, but this time there was a flicker of humor in them, although I had to look hard to see it. I stared back at him with my very green eyes. The air right above his desk where our gazes met must have been aquamarine.

"I guess not," I said.

"No," he replied, "I didn't suppose you would."

"I have to go now," I said, and stood up. "About my job: I'd like to keep it, at least for the time being."

He pretended to be amazed. "I can't imagine why. It's obviously not enough to keep you busy. It doesn't seem to wear you out and send you to bed for a sound night's sleep, the sleep of the innocent."

"Unemployment won't either," I replied.

There was a silence while he digested that. Then, "Well, I don't suppose I have to tell your friend Bixler how we did it. I'll give it some thought."

"Thanks," I said. I went over to his desk to toss my coffee cup into his wastebasket. There were some large, shiny photographs, in color, lying in the clutter on his desktop.

"What are those?" I asked, staring at them.

"The pictures we took of Adam Warren. Want to take a look? You'll recognize them."

No, I didn't want to look, but I couldn't help it. The case had started with this for me, so it seemed appropriate that it should end here, too.

"I didn't know you used color film," I said, swallowing hard. "I thought they'd be in black-and-white." My eyes couldn't get enough of the photographs.

"With the processing we've got now, color's faster and easier."

A lot more real, too. As real as the TV news, because nothing moves in a death scene anyway. The pictures had been taken from every possible angle around Warren's body; they showed his head lying on one cheek, his hair stained with blood where both flowed out onto the floor.

The blood looked very real. I could almost smell it.

I started to feel sick to my stomach, the way I'd felt when I saw this scene the first time. Please, I heard myself say, not here, not again.

My father had looked a lot like that, when he killed himself with one of his hunting rifles. A long time ago, when I was seventeen. I'd found his body, too. I wondered why I hadn't noticed the similarity before.

"Peggy!" someone said loudly, and a hand tightened on my shoulder.

"You don't have to look at them," Hansen said, and started gathering up the photographs.

"I'm okay. I just want to look at that one again." I picked up the one of Warren with his bloody head on the floor, taken from his doorway, showing him as I'd seen him when I found him.

"What is it, Peggy?"

I didn't reply, just kept looking at it. Whatever it was I thought I'd seen, it wouldn't come back. I was too tired to see it, too upset, stunned. I shook my head. "Sorry," I said, "I guess I'm really out of it." I turned away and started toward the door, then remembered something else. "Tell me," I asked him, "is it *Man*sell, or Man*sell*?"

"Neither." He came around his desk, started to put his arm around me, thought better of it. "Nobody calls me that. You can call me Buck, if you want. I'd like it if you would."

I gave him the best smile I had at the moment and headed out of there.

Thirty-two

It was a few minutes before three when I got home, and there was a bee in my apartment. That seemed odd because I have new screens and I'd never had a bee in my apartment before. But I was too tired to think about anything except helping it get out of there and then going to bed. I opened the screen on the window by the telephone a little, to give it a chance to make its own way out.

I'd driven home from Hansen's office in a thunderstorm, but now the storm center had passed to the northeast, leaving only a steady rain.

Since I was there by the phone, and the red light was lit, I pressed the button on the answering machine. I remembered that there was a message from Aunt Tess waiting for me, something about my mother being upset about something. I'd put Tess on hold while I went off to Fred Lundeen's apartment to watch him die. That seemed like a long time ago, but it had only been a little over three hours.

I listened to the rest of what Aunt Tess had to say: my mother didn't want me to keep my father's car; she wanted Aunt Tess to sell it without telling me and send the money to her—it was urgent. She sounded quite upset, Aunt Tess told me.

My mother often gets bizarre notions, most of them put into her head by the evangelists and mystics that prey on the widows in the southern California neighborhood where she lives. I didn't want to spend any more time thinking about it just then. I wanted to go to bed, to try to forget what I'd seen that night.

Aunt Tess hung up. Before I could turn off the machine another voice began speaking to me.

A voice from the dead.

"I guess it can't wait, Miss O'Neill," Fred Lundeen said.

My skin began to crawl.

"Did you try to call me? I was out for a while, walking around. I'm trying to figure out what to do. I don't know what's going to happen next, but I don't like it. I don't think any of them like it, not Jerry even, but maybe Lee. I want to tell you about it now, because I'm scared. It's just gone too far."

There was a sudden noise, not loud, but loud enough so that I knew it wasn't something Lundeen expected to hear, and then he screamed and screamed again and said, "Lee—"

A crash and the start of another scream, farther away but as clear as if it were happening right now, but that scream went nowhere and then there was silence.

I listened into it, rooted there, until in my rain-streaked window I saw something move behind me. I turned. Lee Pierce was standing in my bedroom door.

"Poor Fred," he said quietly, "he never got his chance to tell you all about it, did he? And it was so important to him." He sounded sorrowful about it. He wasn't just mocking me.

I was unable to move. Small noises were coming through the answering machine and I realized they were Lee Pierce's ragged breathing and his listening. Lundeen was dying and Lundeen was dead; his killer was standing over him but he was also standing in my bedroom door.

"Oh," Pierce went on, as if the world made perfect sense, "I suppose Fred might have been about to say 'Leaping Lizards,' but I doubt that even a clever defense lawyer could make a jury swallow that. I think he was speaking my name. Don't you?"

Those words made no sense to me, they were just noise coming out of his mouth, but then the tape stopped with a click and that woke me up. "It was you," I said.

"Yes, and just a few seconds too late. But it's all right now. Everything's all right now."

Pierce's eyes were bright—too bright. He'd strolled into

the living room as he talked, stopping between me and the couch, his hands deep in his raincoat pockets. I noticed, irrelevantly, that the coat was dry, which meant he'd gotten into my apartment before the storm broke. It was dirty, too, from his climb through my bedroom window. It needed pressing badly and so did he. Being able to notice things like that gave me some comfort.

I measured the distance to the outside door, realized I couldn't make it without him getting in my way, and decided to go straight for him instead, up and over the couch.

"Don't do it," he said, as if reading my mind. He brought a pistol out of his pocket and pointed it at me. "We have some time," he said. "Why don't you go sit where you sat the last time we were here—the chair over there—and I'll take the sofa. Old times. Old friends."

I didn't move. I heard the bee buzzing and bouncing off the screen in my bedroom and the rain hitting the bushes in the backyard. I thought that if I didn't move, it would just be a dream, and that felt safer than the reality, so I stayed where I was.

"You'll do as I say." Pierce's voice was sharper, and there was an edge to it I didn't like at all. "And you won't scream," he added, louder still.

I went over to the chair and sat down.

He didn't take his coat off this time. It hung open. Under it he was wearing the jacket and tie he'd worn at his reading, but the tie was pulled away from his throat and the shirt was open. A wing of his colorless hair kept falling down, on the left side of his head.

"If Lundeen hadn't said my name," I told him, "you wouldn't have known who he was talking to. You'd be up shit creek."

He gave me a pained look. "Do women have to talk like that now? But you're wrong, Peggy. I'd have thought of you first. You really upset Fred, you know, telling him Adam was dead. You shouldn't have done that. He gets upset easily. *Got* upset easily, I should say. He started asking questions about you right after you came out to the Beckers' last Sunday. I'd have come to you anyway—if for no other reason than because I'd have no other option." He glanced down at his watch.

My phone rang. We both jumped.

"Who is it?" Pierce demanded.

"How should I know? You want me to answer it?"

"No, don't touch it. Is your answering machine on?"

"No."

"Let it ring then. Who'd call you this time of night?" His voice was edgier than I'd ever heard it. With good reason.

I tried a casual shrug. "Heavy breathers," I told him. "They've been calling a lot lately."

The ringing stopped. He seemed to relax. "Do you mind if I smoke?" he asked me.

He gave me a bright smile—like his eyes, too bright—as if waiting hopefully for a "No, I don't mind."

"Yes," I said, "I mind." My voice was shaking; I was talking to a killer and I was scared.

His laugh would have been remarkably pleasant, if it hadn't gone on for so long. "You're quite an admirable creature, Peggy O'Neill," he said when he'd stopped. "But you certainly know how to make yourself unloved, don't you?"

He took out his cigarettes, shook one up from the rest, pulled it from the pack with his lips, and then tossed the pack onto my coffee table. "A real nuisance," he repeated. "Can you imagine how I felt when I realized I hadn't gotten to Fred in time to keep him from saying my name? I thought he was talking to *you*, not your answering machine. I felt *sick*—to be so close to getting away with it and then have your meddling ruin it, ruin it again! But when I picked up the phone and heard nothing except the noise of the tape, I realized we were going to get away with it—I was going to get away with it—this time, too." He flashed a smile of pleasure at the recollection. It was a humorless, angry smile, like sun glinting off a piece of tin.

He lit his cigarette, sucking in smoke as if it were nourishment he desperately needed. "Of course," he went on, the smoke leaking out among the words, "I still had to get here before you played the tape and called the cops, but I felt sure I wasn't meant to get such a break and then not win. What would be the point of that?"

I didn't know yet, so I couldn't give him an answer. I was looking at the cigarettes on the table, thinking about them even as I listened to him talk. They made me think of the photographs I'd seen in Hansen's office.

The match he was holding was still burning. He noticed it and shook it out and dropped it on my carpet. He immediately thought better of that, however, and keeping one eye on me, bent down and picked it up. "I ran," he went on, "leaving poor Fred to finish dying on his own. I'd just gotten into my car and was about to drive over here—when guess who pulled up in front of Fred's apartment! I laughed so hard, I was afraid you'd hear me! What could be better? You'd be *there* trying to get a name from a dead man, and I'd be *here,* at your place, getting it from a tape." The symmetry of it seemed to amuse him. He got up suddenly, went behind me to my kitchen and took a saucer from the drying rack, came back, and put it on the coffee table to use as an ashtray.

"Why didn't you follow me in," I asked him when he returned, "and just kill me at Fred's right then?" I wasn't very interested in the answer, since it didn't matter now anyway, but I wanted him to keep talking while I worked something out. My eyes stayed on the coffee table, on the pack of cigarettes lying there.

"I considered that, Peggy," he said, "but how could I know what you'd do once you were in the building? You might have called the cops from the apartment of that man who helped you get inside. Or you might have had that gun of yours with you. Oh no, this is better. Every way you look at it, this is so much better."

"But once you'd gotten in here," I said, "you could have just taken the tape and left. You didn't need to hang around here waiting for me. Because now—"

In a sudden flash I remembered what it was that was bothering me.

When I'd found Adam Warren's body, there'd been a pack of cigarettes lying on the floor next to him, in his blood. But they weren't in the photographs Hansen had just shown me of the murder scene. Pierce must have picked them up while

I was busy with Doris Parker, before the men from homicide had gotten there and taken their pictures.

"That's right, Peggy," Pierce said, finishing the sentence for me, "because now I'm going to have to kill you. But I was going to kill you tonight anyway. Or rather," he added, flashing that quick glinting smile on and then off as if using a switch, "Doris Parker is."

Thirty-three

I shook my head, as if the bee were in it instead of buzzing around the room. I was too busy working it out to pay much attention to his last words.

When I'd first seen the cigarettes next to Warren, I didn't think anything about it, because when I'd taken that class from him he was a heavy smoker. If homicide—Hansen—had thought to show me those photographs as soon as they'd been printed, I'd have noticed that the cigarettes were missing. I've got a good visual memory. The case would have ended then, and I wouldn't have been sitting there in my living room with Lee Pierce and his gun.

I realized something else.

"That's why you came over that night, when you learned I was starting to ask questions about Warren's murder. You were playing with your cigarettes, on the table there, and watching me to see how I'd react." I recalled how he'd batted them back and forth between his hands. I had thought it was just because he needed one. "You were playing with me, too," I added.

"It was even the same pack," he said, "although I'd wiped off the blood. I didn't want to make it too easy for you, after all. But you didn't catch on."

"I couldn't catch on," I said, angry with him for being so stupid, "because I didn't see the police photographs until tonight. I had no idea those were your cigarettes lying next to Warren, and I never knew they weren't still there when homicide arrived."

Pierce shrugged. "I couldn't know that, could I? And I

couldn't be sure that you wouldn't see those photographs someday and remember the missing cigarettes. Christ, Peggy," he said, leaning across the coffee table at me, his crazy eyes pleading for me to understand, "I never wanted to kill you. *Never*. But you wouldn't leave Adam's death alone. And I was afraid that sooner or later, you'd remember the cigarettes. Why wouldn't you leave it alone—I asked you to, you know—why couldn't you let it be a computer thief?"

I didn't reply, just sat there feeling sick and disgusted at myself for having allowed him to sneak into Warren's office and take the evidence that would have convicted him, while I was kneeling beside Doris Parker.

A long piece of gray ash drooped from Pierce's cigarette. He noticed it and tapped it into the ashtray. It wasn't because he was a tidy man, I realized, that he wasn't using my rug as his ashtray. He wasn't planning to leave cigarettes at the murder scene this time, too.

I thought of the phone call I'd just received, wondered who it could have been calling me so late. It might have been Al, calling to ask why I hadn't returned his call. He can be a pest sometimes, when he's depressed over his kids. Or it might have been Hansen, to give me the latest on Doris Parker or even to make sure I'd made it home safely. If it was either of them, what would he do next?

"Do you think murder comes easy to me, Peggy?" Pierce asked, bringing me back to now. "I hoped I'd never have to kill you, that something would turn up. I was so enamored of your red hair and green eyes. I still am. I told you the last time we sat here talking that I'm tired of girls who write slack verse and wear taut smiles. Girls who just want my *blessing*."

Yesterday afternoon, I recalled, less than twenty-four hours ago, he'd asked me for a date—asked me to attend his poetry reading, too. He'd asked me out the last time he was in my apartment, had even asked me to go to Ireland with him. I wondered if he would have killed me if I'd gone out with him. I wondered if the real reason he was going to kill me now was because I didn't like him.

"Did Marilyn Parker want your blessing, too," I asked, "want to show you her paintings? Did she write poetry, too?"

"Marilyn? Marilyn's death was just what it appeared to be, Peggy, a hit-and-run accident. She wasn't my girl, she was Adam's."

"And Warren ran over her."

Pierce didn't answer me for a few seconds, just stared into space, but not far enough for my purposes. It was much too big a jump. I watched the cigarette burning in his hand. He seemed to have forgotten it. The bee did a turnaround the room, but stayed away from us. There were all sorts of possibilities, I imagined. The cigarette would burn him, the bee would sting him, he'd drop the gun, I'd jump him. Pierce's eyes tried to follow the bee, then gave it up and came back, suddenly weary, to me.

"No," he said finally. "No, I was driving."

"You killed her!"

"It was Adam's fault, really. He was too drunk to drive."

"Drunk? Or high on drugs?"

"What difference does it make? Both, I suppose. He liked cocaine, but he liked Scotch better. He'd done a lot of both that night. And he couldn't control either."

He fished another cigarette out of his pack, lit it from the first one, and then stubbed out the butt. His gestures were jerky, as if he were having to work to keep his hands from trembling.

On Christmas Eve, he told me, Adam Warren had been mixing cocaine and Scotch and suddenly turned nasty. Jack Becker finally told him he had to leave. He'd started to go, dragging Marilyn Parker with him. Marilyn didn't want to leave, and some of the other people at the party didn't want her to leave either—especially Jack Becker. It was an ugly scene. Pierce intervened. "The peacemaker, always the peacemaker, Peggy," he said to me sadly, as if being a peacemaker were a thankless role, "and look where it got me. Look where it got us, you and me, Peggy. Adam's fault really." He glanced at his watch. It was the second time. I wondered why, because he didn't seem to be in any hurry.

Pierce drove Warren's car. He wasn't in the mood to spend

the rest of Christmas Eve there anyway, and he was afraid of trouble if Warren got into an accident.

Pierce got into the accident instead. Once they got on the freeway, Warren turned really abusive, started venting his rage on Marilyn, trapped in the backseat with him. Pierce tried to get him to calm down, but it was snowing and the roads were slippery and he wasn't in any condition to be driving either. Happy holidays!

Then Marilyn had had enough and started in on Warren, and as they left the freeway she hit him. Warren lost all control then. He hit her back, hard, and Marilyn started to scream. Pierce watched them struggling in the rearview mirror. Marilyn shouted at Pierce to stop the car and let her out and, finally, fed up with both of them, he did. She got out and started running through the snow, in the headlights of the car. Then Warren got out too and ran after her, probably because Marilyn was so poorly dressed for the weather. "As crazy as he was," Pierce said, "Adam knew better than to let her try to walk home dressed like that. What if she'd been picked up by the cops? And maybe he cared about her, too," he added as an afterthought.

I remembered that one of the things that had thrown the police off was that they'd assumed Marilyn had come from a house in the neighborhood where she'd been killed, because she wasn't wearing an overcoat and boots.

Pierce sat and waited for about a minute, but Marilyn kept running, with Warren in pursuit. They were maybe fifty yards ahead of him when Pierce took off, intending to leave both of them out there, struggling down the snowy street.

He was still accelerating in Warren's new car when he caught up with them.

"And then," Pierce said, his eyes wide, shocked at the memory, "the crazy bitch jumped in front of me." His eyes burned into mine, blazing with indignation at the behavior of the crazy bitch, demanding sympathy and understanding.

"Warren *pushed* her?" I asked.

"No! No, she jumped! Don't you understand? They weren't even struggling, she just jumped! It wasn't my fault, she committed suicide. The bitch was trying to ruin my life. Later it was Adam who tried to ruin it, but then it was her. It wasn't my fault," he repeated. He looked at me, then looked around my apartment as if searching for somebody more understanding. But we were alone, the two of us, with our ghosts.

I had an image of Marilyn Parker, high as a kite, confused by the headlights rushing at her, and at the same time I saw the self-portrait she'd done for her mother, hanging on her mother's wall. Like some shy animal, I'd thought. The kind you see dead on highways.

I said, "You were just out for a Christmas Eve drive, you happened to cruise past an eighteen-year-old girl who was staggering down a snowy street, fighting with a distinguished professor, all three of you stoned out of your minds. What does it sound like, Pierce, hitting a kid, a crazy bitch, like that?"

I expected him to pull the trigger, but at that moment I didn't care. I spat the words at him. Instead of shooting me, though, he waited a moment, got his face under control, and said, softly, "I hit a dog once, a big one. It sounded like that." He seemed to drift off for a moment, at the thought of the one killing or the other. He took a long drag from his cigarette. I pulled my legs back slowly, tensed to jump at him. I wanted to hurt him, badly, only in part to save my own life. He noticed what I was doing, shook his head at me, and gave me his tired smile.

"That's an ugly story," I said softly, keeping my legs where they were. "Do you find it easy to live with?"

"It was an accident. I wasn't going to let it ruin my life. I'm not going to let anything ruin my life."

"Except the important stuff—booze and drugs. People like you make the accidents happen. And anyway," I added, "she might have lived. You left her there to freeze to death."

"Yes," he said, almost hissing it in his eagerness to miss my point, "and once we'd done *that*, there was no going back. Adam should have known that." He glanced at his watch again.

"How did Fred Lundeen fit into it?" I asked. "He didn't look to me as if he belonged out there at the Beckers'."

"He was our tester," Pierce said.

"Your what?" That wasn't a word that made any sense, not in this context.

"Tester." Although he seemed to be in something resembling pain, Pierce laughed at my puzzlement. "He tested cocaine for us, determined its quality before I'd buy it. He was a chemist."

"You're a drug dealer?" I asked.

"You could call it that, if you need a simple job description. It started out with me bringing in a little coke now and then from Europe, just for fun, for recreational purposes, just to share with a few friends. It was pretty safe. After all, I'm Lee Pierce, aren't I? I go to Ireland regularly, well-publicized trips, sometimes even on government grants—to read poetry, give workshops, lecture. Just an eccentric 'bard,' spreading American culture abroad." He laughed. "The customs people never go through my luggage with a comb, and they'd have a hard time finding anything if they did. What do people smuggle in from Ireland anyway, besides a little whiskey—shamrocks?"

"But it's bigger than that now."

"Oh, yes, it's bigger now. It was amazing to me how big it got, and how much bigger it's going to get. Now I just make the arrangements when I'm in Europe. Fred tests the coke when it arrives in this country, in Florida. He's very good at what he does."

"*Was* very good at what he *did*," I said.

"Yes."

"And Adam Warren was involved in drug smuggling? It doesn't seem likely."

"No, not Adam. He didn't know anything about that. I don't know what he suspected. The drug operation was Jerry's and mine. Jack doesn't ask where the cocaine comes from, or the money that lets him live the kind of life he lives out there in Arcadia. He thinks he can afford it on his salary and his royalties, and what Jerry makes as a therapist and marriage counselor." He gave a short laugh. "Well, he's partly right, since a good part of Jerry's therapy involves drugs. I mean, we don't exactly sell it on the streets, do we? Jerry's practice provides us with a nice reason for people to be coming and going at regular intervals. She has a sliding fee scale, too, of course, which is convenient when the tax man calls."

"I suppose Jack Becker didn't know you'd killed Warren either?"

Pierce shrugged. "There's knowing and there's knowing, Peggy."

"Trying to quit using drugs can be a dangerous thing," I said. "In Warren's case it was fatal."

"He developed a conscience. At first it didn't bother me much, I just laughed at him because he had as much to lose as I did. Christ, Peggy, we'd gotten away with it! Nobody connected us with Marilyn Parker's death and we didn't have to worry about the people out at the Beckers' either. Most of them didn't even know who she was. But Adam—Adam couldn't handle it. I don't think he *liked* success! He just got worse, the more obvious it became that we were going to get away with it. I didn't realize how bad it was, not until the day I had to kill him."

Warren came into Pierce's office that afternoon and told him he'd decided to go to the police. He told Pierce he was going to tell them that he—Warren—had been driving the car and had killed Marilyn Parker. He was going to leave Pierce out of it entirely. He'd already told that story to Doris Parker, in her office the day before.

"He was going to make—*amends,*" Pierce said, spitting the word out. "Amends! That's the word he used. He was going to make amends for both of us. Fine! But the trouble with that, Peggy," he explained, wagging his pistol at me like a long hollow finger, "was that Adam wasn't a good liar. I couldn't trust him, he was too close to collapse. And when he told me he'd already talked to Doris Parker about it—told her he'd killed her kid—I almost killed him on the spot. Luckily she threw him out of her office, told him she didn't want to hear anything about it."

And so Pierce persuaded Warren to wait, promised to go with him to the police and tell them the real story, the whole truth. He had trouble keeping his eyes off the hammer lying there in the clutter on Warren's desk, trouble keeping his thoughts to himself. And later in the afternoon, when most of the students and faculty had left the building, and his office, like Warren's, was full of the rock music coming from across the street, he'd gone next door and killed Warren.

"Adam was a humanist," Pierce said, his voice tinged with both sadness and scorn. "He wasn't capable of believing that anybody could really kill another human being—not in cold blood anyway. Killing him was the easy part."

He wanted to make it look like the work of a thief, but there wasn't much time.

"I knew someone could come in at any time, Peggy," he said, "and I was willing to take that risk—it excited me—but I had no idea Adam had just called the campus cops and that you were on your way. And when that music suddenly stopped, I thought I could hear myself breathing. I thought I could hear Adam's office crying 'murder!' and I thought everybody in the building must be able to hear it, too."

He stopped then, perhaps to relive the murder of Adam Warren, feel the heat of the afternoon in Frye Hall, hear the rock music coming from across the street, and smell again the blood.

My apartment seemed very quiet all of a sudden. The rain had stopped—I didn't know when—and a cool breeze was blowing in through the window I'd opened to let the bee escape. The bee was gone, too.

"I had to kill Adam," Pierce said, breaking the silence, as if we were two old friends reminiscing over ancient accomplishments. "No matter how much I loved the man, I had to kill him. He was out of control."

"You did a good job," I said, "except that you forgot your cigarettes."

"I had so much to do," he said, his voice so soft now that I had to strain to hear him. "I was in a hurry. I knew it when they fell out of my pocket—when I bent over to make sure Adam was dead. I meant to come back for them, when I'd have time to wipe off the blood, but then the music stopped and I panicked and forgot them." His face brightened suddenly and he said, more loudly, "But then, if I *had* remembered them, and stopped to pick them up, you'd have met me coming out of Adam's office, wouldn't you? Oh, I've been lucky, Peggy, very lucky."

I asked him why he'd tried to kill me in Frye Hall.

"I told you, I was afraid I'd have to kill you sooner or later. You knew about the cigarettes. That was a loose end I didn't want to live with. You were walking around with a piece of the puzzle—no, you were walking around with the answer itself—and I didn't like that. You were also becoming so tiresome—you wouldn't let it alone. The police hadn't shown any interest in Marilyn Parker in connection with Adam's death. Why did you? But trying to kill you that way, in Frye Hall, that was Jerry's idea. Doris Parker saved your life. If she hadn't shown up sooner than I'd expected, I'd have finished what the stairs were meant to. You were lucky, that time.''

"Adam Warren acquired a conscience and Fred Lundeen got scared," I said. "A poet's life is hard, isn't it?''

"Fred was just out of control, Peggy," Pierce replied matter-of-factly. "It was business, his dying. It really had nothing to do with Adam Warren''—he waved his pistol around—"with any of this.''

"Then what did it have to do with?''

"He used too many drugs. They took him over. And he didn't like it when the operation started growing so big. He must have guessed that he was outliving his usefulness to us. And maybe he overheard something Jerry said, I don't know. But he didn't like the killing of Warren, which he learned about from you. And when he found out you were a cop— even just a campus cop—that scared him, too. He'd been in jail before. But you aren't responsible for his death, if that concerns you. We'd begun worrying about Fred before you stuck your nose into it. We'd pretty much stopped using him, in fact, and he was getting upset about that, too. Your meddling just moved the date up a bit, that's all. 'Fred Lundeen. Born and died.' ''

Whether I'd been responsible for Fred Lundeen's demise earlier than planned or not didn't bother me very much. I was thinking of Doris Parker. The cops were out looking for her, and sooner or later they'd find her. Whether she could be tried and convicted for murdering Warren and Lundeen, I had no way of knowing. Maybe there'd be witnesses who could place her somewhere else at the time Pierce killed Lundeen. In that case she'd probably be off the hook. But something told me that wasn't very likely: why would Lee Pierce and Jerry Becker try to frame Doris for Lundeen's murder, if there was a good chance she'd be able to account for her whereabouts at the time he was killed? Lee Pierce might be crazy enough to play something like that by ear, thinking he was destined to win, but I doubted that Jerry Becker would.

I asked Pierce how he was going to pin my murder on Doris Parker.

"Let's let it be a surprise," he said, and wouldn't meet my eyes.

"Are you sure you want to go through with it?" I asked him.

His eyes came to mine, startled. Then he shook himself, tried out his grin, but abandoned it when it wouldn't work. "I don't have any choice," he replied. "I have to be free, to write."

"On drugs," I said. "How free is that?"

He'd been slumped in the couch, but now he straightened up. "As free as I can get now," he said.

So I realized I wasn't going to save my life by getting him to give up—at least not without a lot more time, and I was sure I didn't have that.

"It's a terrible thing, isn't it," I said to him, "when a poet runs out of words."

"I haven't run out of words," he answered. His voice was level, reasonable at first, but his eyes started to grow angry again. "Oh no, Peggy. The irons are hot. Haven't I told you that before? I'm at the beginning of something wonderful now, something tremendous! I wish you could be here to see it—and I wish Adam could be here to see it even more. Oh, Peggy, believe me!" I believed he was at the beginning of something serious, yes: killing me. He added: "It's something that's going to throw all my earlier poetry completely into the shadows."

I said to him, "I was at your reading tonight, Lee. Last night," I corrected myself, for I could see that it was getting light outside. "I was standing in the back row, in those shadows with your earlier poetry, listening. It was really boring stuff. Those new poems, Lee—they were empty and pretentious exercises, and I finally had to leave. It was either that or fall asleep on my feet. Other people were leaving, too, and I heard one of them say that your poetry was"—I groped for Arthur Fletcher's formulation, and crooned it at him slowly—"like masturbating in a hall of mirrors. Frankly I didn't think it was *that* good."

His face was only basted to his skull, not properly sewn, and now it started to come apart. He forgot himself: forgot that he was a good ten years older than I and had spent a lot of those years poisoning his body. Forgot, if he'd ever known, that I'd spent a lot of time learning to do things with my body that women never used to know how to do at all. All he knew, at that moment, was that I was a woman—a crazy bitch, perhaps, like Marilyn Parker—who'd just bad-mouthed his poetry, bad-mouthed him, and he was a man and that's really enough. *That's all she wrote,* my father used to say on those regrettable occasions when he had to hit a woman, as he balled up his fist.

He jumped up, faster than I'd thought he could, and came around the coffee table, making noises that would have been acceptable in an animal in a cage but, in a man, were both horrible and completely stupid.

I got up fast, too, and came to meet him, ducked, and turned under the pistol he'd raised above his head and was bringing down at me. I slammed my right elbow into his side with all the rage and strength I had, a low elbow strike, something as easy to learn as riding a bike and just as hard to forget. The gun went off and something exploded across the room and something gave in Pierce with a crack I could feel shudder all through my body. I pulled back my arm, reversed my fist, and slammed my elbow into him again, this time into a face that was falling to meet it.

Whoever was at my door was trying to break it down. I spun around and kicked Pierce in the side of his leg with the heel of my shoe, and I heard the leg break with the sound of a broomstick snapping. He fell screaming and I kicked the gun away from him and then went over to get it.

"Leave it there."

I looked up and Doris Parker was standing just inside the door. She had a hand to her mouth as if she were about to scream. Next to her and slightly behind her was Jerry Becker. She held a gun and it was pointed at me.

I knew all at once, without any thought at all, that Pierce

and Jerry Becker planned to kill me and pin my murder on Doris Parker, too. It was as clear as if it had already happened, and I was watching it. I could even see myself dead, Doris Parker dead, too, and her death made to look like a suicide.

"Move away from the gun, Peggy," Jerry Becker said, "quickly."

I started to move toward her and I didn't intend to stop until I was dead.

Al's head appeared in the doorway behind Jerry Becker, like a full moon in a pale sky.

"What the hell's going on in here?" he hollered, and when Jerry turned, Al looked at the pistol coming around at him and took it. He's a big man and he didn't seem to be moving fast at all. He never does. From where I stood, it looked as if he were plucking from Jerry Becker something she was offering him, something she wanted him to have because she no longer needed it.

I don't think she knew how he did it either, but by the time I got to them, Al was holding the pistol in one hand and Jerry Becker's arm in the other.

Doris Parker, of course, was fainting again and I stood back and let her. My carpet's deep.

Thirty-four

"I saved your bacon," Al called after me as I padded toward his bathroom.

"What?" I was still sleepy.

"Your bacon," he said, trying an alternative construction, "I saved it." He said it with great satisfaction, as if he'd planned for, studied and rehearsed for, the moment when he appeared in my doorway and saved me from being shot by Jerry Becker.

"I know you did," I said, "but I have to go to the bathroom now. I'll be back." I closed the door behind me. He said something else, but I couldn't make out the words, so I hollered out to him to wait until I was through.

I'd spent what remained of the night at his place, although it was almost five A.M. by the time we left my apartment. Lieutenant Hansen didn't even take a full statement from me, just got the facts he needed then and told Al to take me away and bring me downtown that afternoon at one.

When the toilet stopped flushing and I'd opened the bathroom door to hear better, Al went on: "I said, it would have been such a waste—Jerry Becker killing you. By turning your apartment into a karate studio and shooting gallery, you'd spoiled their plan to make it look like a murder-suicide, so what good would it have done to kill you? But my guess is, she was too involved in the moment to see it that way. She didn't seem like a reas—are you using my toothbrush?"

When Pierce's gun went off and things—Pierce among them—began shattering right and left in my apartment and going bump in the night, my landlady and other neighbors all dialed 911, probably simultaneously. I suppose the system is built to withstand that kind of overload. The police, their sirens screaming, started arriving about three minutes after Al did, which wouldn't have given Jerry Becker enough time to carry out Lee Pierce.

"Yes," I replied, somewhat frothily, "I am."

"That's disgusting. I'll never use it again."

"Yes, you will," I said, "and soon." I spat and rinsed and went out to see what he was doing. He was at his kitchen counter, making coffee. Neither of us was wearing any clothes, but it was only 11:30, so we had lots of time to get dressed before we were due at Hansen's office. "Thanks for coming over last night," I said, "and for saving my bacon."

"That's okay. My reasons for coming over weren't exactly heroic, you know," he pointed out, and actually looked ashamed.

"I know," I said, "and my reasons for coming over here this morning weren't exactly unselfish either."

"Right," he said, pleased that I'd seen the light. "You could have checked into a hotel if you'd wanted to sleep alone. But nobody's perfect."

He went into the bathroom and I sat on the edge of the bed not thinking of much of anything until I heard the shower running and then I knocked and went in and climbed in with him.

Al and I drove downtown that afternoon and gave our statements to a stenographer and then Hansen filled me in on what I didn't already know. Some of it, at least, since he didn't know everything yet himself. Lee Pierce was doing quite a lot of babbling, and so was Doris Parker, and not all of it made sense. Jerry Becker was keeping a stony silence and her lawyers were filing briefs detailing police incompetence and brutality and demanding bail.

What I was most interested in knowing was how Jerry Becker had gotten Doris Parker to leave her cabin and accompany her back to town.

According to Hansen, Jerry had driven up there right after Lee Pierce's poetry reading. She told Doris she was a police officer and that Doris was wanted for some questioning back in town. Doris balked at first—they'd tricked her once before, into thinking Hansen wanted her at Frye Hall the night I'd fallen down the stairs—but Jerry showed her a badge, one she'd probably taken from her husband's collection. She also told Doris Parker that the police knew what she and Adam Warren had been quarreling about in her office the day before Warren was murdered. That convinced Doris that Jerry really was a cop and that she was in real trouble.

"I can't figure out how Jerry Becker knew what Doris Parker and Warren had quarreled about," Hansen said. "Parker doesn't know, Pierce doesn't make sense, and Jerry Becker isn't talking."

"Warren told Pierce," I said, "at the same time he told him he was going to the cops to confess to Marilyn Parker's death."

"Is that in your statement?"

"No," I replied. "I forgot."

Hansen made a note.

Al said, "I can understand why, once they decided murder was a viable way of solving problems, they had to kill Fred Lundeen. He was losing control and getting nervous, especially after Peggy barged in on them in their hot tub. But why did they want to kill Doris Parker and Peggy? What's inside the heads of people like that?"

"Chemicals, mostly," Hansen said.

Mixed with fear. They were probably afraid I'd learn about Fred's murder and connect him to the Beckers, since they didn't know I wasn't keeping some kind of contact with homicide. And, of course, Lee Pierce was worried about me discovering that he'd picked up the cigarettes he dropped when he killed Warren. Those cigarettes, apparently, were vivid in his mind, lying there in Warren's blood, next to Warren's body. I had no trouble understanding that, since that picture was still vivid in my mind, too. I should have noticed that the cigarettes were missing as soon as I saw the photographs in Hansen's office—but I'd been too tired.

Since Doris Parker was the most likely suspect in Adam Warren's murder, they decided to add Fred's death and mine to her list of crimes.

Al asked Hansen what Lee Pierce was doing while Jerry Becker was driving up to get Doris.

"Apparently he went to the party in his honor after the poetry reading and then left early. We've found witnesses who've been more than happy to sign statements to that effect. He sneaked off to kill Fred Lundeen and then went over to Peggy's, waited for her to come home from work."

Al chanted, "They killed Adam Warren because they'd killed Marilyn Parker, they killed Fred Lundeen because they'd killed Adam Warren, and—"

"*Stop it,*" I said, my voice rising. "I don't want to hear any more about it."

Hansen looked over at me then and said, "Peggy, their plan would have worked. Damn it, it would have! Jerry Becker got Doris Parker to go with her with no trouble at all. And you and I, we sat here yesterday morning, right where we're sitting now, at about the same time Jerry Becker was conning Doris Parker into coming back to town with her, and we created a fiction—a *fiction*—in which Parker was guilty of both Warren's and Lundeen's murder. And if I'd found you and Parker dead, an apparent murder-suicide, it would just have strengthened the fiction we'd created. I would have finished the story for them while they sat back and laughed!" His words made him go a little pale.

"But without me here to help," I said gently, "it wouldn't have been as *good* a story."

He gave me a disgusted look for trying to make light of it, but I couldn't help it. It was either that or shout again. "Let's quit now," I added, getting up. I gave Al a hand and pulled him to his feet.

"Frankly," Hansen said, getting up, too, "the only mystery left for me is why you stayed involved so long, Peggy. Why you lied and cheated your way until you nearly got yourself killed."

Both men looked at me. I thought of telling them one thing or another, for example about my father who killed himself and my brother who fried his brains on drugs and my mother who doesn't believe any of it happened, but I didn't know where to begin. It wasn't the time or the place anyway.

So I lied some more. My eyelids don't flicker when I lie; I think maybe I've mentioned that before. "I didn't handle it very well when I found Warren's body," I told them. "I made every possible mistake. I just wanted to make up for that.''

Hansen gave me a long look, a smile, and then a shrug. He picked up the little tape cassette from my answering machine. ''We're going to need it as evidence,'' he said, ''but there're other messages on it, besides those from the Other Side or thereabouts. One's from Al here, which I don't suppose you need anymore. The other's from somebody who sounds like what used to be called a maiden aunt, but I suppose there's another name for it now. Aunt Tess. She says your mother doesn't want you to have the car, whatever that means. She wants this Tess to sell it behind your back and send her the money, as soon as possible. Sounds sinister to me.''

I told Hansen I'd heard the message.

''What car's that?'' Al asked me.

''My dad's car,'' I said, ''from when he was a kid—it was a long time ago.''

''Must be a classic,'' Hansen said. ''Valuable?''

''Well,'' I told him, ''I know a blind mortician who's willing to shell out a lot for it. Apparently he's got a rich customer who's dying to be buried in it.''

''That's terrible!'' both men exclaimed at once.

I thought it was kind of funny, myself.